# FOR LOVE AND MONEY

## G.A. HAUSER

Linden Bay Romance, LLC
Palm Harbor, Florida 34684
www.lindenbayromance.com

First Linden Bay Romance publication: May 2007

# Chapter One

Dr. Jason Phillips sat with his mouth hanging open as he gaped at the picture on the television screen. A Hollywood premiere, his ex-lover walking up the red carpet with the Italian model 'Vincienzo' on his arm, it was all too much to take in. How had he made it? How had he succeeded in a career that had been the ruin of many a young man?

Sitting in the lounge of his stately manor in Carlisle, England, over five thousand miles away from the lovely Ewan Gallagher, he wondered if he would ever get the answer to that question.

When a shadow passed the room entrance, Jason cringed. That woman. That 'thing' he married. Priscilla Farnesworth Prescott. All in the name of money. Once he had thought he had sold his soul to that lovely male actor; now he was quite certain it had been to his late Aunt Margerie Witcomb. He had made a deal with the devil. This sham marriage for over five million pounds in property and assets and a fat corgi named Willie.

As he gazed around the sterile room, untouched since his aunt's hands had lived, the old mongrel snoring under his chair, he knew it had not been worth it.

Wiping his eyes again as the water filled them, Jason wondered two things: how he had missed the plane that day, and why Ewan had climbed on board without him?

Fate. Fate and blind ambition drove both decisions.

Priscilla stuck her mousy nose into the room. "Should I at least get Charles to make you some tea?"

"No." He rose up, shut off the television with the remote and passed her in the hall.

Scuffing his feet along the expensive tapestries that lined the upper floor, Jason closed himself into the study attached to his private bedroom and locked the door. Moving as if he were already dead inside, like he had been ever since that lovely man left his life, he approached a shelf with tiny ceramics on it. When he had quit his job at the hospital, he had his collection of mice relocated to his home from his office.

Reaching for one out in front of the rest, he lifted a miniature brown mouse on a green leaf. At the touch of the delicate item, he almost felt Ewan's presence. It had been a gift from Ewan during their weekend away in Windermere. Ewan still had a cast on his left leg from breaking it. Hit by a car one wet winter night so long ago, it was what brought him to the emergency room in the first place. Where fate decided they should meet.

Sitting in front of the computer, setting the mouse down beside its electronic counterpart and pad, Jason booted up the hard drive.

"Vincienzo?' Jason scoffed out loud the name of the young runway model Ewan had had on his arm. "Where the hell did he find him from?" It angered him. Ewan was so damn comfortable being out. Openly gay! There he was walking with a gorgeous Italian stud on his arm right in front of the world. If only Jason had the same guts.

Ewan had accused him of being weak. He was so damn right.

When the screen lit up with lists of fan sites from entering that Ewan's name, Jason opened his mouth in awe.

"Bloody hell!" The amount of movie chat rooms, galleries of photos, posters, and biography descriptions were beyond belief.

One by one, Jason entered them. When he found a site containing information about Ewan's current film, '*Murphy's Hero*', he read the fine print.

"...April 27$^{th}$, the London premiere of *Murphy's Hero* will be shown in Leicester Square..."

Jason checked his watch for the date. It was one week away.


After almost three hours of reading everything there was to read about the famous Mr. Gallagher, Jason shut down the computer and stood to stretch his back. Checking the time, seeing how late it had become, he assumed Priscilla was in bed, and then shrugged, knowing he didn't care.

Finding his file cabinet, he unlocked it, leafing through the documents. Aunt Margerie's will was in a separate folder. Taking it out, sitting with it on his bed, he read it again, the fine print, the conditions. If he violated them, only his parents would be left to fight the battle to get his inheritance back. If he left Pricilla, divorced her, then by the contract of his old Aunt Margerie, he would lose everything she left to him. When they found out he was gay, they had blackmailed him into a bad arranged marriage. Would they bother?

Shoving the paperwork to the floor where it scattered like feathers across the polished wood, Jason clenched his fists and snarled, "Go ahead and fight me," he challenged his parents, "I'm sick of this charade! I want my lover back!"

Then, with the reality of his situation beginning to grip him like a strangling hand around his throat, he wondered, *would Ewan even want me back*?

# Chapter Two

The ending credits moving up the screen, Ewan ran his hand through his long hair and felt the exhaustion creeping up on him.

As people stood, clapped, and began chatting about the wonderful storyline, Vincienzo leaned against Ewan's shoulder and purred in his ear, "We go back to hotel? Yes?"

Rising up as several fellow actors came to shake his hand, Ewan only glanced back in distraction as his lover pouted, wanting his reassurances.

"Brilliant!" Dennis Foreman clasped his hand enthusiastically. "I'll have my man call yours! I've some ideas for a new script I want you a part of."

"Aye, right. Cheers." Ewan smiled at this popular movie producer, nodding, trying to hide the empty hole in his heart.

The bodyguards had formed a line to usher them into their waiting limousines. Vincienzo held Ewan around the waist as the screaming of the fans covered even the loudest motor engine.

Hearing his name being cried as he bent low to climb inside the car, Ewan waved quickly as he was shoved from behind. The door shut and the vehicle jolted into motion. Through the tinted glass he tried to wave, but had no idea if anyone could see through it.

"Why you no talk to me?" Vincienzo nuzzled closer.

Growing weary, Ewan set him back. "I'm shattered, love. Yeah? I need some sleep."

"You no love me. You no call me *love*-!" He crossed his arms and pouted.

"I don't want you coming back to my room tonight, Vee. Please. Let me ring you tomorrow."

"Que cosa?" he shouted, "Why you do this? We make love tonight!"

"No. We don't." Ewan leaned to the driver to say, "I don't care where you take him, just please, don't drop him off with me."

"Right, sir."

Hearing every word, Vincienzo went into a string of Italian expletives, furious with the terrible treatment.

When his hotel appeared, Ewan gave his lover one last comment, "Bear with me."

"No! You go bear yourself! I'm finished!" He waved his hands dramatically.

"Suit yourself." Ewan climbed out when the doorman opened the back of the car.

Nodding to the few employees who rushed to attend him, Ewan was shown to his room, his door opened for him, then he was handed the key.

"Would you like anything, sir?"

"Yes, some ale. Cheers." He closed the door on the bellboy's nod of understanding, and loosened his tie.

He knew there were hundreds of parties to attend and he would get flack for not showing up. Especially the one for the cast and producer, but, he was too tired. He just wanted some peace.

Before he had stripped down, a soft knock was heard. He opened the door to a tray of ice cold beer.

"Lovely, cheers." He waited as the man set it down,

paused for any further instructions, received none, then left.

Locking the door behind him, Ewan took off the rest of his clothing and poured the bottle into the frosty mug. Moving to the window, he gazed out at this lonely city filled with light, and felt sick to his stomach. The cure for his ache? Thousands of miles away on a tiny isle called Britain.

# Chapter Three

"What do you mean 'going out of town'?" Priscilla crossed her arms anxiously. "Where? For what reason?"

Packing his small suitcase, Jason restrained the urge to scream—It's none of your business!— and lock her out. But she was his damned wife, after all. "Just for the weekend. I want to go to London for a convention."

"Convention?"

"Yes. A doctor's convention." He avoided her and moved to his dresser for some more clothing.

"Why is this the first I've heard of it? Did you know before today?"

"I just forgot to mention it. An oversight on my part."

"Can't I come? I'd enjoy a trip to London. I've never been there!"

His back becoming rigid at the idea, he didn't meet her eyes when he said, "No. Not this time. It's for men only."

"Men only?" she gasped. "How amazing. Only men doctors?"

"Yes. I'll take you to the next one. Next year." Going to his en suite bath, he began gathering his toiletries.

As she watched him get ready, she appeared a forlorn

little girl and waited for him to come back to the bed where the suitcase was lying.

After he had dropped his things in it, she ran her hands up his arm, feeling his powerful muscles under his cotton shirt. At the touch, he froze.

"Jason," she purred, "Maybe we could try again, when you get back?"

Closing his eyes as the revulsion surfaced, Jason's mouth formed a tight line. Catching her left hand as it moved down to his pelvis, Jason shook his head. "It's no use, Priscilla. I can't make love to you."

"How do you know? Maybe if I dress up, role play—"

Trying to find a little tenderness for her, Jason turned his body and held her arms in both his hands. "Dear," he whispered, "I appreciated you trying, honestly. But, it's dead. I've tried myself to bring it to life, and it's useless."

"Can we just lie naked together?" She leaned against him, craning her neck up to his height. "A year we've been married and I've seen you naked only a handful of times. Mostly in the shower—"

"Cilla…" he sighed, "Please."

"But—you're my husband, Jason. If I can't hold you, who can I hold?"

Pushing the suitcase over to make room, Jason sat with her on the bed. "If you want to find a man who—"

"No! Jason, I would never!" she gasped in shock.

"Listen to me, lovely… You go and get what you need. I won't stop you, nor will I be angry. You're a young healthy woman. You should have your urges satisfied."

"No! Jason! How can you say that?"

Cupping her face gently, trying not to see her as repugnant, Jason whispered, "But, you must. If you want children, you must find a suitable man to have a physical relationship with."

Biting her lip, she whispered, "Are you telling me you will never be able—"

"Never. It's broken, my love. I cannot get an erection.

Now, let me pack, get myself on the road, and then I'll be back home again soon. All right?"

She closed her eyes and leaned forward. Swallowing down the black water in his throat, he kissed her quickly, not wanting anything to do with her tongue.

After that kiss, she sat back and smiled sweetly, reassured. "Will you call me? When you arrive?"

"Absolutely." He stood and closed the case, snapping the locks.

She followed him down the stairs to Charles who was waiting with his jacket. "You know, Jason, Willie's taken poorly. I think I need to get him to the vet."

"He's so bloody old and in agony. Just have him put down." Jason took his coat from the valet.

"Oh! Jason! No. Not unless he can't be helped. He's a good little boy."

"Whatever, you decide."

"I'll miss you…" She pouted.

"Now, you remember what I told you." Jason slid his leather jacket on and made eye contact with his wife. "You get busy on what we discussed."

"Jason!" She looked over at Charles.

Peering at him slyly, Jason added, "Maybe Charles knows someone suitable."

As the old man tilted his head curiously, Jason laughed to himself, leaving the two of them in awkward silence behind him.


He didn't remember how long of a drive it was. Three hundred and fifty miles and seven excruciating hours later, he was pulling in front of the five star hotel near Regent's Park. Immediately assisted with his luggage and car, Jason was very glad to be able to afford the luxuries of the upper class, and not deal with the abusive self-service motor lodges.

"Thank you." He attempted a smile, though all he could

think of was sleep.

"Certainly, sir. This way, sir."

He followed a red-coated man inside the crystal and brass lobby. Approaching the desk, he removed his wallet and thanked the concierge for his help.

"I've a reservation. Dr. Jason Phillips."

"Yes, sir." The conservatively dressed gentleman searched for his paperwork. "Here we are, sir. Four nights?"

"Yes." Jason handed him his credit card.

"Just for one, sir?"

Raising his light eyes to this older gent, he whispered, "Yes."

"Very good, sir." The man nodded to the bellboy again and handed him the key. "Enjoy your stay, sir."

"Thank you." Hardly creating any sort of amiable expression on his face, too tired and anxious about this insanity to feel kind, Jason followed the red-coat to his room.

It was more than adequate, with a large queen sized bed, a sitting area, a balcony, an enormous bathroom and shower. He handed the man a tip and then stood still, trying to gather his thoughts.

As he opened his jacket and kicked off his shoes, he moved to the window, gazing out at the madness of the twisted lanes of London. Unbelievably, he'd not been back here since his medical school days, when he was attending college in Cambridge. And then only a handful of times did he venture into the heart of the city.

Intimidated, yet certain he could manage, knowing a little about the underground, he tossed his clothing on a chair and prepared to nap. He was completely exhausted.

Ewan hadn't been on a plane for over a year. Seated in fist class on a British Airways flight, he sipped a beer and tried to relax for the long crossing over the Atlantic. He was anxious to get back on English soil. Though the year had gone better than he could have imagined, he missed the UK, his mother, and his mates.

Disturbing him from his thoughts, the hostess asked him if he would like another beer. "No, ta. But another pillow would be lovely."

She found one in the overhead compartment and smiled invitingly into his handsome face. Ewan thanked her, ignored the obvious flirt, and nestled in to try and sleep.

He sighed deeply. The things he had sacrificed to get to Hollywood frightened him. *Oh, Jason...* he moaned silently. *My love, my baby...* a lump came to his throat. *I should get me arse up to Carlisle. See you and Mum.* Trying to think of when and how to do it with the noose of a tight schedule around his neck, Ewan dabbed at a tear threatening to roll down his cheek. "Aye, you'd not want to see me," he mumbled, "You and your new wife, yeah. You should have come with me, love," Ewan groaned. *Me—you—in LA in me big house. Oh, why did it have to be this way?*

When a full blown shiver of a sob washed over him, he brought the blanket up to his chin, knowing he would die of embarrassment if anyone found him weeping.

He had cried so many nights, he should be finished with the tears. But every time he imagined that incredible man, he welled up and burst into sobs. What was it about him?

And if they did meet again? Would it be cold, distant, horrible?

"Aye. Tea with the wife. I couldn't do it, Jason. I couldn't do it." Ewan closed his eyes and felt the hot tears run down his cheek.

# Chapter Four

In the cool wind of that April morning, Jason stood in Leicester Square staring up at the marquee. Men were erecting barriers to keep the fans back. A canopy and red carpet were being set up. His hands deep in his pockets, Jason took in the appearance of Ewan's face on the massive *Murphy's Hero* poster advertisement. That adorable grin, the Roman helmet shoved up on top of his head, all that long luscious hair spilling out of it. And his handsome blond co-star? Gorgeous Brad Pitt. Who would have ever imagined it?

His deep sigh jetting out like a steam cloud in the cold air, Jason lowered his head and made his way to a coffee shop.

The time zone change of eight hours was enough to kill him. Stumbling into his hotel, the red-coated bellboy hauling his bag, Ewan kept his hat on and his hair tucked under it, trying not to be recognized. Once he was at the front desk, he took the hat off and his hair fell softly around his face to his shoulders. "Aye, you got a room for me, mate?"

"Of course, Mr. Gallagher."

"Good. I'm knackered."

"Long flight, sir?"

"Not half—" He tried to laugh, was too tired, then followed the man to his room. Once inside, he stripped and dropped down on the bed, snoring before his head hit the pillows.


Blowing the steam off his latte, Jason imagined living in London. It had its pluses and minuses. At times he felt like a country bumpkin, the rural family physician from up north. Carlisle. No one ever even heard of the place. Newcastle, yes. Carlisle?

Checking his watch, he found it was after ten o'clock in the morning and just remembered he was to have called Priscilla. "Fuck." He did not want to, nor was he happy he had forgotten. "Christ, just leave me. Get fed up with the sterile marriage and go away!" he grumbled. Impotent. Ha. He didn't have to do more than think of that gorgeous man to get an erection. Just staring at that movie poster there in the square was enough.

The memories of that body, that heat, washed over and over him until he was dizzy with it. He had never had sex like that before, or after, in his life. Though he did consider having an affair, where was he going to find another man like that in all of Carlisle? Well, quite frankly, none existed.

Sitting by the window, eyeing the few brave souls who decided to camp overnight near the ropes to see their favorite stars, Jason felt very numb inside. He'd simply be one fan in thousands tomorrow night. Ewan would never even know he was there.


After sleeping for three hours, Ewan forced himself to get up and try to acclimate himself to the time zone even if it killed him. Rubbing his face and sitting up, he moaned in agony and scuffed to the shower to wake up.

Within an hour he was dressed and handing his key to the man behind the desk.

"Shall I get you a taxi, sir?"

"Aye. That'd be lovely." Ewan began gathering all his hair up to hide under his brimmed hat, then wrapped a scarf around his face.

The gentleman smiled wryly. "The fans giving you no peace?"

"I don't even want to deal, yeah? I'm still a bit lagged."

"Could I phone someone to escort you, sir?"

"No! I don't want a bloody baby-sitter. I've been fine on me own. Just need the damn hat, yeah?" He adjusted it in the reflective glass behind the man.

"Yes, sir. Your cab is outside presently, sir."

"Cheers, ta." Ewan took another look at himself, made sure only his eyes were visible, then covered them with sunglass and went out to the waiting car.


The cup empty, his nerves frazzled, Jason rose up and tossed it in the trash, then closed his jacket and tugged on his gloves. Thinking of going back to the hotel to call Priscilla, he passed through Leicester Square again to gauge the number of people already setting out blankets. Police constables had begun to linger in anticipation of the mob.

Finding himself behind a man with a brimmed hat, glasses, and scarf covering his face, Jason moved aside to stop the man from blocking his view. If he thought that was bad, just wait. He'd never even get near the ropes on opening night. It did occur to Jason to start finding a spot now, like the rest, but he just couldn't face a night sleeping on the pavement. The luxury hotel was a must. He'd take his chances and just be aggressive about shoving through. What choice did he have of ever getting close to that man again?

*For Love and Money*

As he lost himself in thought, the man with the hat stepped back, almost bumping him. Jason dodged out of his way, and then lowered his head, resigned to try and get something positive out of the city while he was there.


Ewan gazed up at the marquee in awe. London. Leicester Square. His face. Unreal.

Raising the scarf higher on his nose so only his eyeglasses were revealed, he found some fans already setting up and couldn't believe the dedication, or insanity, of them.

Backing to get a good look at it, he almost hit someone, turned his face away quickly to avoid their gaze, and waited until they moved on. Checking behind him, he found the man had left, sighed with relief, and then dissolved into the underground to kill some time.


Twilight came, bringing a sense of tranquility to the lavender sky. Jason had intentions of ordering from room service and making it an early night. Checking in at the desk, the nice man behind the counter remembered his room number and handed him the key. "Will you be needing anything, sir?"

"Yes. I'll be ordering from the menu in the room."

"Yes, sir. May I recommend the lobster/filet mignon combination, sir? With some French wine?"

"Thank you. I'll have a look." Jason had no appetite for a heavy dinner. His nerves and stomach were shot.


Coming in from the blowing wind, Ewan took off his hat and scarf and made it to the desk. "Ta…" He took the key from the man behind it.

"Will you be needing anything, sir?"

"Just room service, yeah? In a bit." Ewan opened his

jacket in the warmth of the lobby.

"May I recommend the lobster/filet mignon combination? With some French wine?"

"Oi?" Ewan turned up his nose. "No, ta. But if ya can get a nice cold ale on the way, I'd appreciate it."

"Very good, sir," he nodded.

Ewan found the red-coated man in the elevator holding the door for him. He hustled in and thanked him.

On the ride up, it was silent. Maybe he should have brought Vincienzo. He wanted some company. He thought he'd appreciate the solitude, but it seemed slightly lonely. That was an emotion he hadn't felt in a very long time. Well, at least not on the outside. Companions he'd had plenty. Soul-mates? One.

"There you go, sir."

"Cheers." Ewan nodded and strut down the hall.

He stuck his key into a lock and it wouldn't turn. When he looked up, he realized it was the wrong room number. It was 303, his was 301.

Shaking his head at being so stupid, he knew he should remember that number. It was the same room number he had when he was in Carlisle General hospital, over a year ago.


Jason heard a noise at his door. Setting the menu down, it sounded as if someone was trying a key in his lock. Pausing, listening, he waited. When it stopped he opened it. No one was there.

Trying not to believe he was going mad, he sat back down at the desk and lifted the menu once more. "Yes, hello, I'd like to order some food, please."

Once he had finished that task, he flipped on the television to see if he could find some news regarding the premier.

A knock at his door startled him, then he remembered his meal.

Opening it, he found a loaded cart and a bellboy. "Christ! I didn't order all this!"

The man laughed softly. "No, sir. Some of it's for the gentleman in 301. You both ordered the same thing, ironically."

"Oh. Come on and bring it inside." Jason opened the door wider, allowing him to lift a heavy silver tray and carry it to the table in the suite. Finding his wallet, Jason took out a five and waited until the man was done, then stuck it in his palm, showing him out.

"Thank you, sir."

"No problem." Jason managed a small smile, then before he closed the door he asked, "Oh, just one thing. Where is the pool and spa?"

"All the way down to the basement, sir."

"Great."

Winding down, the last of the ale consumed, Ewan flipped on the television while he lay in bed. The news had a clip showing the manic fans who had camped out for the night at the theater. "What bullocks," Ewan shook his head sadly. "Go home!" Changing the channel, he found a replay of the last of the *Lord of the Rings* trilogy. Nestling into the blankets, his eyes becoming lazy as he watched, he recalled very nearly getting to meet his idol Viggo once but missing the chance.

Yawning, he heard some noises next door, a door closing and then the shower starting. Vaguely he wondered if it was anyone from the movie. They were spread out all over the city. He had wanted to book his own room. Last thing he wanted was to be in the middle of some wild drug party. No. After the premiere he wanted nothing more than to relax in peace.

You can take the boy out of Carlisle, but you can't take Carlisle out of the boy; he smiled smugly.

The hot water felt wonderful after swimming laps. Jason turned off the tap and stood dripping. He hoped he'd get a good night's rest. He was anxious for tomorrow to come and to see if he could get a glimpse of his ex-lover.

Stepping out of the shower to dry off, he imagined Ewan was waiting in his bed for him. He would be giving him that very naughty look of his, craning his finger to come closer.

And Jason would push open those long muscular thighs and lie between them, smothering his face into Ewan's long fragrant hair.

Coming around the corner, Jason found the bed empty. Some low noise was heard from the television in the room next door. He dropped the towel and lay back under the sheets, the pillows soft and comforting. Moving his hand between his legs, he imagined that fantastic male once more, his image neither fading nor tarnishing from the time passed.


At the sight of the lovely Aragorn, Ewan felt a twinge of excitement. Finding himself almost erect, he nudged the blankets off and tried to come, thinking of that gorgeous male. But, another face kept intruding. His handsome doctor. Closing the television, he shut his eyes and masturbated, envisioning his ex-lover with perfect clarity. His back arching as the orgasm rushed upon him, Ewan didn't remember the last time he had to please himself. Vee was so willing. Ironically, it wasn't his Italian lover he was thinking of. Without the slightest twinge of guilt, he climbed out of bed to clean up, then dropped back down to try his damnedest to dream of his old flame.


Gasping, Jason came, only to have the intense feelings drop down to sadness instantly. After getting out of bed to wash up, he lay back down, dabbing at the tears that threatened. He just had to meet up with him again. He had to tell him he was sorry.

# Chapter Five

Fretting about how the evening would play out, Jason was rushing underground to get the tube. When he found thousands of others doing the same, all trying to squeeze onto the few cramped cars, he groaned and knew this was a fool's folly. He'd be better off writing a fan letter than this!

Moving with the mob to the main entrance of the theater, already jammed hundreds deep, Jason knew this would not work. Even if he spent all his efforts getting near the front, which he would do, he knew no one would be able to pick him out of this type of wild horde. Not even Ewan's brilliant blue eyes had that kind of magic.

"Bloody hell!" The jostling was driving him crazy. No where in Carlisle had there been this kind of event. Even the football matches seemed less psychotic.

Only twenty rows back from the ropes, Jason found the going a bit tighter. His polite, "Excuse me," wasn't working any longer.

"Who are you?"

"Me?" Jason touched his chest and peered behind him.

"Yeah. Are you someone?" The girl snapped her gum and then pulled it out of her mouth like taffy with her fingers.

"No. I'm not."

"You look like someone."

"Unless you've been a patient at Carlisle General Hospital, you won't know me, love." He strained to try and get past her, a few more rows up.

"You a doctor?" she laughed.

"Yes. And a lot of good it will be if someone needs me."

As if that were her cue, she started shoving people aside roughly, shouting, "Let the doctor through!"

At this strange turn of events, he allowed the small but effective girl to plow a rut in the field of bodies.

When the first limousine pulled up, he couldn't believe the crush. The sensation of being crammed into everyone around him actually frightened him. Top that with the hysterical screaming that was so loud he couldn't hear his own thoughts. It was getting more and more futile.

One by one, stars and starlets passed by, waving, some stopping to sign autographs, but most were ushered quickly into the theater. Jason was straining to see him. The amount of people passing on the red carpet surprised him. He had expected only a few, when in fact there were hundreds who were able to get special tickets to see the film aired.

Then something caught his senses. The name 'Ewan' began being chanted. Straining, leaning against the backs of the people in front of him, as the ones behind him did the same to his row, he knew Ewan must surely be getting close. Swallowing, thinking of what to do or say to get him to notice him in this mayhem, Jason felt a very rude hand move between his thighs. Choking in shock at the assault, he attempted to look over his shoulder and found the little lady who had helped him previously, more intoxicated than before, and certainly bolder.

"Nice arse, doctor!" She squeezed his bottom.

"Kindly remove your hand!" he ordered.

With a very wicked smirk, she obeyed, then did her best

to get shoved into his back.

By the time he turned around, they were shouting another star's name. Could he have missed him? No!!

"Did Ewan pass?" he shouted frantically at the man standing near.

"What?" he screamed back.

"Ewan Gallagher! Did he pass just now?"

"Yeah! You just missed him!" The man nodded, then rose up on his toes to see who else was coming.

Jason was gutted. All this way! All this effort! Only to have a slapper stick her hand up his bum and distract him! *No!! no, no, no, no...*

Completely defeated, he shoved his way, very violently, out of the crowd, causing several people to slam into others and almost inviting a fight.

Finally outside the nightmarish circle, he held back his anguish and disappeared into the underground.

Sitting alone on the tube, the throng still screeching above ground until the last star had passed, Jason rode back to the hotel, trying his best not to burst into tears.

"Good evening, sir." The man behind the desk handed him his key.

"Thank you."

"Anything we can do for you, sir?"

"No." Turning his face away before the man noticed his red eyes, Jason was given a lift in the elevator. Then when he was inside his room, he changed into his work-out clothing, deciding to have a run on the treadmill. It was too dark to venture in the park, though the idea of getting himself beaten up or mugged for his stupidity was almost appealing.


Growing bored, having seen the film too many times, Ewan excused himself out of his row on the pretext of taking a pee. After the grumbles of protest for disturbing the spectators, he found his way to the front lobby and searched for a limo driver.

"Where you off to?" Adam, his current minder, grabbed his sleeve.

"I'm knackered. Going back to the hotel."

"You just don't disappear. We've a tight schedule, Ewan, and you've already angered several of your contacts simply because you chose your own accommodations."

"Piss off! No one owns me!" Ewan wrenched out of his grip.

As he watched Ewan walk away, Adam laughed callously, "That's where you're wrong, pretty boy!"

"Back so soon, sir?" The man behind the desk was surprised to see Ewan removing his hat and scarf as he came up to meet him.

"Aye. Seen it too many times. It's just for the publicity. I can't be arsed. Part of the contract, yeah?" He took the key that was handed to him.

"Of course, sir. I understand. Anything I could get you?"

"An ale would be lovely. Cheers." He nodded and found the elevator man holding the door.


Jason jogged up the four flights of stairs and imagined a hot shower, ice cold water, and a refreshing salad for dinner. Then, maybe, just maybe, he'd get up the courage to phone home.

Coming through the stairwell, he took his key out of his shorts pocket to have ready. When he raised his head to his destination, there was a man in front of his door, trying a key in the lock.

Checking the number on his own key, seeing it was indeed his door the man was standing in front of, Jason cleared his throat and asked, "Are you at the right room, mate?"

Completely preoccupied with his thoughts and unaware of his surroundings, Ewan started at hearing someone close by. He jerked his head up and read the number. "I did it again!"

That Northern accent! Like a fingerprint, Jason knew it immediately. "Oh, my fucking god…"

Spinning around, Ewan gaped at him in shock. "Jason!"

"Ewan!" Jason didn't know what to do. He was covered in sweat and imagined he looked like crap from the work-out.

"How? How the bleedin' hell?" He embraced him tightly.

As Ewan's tuxedo-clad arms wrapped around him, Jason closed his eyes in relief and complete wonder. Fate. Once it had betrayed them, but now here it was, putting them right next door to each other. His body engulfing that incredible male, Jason groaned despite himself, pressing his very excited cock into Ewan's hips.

Setting back to see his face, Ewan sighed, "Oh, you're still smashing! Yeah? Exercising? Oh, look at the body on you! Horny as ever!"

"I'm a sweaty mess." Jason laughed, the blush hot in his cheeks.

"Since when have I minded your sweat on me? Eh?" Ewan laughed.

"Can you come in?" Jason gestured to his room.

"Yeah! Of course!"

As Jason's hands shook, he opened the door and showed Ewan in.

"What are you doing here? Did you come to the premiere?" Ewan stood very near him, taking off his jacket.

Tossing the key on the table, Jason crossed his arms over his chest selfconsciously, feeling very intimidated by Ewan's success, though in the past it was more likely Ewan who would be the silent, dreamy one of the two. "I was there. Couldn't get near the place without pushing every git over. A flamin' drunk slapper had her hand on my arse!"

Ewan laughed.

"Then I missed you! Was telling her to get her finger

out of my fucking anus, and you had passed! I was hoping to wave and catch your attention. I was gutted, Ewan."

Trying not to explode with laughter, Ewan giggled, "Her finger in your anus?"

"Close! Jesus, the things they think they can get away with in that crowd."

"Aye…well, my handsome doctor, you have *my* attention now."

At that very seductive comment, Jason went mute.

A smile on his lips, Ewan stood still, staring at him.

"Right." Spinning around, trying to think of what to do next, Jason finally sighed, "I need a shower. Uh, you want to call room service?"

"I can, aye. What do you fancy?"

As he said that last line, Jason found Ewan's light eyes flicker to his crotch. "Uh…anything. You know, something light."

"All right. Beer? Or wine?"

"Wine. Italian red." The moment Jason said 'Italian', his face went into a crimson flush, thinking of Ewan's model lover.

"I remember." Ewan smiled sweetly removing his bow tie to try and get comfortable.

"Right." Jason hesitated, trying to make sure this was real and that if he left the room, Ewan would not vanish. "You'll be here? When I get out?"

"I'm not going anywhere, love."

"Be only a minute…" Jason began backing out of the room. "You want to go next door to get into something comfortable?"

"No, I can get comfy here." Ewan started opening the top buttons of his starched shirt.

"Right."

When Jason finally left, Ewan shook his head, and picked up the phone. "Oi? This room service? Yeah, it's Ewan, look, I want two meals sent to 303, not 301, yeah? Me and the doctor are having dinner together tonight." As he ordered their meal, he grinned mischievously in the direction of the shower.

Jason was under the spray, scrubbing as quickly as he could. His mind was going haywire. Where do you start? How do you backtrack twelve months and try to explore what went wrong? It seemed almost impossible to want to bring up that horrible mistake and ruin a lovely night.

Closing the taps, Jason stood still, dripping for a moment, to think. When he looked up, Ewan was in the steamy tiled room. His shirt sleeves had been rolled up, his collar opened low on his chest.

Swallowing his intimidation, Jason moved the sliding doors back to see him.

When he did, Ewan hissed through his teeth, "Oh, Jason…you are too lovely." He reached out to cup his face and kissed him, moaning at the taste of his lips.

Jason savored the kiss then sighed, "No. I'm just a bloody old prat."

"Old? Compared to whom? The slapper that stuck her finger up your bum?"

"No…to an Italian model," Jason mumbled sheepishly.

"Oi?" Ewan perked up. "Vee can't hold a candle to you! You're only thirty-seven, Jas! You're joking! Yeah?"

"Vee?" Jason peered out of the shower stall.

"Vincienzo. Vee. He's nothing. Just an escort."

"Exactly. Male escort." Jason shook his head and grabbed one of the soft white bath sheets, stepping out and rubbing it over his head.

The sweet expression on Ewan's face changed to anger. "Don't even get us started on betrayal, love. You've got me beat, hands down, yeah? Lovely gold ring on your finger." He nodded his head to it in disgust.

Jason paused in what he was doing and looked down at it. He twisted it off and threw it in the sink. "Means fuck all. Haven't so much as touched the wench."

"Wench? You mean wife, don't you?" Turning his back, Ewan left him standing there.

## For Love and Money

Trying not to be cut to shreds by him, Jason threw down the towel and stormed out, confronting him. "I told you! It was just to get the money! How many times do I have to say it?"

"And do we need the money now, Jason?" Ewan faced him, hands on his hips.

Grappling with logic, Jason made some small sounds of frustration, then ran his hand through his wet hair in agony.

Ewan softened. "Love, you could have been the one to wait, yeah? One year, and look at me. I've got all we need. You had no faith. You thought I would fail."

"No." Jason tried to control his emotions. "Inside, I knew you would never fail. You've got everything a man needs to succeed. I just was afraid of that success."

"Afraid?" Ewan's eyes flashed over Jason's naked body.

"Yes. Look at you! You've passed me by! That glorious young male that I fell in love with, he idolized me! Christ, Ewan, the pining you did over me when you were in my care! Look at the role reversal!"

"You don't know what you're bloody talking about!" Ewan shouted. "You think I haven't been sick over losing you? Thinking of how to patch the bleedin' hole in me heart! I tried to contact you! You were bloody moved out so fast, I lost you! You couldn't wait to marry! Don't talk to me about passing you by!"

"I've not touched another human being since you left!" Jason's emotions welled up.

"Right!"

"I told her I was impotent! We sleep in separate rooms, for fuck's sake!"

When Jason choked in a sob on the last line, Ewan blinked his eyes at him in shock. "You haven't had a shag in over twelve bloody months?"

Wiping his eyes roughly, Jason glared at him. "Yes! She's revolting! Christ, you don't hear a thing I say!"

Sitting down, Ewan folded his hands in his lap and kept

quiet.

When there was a knock at the door, they both stared at it in irritation.

"Oh, must be room service," Ewan whispered. "You get your naked butt hidden. The bloody bellboys all want a piece."

Jason nodded and grabbed a white terry cloth robe, leaving the room.

Ewan opened the door to allow the bellboy to push the tray in, set up dinner and leave. Ewan poured his ale and then a glass of wine for Jason. "All right, love, he's gone."

Coming back out, Jason took the glass from his extended hand and thanked him.

In silence they sipped their drinks.

Finally, Jason said, "Are you and 'Vee' serious?"

"No. I don't get serious any longer. My heart isn't capable." Not meeting his eyes, Ewan sat down near his meal.

"What does that mean?" Jason sat across from him on the soft overstuffed chair.

"You're not thick, Doctor, figure it out."

"Me? I destroyed your heart?"

"Aye. If you think I'm going to be hung out to dry again, you're mad." He set his beer down and lifted a fork.

"So? Casual flings instead?" Jason watched him eat, wondering if he had the appetite.

Glaring at him over the food, Ewan snarled, "I resent that completely."

"Well, this 'Vee' bloke—"

"He's sniffing around me, yeah. You think because I'm in LA and famous I've lowered me standards? You don't know me at all, Jason." He went back to his food.

Stabbing at some of the salad with half a heart, Jason whispered, "I can't help but be jealous, Ewan. They all have what I want."

"Jealous?" Ewan choked at the irony. "Of what? No one has what you've got!" he shouted in rage.

Jason tilted his head curiously. "What I've got?"

"You may have gone to years of med-school, yeah? But you're thick as shite." Ewan continued eating.

"You? Are you telling me I've still got a hold on you?"

Chewing spitefully, Ewan swallowed and shouted, "Why didn't you get on the bleedin' plane! You left me there to wait! I boarded alone! Took our dream holiday, alone!"

Jason dropped his fork and leaned across the table to him helplessly. "It was the timing! My fucking aunt died before I even got to her manor! Ewan, what was I to do?"

"Did you take the next flight the next day? Meet me at the hotel? Eh?" he shouted, "No! You bloody got married! Left me to me own in a strange place! During a vacation that was supposed to be ours! You said you loved me!" He finally broke down.

"I did! I still do!" Jason rushed to his side, brushing his hair back from his face.

"No! How could you 'ave? You never called, never came over!"

"I waited for you to get back!! I rung your mum! She didn't know where you went, either! Oh, Ewan I was gutted!"

"You gutted? You left me! You left me for the flamin' money and some nasty bitch who now owns your name! She's got your bleedin' name!"

Grabbing his face in his hands to make him search his eyes, Jason paused until he had that furious glare all to his own. "And my name will be scratched off her very soon. I've every intention of divorcing her, Ewan. We never consummated the bloody marriage! I've been shoving her into having an affair! I have been yours since that day you left England! Do you hear what I am saying?"

Biting his trembling lip, Ewan said, "You had no faith, none, in your Ewan. I know exactly what everyone back home thought, yeah? I'd come home defeated. Broken. Begging the fat arse Darren for me theater job back— Oh, I know. I know."

Holding that smooth jaw tightly, not letting him turn away, Jason was close enough to kiss those lush lips. "I'm sorry, love. That may be the truth. I still don't know how you did it. I'm so glad you got your dream. But we both were a bit blind back then. Not just me with money. You. You wanted this fame with everything you owned. Don't put it all on me, love."

Ewan's anger seemed to break suddenly. It was as if Jason could tell something changed. Finally he sighed. "Aye. You're right, Jason. I did need this fame. I did leave you because of it. It's the honest truth, love."

Softening completely at the confession, Jason moved even closer to him on the couch bringing his cheek to rest against Ewan's. "God, I've missed you," Jason moaned, stroking back Ewan's long hair. "A day has not passed that I have not thought of you, wished I could speak to you."

Releasing his tight back muscles, Ewan rested his body against Jason's. "Aye. The same here, love. I did try to find you. You have to believe me. I even rung the hospital. It was useless." Opening his eyes, Ewan glimpsed down at the open white robe Jason was wearing. His solid thighs were revealed. Runner's legs. Powerful and long. Very slowly, he moved his left hand down, gently pushing back the fabric to expose him.

"No. I didn't expect them to give out my home information, Ewan. The day Margerie passed on, I gave my notice. Just telling that prick, Edward Butts, I was leaving, gave me great satisfaction."

"Aye," Ewan laughed softly, "I bet it did. I know how much you hated that place, Jason." Secretly having pushed the robe aside, Ewan had a grand view of Jason's erection.

"I did, love. It was one of the motivating factors in my decision." Jason gently moved back to see Ewan's face. When he noticed his eyes flicker downward, he glanced at his lap, then back up to Ewan's smirk. "You naughty boy!"

Ewan burst out laughing. "You think a year has made a

difference? Yeah?" he roared with laughter.

Hearing that wonderful sound, Jason's heart burst with pleasure. "Oh, my love. I adore you."

"I'm sick of this bloody talk. All you wanted to do on our weekend in Windermere was talk! Yeah? I wanted a shag-fest, you—a chat!"

"No! That's not true! Believe me! I wanted your arse! Make no mistake! But I just wanted you to know where I stood."

"Yeah?" Ewan challenged, "And now? Where do you stand now, Dr. Jason Phillips?"

Slowly moving his eyes back to his lap, Jason then met Ewan's bright gaze to whisper, "I'm through talking."

"Brilliant!" Ewan dove on him, pushing him back on the couch, finding his mouth.

Groaning in pleasure, Jason wrapped around him, squeezing him tightly, amazed he had this lovely male back in his arms. It just didn't seem possible.

Parting from their kiss, Ewan smiled down at him wickedly, his hand already holding Jason's cock. "A year? That's a lot of wanking, love."

"Not half," Jason breathed in frustration. "I'll probably suffer premature ejaculation! I'm so bloody pent up!"

"Spurt for me, love." Ewan wiggled on him excitedly. "No need to hold back for me. I'm no bloody bird!"

"Take this off." Jason tugged at his shirt.

Jumping to his feet, Ewan wasted no time stripping. As he did, Jason rose up, intent on getting them into the bedroom.

Watching as that gorgeous young matinee idol dropped his clothing to the carpet, Jason could not believe this man was once his. "You are so fantastic, Ewan…" he moaned.

"Aye! Took the words out of me mouth, love!" Ewan was down to his socks, yanking them off quickly. When he was naked, he straightened up and opened his arms to his lover.

Moving to him slowly, Jason got close enough to attack

31

him, then lifted him over his shoulder and carried him to the bedroom.

Ewan laughed wildly. "Oi, it brings back memories!!"

Throwing him on the bed with a bounce, Jason shrugged off the robe and crawled over to lay on top of him.

"Still hot on raping me, doctor?" Ewan purred, wrapping his legs around Jason's hips.

"Oh, yesss…" Jason kissed him.

"Want your toyboy?" Ewan teased.

"Oh, yesssssss…" Jamming his hips into Ewan's in simulated intercourse, Jason knew he was already very close to an orgasm.

"Why don't you take your toyboy?" Ewan purred, opening himself up.

Jason knelt between Ewan's knees, staring down at him. Intruding thoughts were distracting him. Jason wanted to use protection. He'd no idea what Ewan had been doing for the past year.

Seeing him hesitate, Ewan reached out to play with him. "Jason?"

"We could use some lube…and…" Jason focused on Ewan's hand as it teased the tip of his cock.

"And? A rubber?" Ewan asked.

"Yes."

"Right." Ewan nudged him off, then reached for the phone by the bed.

"What the bloody hell are you doing?!" Jason cringed.

Ewan held his hand up to quiet him. "Yeah, uh, room service? It's Ewan here. Look, could you bring some lubrication and contraceptives to room 303? In a hurry? Cheers."

When he hung up Jason was gaping at him.

As he stared at Jason's expression, Ewan began to laugh. "Jason, love! I'm a Hollywood star. Yeah? You think they aren't used to us making odd requests?"

"I don't believe it!" Jason tried to find humor, but only felt humiliation at the moment.

"Yeah. About this rubber. Me again?" Ewan pushed the hair back from his face.

Jason shifted to a more comfortable position on the bed, then sighed, "Well, I've been bloody celibate."

"Aye…I see." Ewan rubbed his jaw.

"You?" Jason wanted to know the extent of Ewan's sexual affairs. Had to know, actually.

"I thought we were through talking?" Trying to wiggle off the hook, Ewan reached for Jason's cock again.

Jason moved his hips back, preventing contact temporarily. "Ewan," he sighed wearily.

Resting back on the pillows, Ewan combed his fingers through his hair. "All right. You want to know the pathetic truth?"

Though he nodded, Jason wasn't sure he was ready for it.

"I do have sex occasionally with Vee. Always protected!" Ewan clarified loudly. "Though not as often as you would think. No. Vee's always up for it, but, he's not you. He doesn't get me as hot as you do." Ewan shouted, "You believe what you want! Yeah? If you don't, why am I even going on about it?"

"All right! Keep your 'air on!" Jason calmed him down. "Okay, some protected sex with Mr. Vee. Who else?"

Very reluctant to delve into places he had not been willing to go before, Ewan was silent. When there was a knock on the door, he hopped out of bed quickly and grabbed Jason's robe.

Opening it to a very sly smile on a bellboy's face, Ewan took the small bag and whispered, "You'll be discreet, yeah? I trust this hotel has some ethics."

With a reassuring smile and a nod, Ewan told the boy to wait, then found his wallet for some financial reassurance. "Here." He handed him some cash. "No interview with the bloody *SUN*, yeah?"

"Yes, sir." The boy tipped his cap and left.

Locking the door behind him, Ewan headed back to the

bedroom to find Jason lying on his back, his hands behind his head, deep in thought.

When he set the bag down on the night stand, he just noticed something he hadn't spotted before. Lifting a small porcelain mouse, Ewan stared at it in awe.

Tilting his head, Jason watched his reaction closely.

Sitting down, the brown mouse in his palm, Ewan dabbed at a tear and choked up. "You...you brought it with you?"

"Aye. I did," Jason replied.

As the memories and images of his life washed over him, Ewan cuddled against Jason and cried.

Jason was very surprised at the response, cradling him and calming him down. "Shh, baby...shhh...no need to upset yourself."

Through his jerking breaths, Ewan stammered, "I...I did what I said I would never do..."

"What, love? What did you do?" Jason took the little mouse from him and set it back down, then dug under the robe to find his skin, bringing him to lie on top of him. As he kissed his tears, Jason whispered, "It's all right, love. Please, stop crying."

"I sucked a bloody cock for it, Jason!"

"Shhh, all right, love." Jason did have his theories on how Ewan had climbed the star ladder so quickly.

"It was so revolting I almost died..." he hiccuped and tried to stop sobbing. "The worst fat slob you could meet. He got me in. He got me bloody in."

As his crying intensified, Jason wrapped around him, rocking him gently. "All right, love. It's over. You don't have to do it again, love."

The confession of the deed wracked Ewan's body with its wailing sobs.

"Shhh, all right...stop this crying. Ewan, please." Jason shook him by the shoulders, then lifted him up off his chest to see his face. "It's past. It's done. Don't upset yourself." Then he began kissing his wet cheeks, his eyes, his jaw, purring, "I love you, I love you…"

At the kindness and devotion, he broke down like a little boy, in his arms. "Don't leave me. Don't ever leave me again."

"Shhh…" Jason wrapped his strong arms around Ewan's back and squeezed him as hard as he could. "I'll do everything in my power to be with you…"


As the hours of night moved by, Jason cradled a motionless Ewan in his arms, wondering if he had fallen off to sleep.

The reunion was nothing like what he had dreamed of. Back in Carlisle, in his private bedroom, he had imagined them embracing, ripping each other's clothing off, and making mad passionate love.

But, though the sex had been put off, there was something more poignant about the emotional bonding taking place than what the physical love could have produced. That sense of deep love and devotion was real, not some trick of euphoric recall. The fact that they did want to be together again, at any cost, was reality, not a fabrication of his deluded mind.

Yet, the same problems existed. Ewan lived in the United States now. How long would it take him to sell the manor in Carlisle, auction the contents, divorce the shrew, and move?

Thinking about those details made Jason's head ache. Even considering vocalizing his request, that Ewan stay with him until it was finished, was impossible. Ewan had obligations. Big ones. His time was very carefully orchestrated. He was expected back in LA, lord only knew how soon. For all Jason knew, they had only hours left to be together.

Feeling Ewan stir, Jason pushed back his long dark hair to see his face. "Did you sleep?"

"Aye. A bit." Rubbing his forehead, he asked, "What

bloody time is it?"

Jason craned his neck to the clock on the stand. "Only nine p.m. Do you have to be up and off early?"

"Aye. I do."

"I had a feeling."

"I'm scheduled back at the studio day after tomorrow." Leaning up, Ewan moved to snuggle by Jason's side to be able to touch his chest and abdomen.

"No time. We have no bloody time," Jason groaned.

"Come with me."

Though the thought was very tempting, he knew he had to fix things up in the UK first.

As he hesitated, Ewan sighed. "Aye, same problem as last time."

"No. It isn't!" Jason corrected abruptly. "All I need is a few months to get the estate sold, and a flamin' divorce."

"Yeah...right." Ewan laughed sadly, then toyed with Jason's flaccid member.

"Listen to me! I will do it! I will get out and be with you! Just let me get on with it!"

"Aye...truth is in time. We'll see, yeah?" The fingering had brought Jason's cock to life. "Impotent?"

"Have you seen it come yet?" Jason peered down at it.

"No. But, it's been very hard, love." Ewan wrapped his hand around it and smoothed up and down its surface. "What a cock you have on you, yeah? Oh, Jason, what a lovely cock."

"Make it come."

"Dirty...dirty..." Ewan giggled. "You want to shag your toyboy?"

"Aye!" Jason laughed, "I do! I'm having a nasty case of déjà vu!"

"No. This time you will. We've got all the gear." He removed the robe, then twisted to the nightstand and grabbed the bag peeking in. "All right. Not too bad. Seems they've some experience." He dumped out the contents.

Jason investigated the lubrication. "Yes, that'll do

nicely." Jason moved so he could lie down on his back in the center of the bed. As Ewan knelt up next to him, Jason inspected the package of lube and tried to see how to open it in the dimness. When he did, Ewan tore open a condom and slipped it on Jason's cock.

"Bloody hate those things," he mumbled.

"You trust me?" Ewan asked.

Hesitating, Jason then asked, "One blow job with a nasty slimeball, and then only Vee with protection?"

"Aye." Ewan nodded.

"The blow job with a rubber?"

Flinching, Ewan shook his head. "No. Naught."

"Have you been tested?"

"Oi!" Ewan shouted, "Use the bloody rubber! You're losing me, doctor!"

Tearing the rubber off and throwing it on the floor, Jason spread the lubrication over himself and then his lover. As he hovered over him, he tried to get over how long it had been since he penetrated someone. Over a year.

While Ewan held his own knees, giving Jason access, he studied his face. "You hesitating because you think I'm infected?"

"No. Just trying to savor the damn moment. Once you leave, I'm celibate again."

"Oh." Ewan smiled slyly.

Pushing in, closing his eyes at the shiver of pleasure, Jason released a low groan of yearning.

"Yeah, take your toyboy…that's it, doctor. He's yours, he's yours…" Ewan hissed seductively.

Stilling his hips, knowing if he moved he'd come, Jason tried to prolong the sensation, but at Ewan's lovely words, it was growing increasingly difficult.

Ewan reached out to touch his arms as they braced him up off the bed. The moment he established a rhythm, Jason shuddered in the climax, pressing deeper inside.

Ewan opened his mouth to inhale a soft breath as he gazed at Jason's face.

Reluctant to pull out, Jason did, then hung his head, trying to recover.

"Oh, you gorgeous thing you…" Ewan unfolded his legs and stretched out, then engulfed Jason's hard body against his own. "Give it here…come on." Ewan nuzzled against him, trying to share the afterglow.

With his face pressed against Ewan's cheek, Jason whispered, "It was perfect. Thank you, love."

Slowly rolling them over, so he was on top, Ewan smiled wickedly at him. "I'm very glad, love. Now, open wide."

Blinking, seeing that impish grin, Jason spread his thighs.

Kneeling back, Ewan made a show of coating himself with lubrication. "Oh, I am looking forward to this!" he giggled. "A year of fantasizing! Wishing it was you I was with!"

Silent, studying him, trying not to think of him doing the same thing with that—that model—Jason moved his gaze all over Ewan's perfect five foot-eleven inch frame.

Getting on target, Ewan leaned on his hands the way Jason had done, then made eye contact with him. "Ready, love?"

"Aye." Jason nodded, his eyes glued to his.

At that acknowledgement, Ewan pushed in, hissing a breath between his teeth at the act. "Oh, yes! Like virgin territory."

Trying to find some humor in it, when he knew it was Ewan's intention not to insult him, or boast his own prowess, Jason raised his hips to meet the thrusts, closing his eyes until he felt Ewan come close, then he watched his expression intently.

Ewan came, thrusting once more, his arms flexing, his veins showing through the muscles.

"Christ, you're gorgeous."

When Ewan opened his eyes slowly, Jason found that loving gaze.

Disconnecting himself from Jason, he lay on top of him and touched, nose to nose. "I adore you. Get a flamin' divorce so you can marry me, Dr. Jason Phillips."

That made him laugh. "Same sex marriage legal in California?"

"Oi! I don't care. I just want you permanently. Yeah?"

"Yeah." He wrapped around him and hugged him tight.

# Chapter Six

Adam Lewis stood before the man at the desk. "Has he checked out?"

Flipping through some paperwork, the man said, "No, sir. Not as of yet."

Grumbling profanity as he walked away, Adam shouted back at him, "301? Right?"

"Yes, sir," the man behind the desk answered, then nodded for one of his red-coated bellboys to follow the furious American.

His arms folded, surrounded by red-coats in the elevator, Adam was fuming. The moment the door opened, he stormed down the hall and began pounding. "Ewan! Ewan Gallagher, open the door this instant!"


Jason opened his eyes. His lover was wrapped around him, sound asleep. A noise of something in the hall was intruding on his slumber.

Feeling Jason stir under him, Ewan woke, then smiled adoringly at him. "Morning, love."

"Mornin'." Jason kissed his cheek.

"I've got one hell of a hard one."

"Yes, you usually do in the morning. Need a piss first?" Jason asked.

"No. I don't have to go at the moment, I'm alright. You?"

"Had a piss already, so I'm fine. What do you fancy?"

"Your bum." Ewan giggled.

"Spoilt, spoilt..." Jason laughed softly.


"He's not answering! Open the damn door!" Adam shoved the bellboy in front of it.

Opening it quickly, he was pushed aside as Adam searched the rooms. "I'll kill him!" Adam growled.

"If I may, sir..." The bellboy tried to get his attention.

"What!" he snapped angrily.

"He had dinner with the doctor in the room next door last evening. Perhaps—"

Adam shoved by him and into the hall. He began pounding again. "Ewan!"


"Ah! That's it, love..." Ewan worked Jason's cock as he pumped, wanting them to come at the same time. The noise outside in the hall was becoming a distraction.

Jason lit up first, grunting at the sensation as Ewan followed soon after, loving the sight of Jason's cum covering his chest and stomach.

When someone entered their private bedroom, they both shouted out in surprise.

"What the hell are you doing?" Adam roared. "Who the fuck is that?"

Scrambling to get unattached, Ewan pulled out of Jason and sat up. "What bloody time is it?"

"Late! Get dressed or you'll miss your fucking plane!" Adam looked around the room. "Ewan, who the fuck is the man in bed with you?"

41

Climbing out, looking for something to slip on unsuccessfully, Ewan caught sight of a lingering bellboy. "Oi! Get the fuck out of here!"

Adam twisted around and raced to shove the boy out.

While he was gone, Ewan pouted at Jason sadly. "Oh, my love…"

"You have to go?" Jason sat up, tucking the blankets around him.

Looking miserable at the prospect, Ewan climbed back over to him and cuddled for some last minute reassurance. "I don't want to. I want to stay a while."

"Maybe? Another day?" Jason asked, then found Adam in the room again.

"Ewan!" he hollered in frustration. "Get your ass out of bed now!"

Climbing back off the mattress, Ewan held his finger up to Jason, telling him one minute, then moved Adam out of the room to the lounge.

"The answer is no!" Adam screamed in anticipation.

"One day!" Ewan whined. "One bloody day!!"

"I'm not giving in to your one night stand, Ewan! Get dressed!"

"Oi! He's no bleedin' one night stand! He's me lover!"

"Vincienzo is your lover, remember?" He found part of his tuxedo and threw it at him.

"Aye! For the PR machine! Not for me heart!" Ewan threw the item of clothing down. "Listen to me, Adam! Jason's me true lover! Yeah? The one I had to leave a year ago! He's the one that means something to me! I don't care who you try and pair me up with to look pretty! Jason's me lover!"

"Whatever! Get dressed! I'll not tell you again! If you miss this plane, you're not the only one who'll have your head removed! Jack will kill me, too!"

"One day!" Ewan begged. "It's not like we have a film schedule, yeah? It's just more of this shite! More publicity for the film—"

"Exactly! Letterman's Show! Oprah! Now, get some fucking clothing on, or I will drag you out of here naked!"

Behind the wall, Jason had slipped the robe on and listened. His mind blank, knowing they would inevitably be separated, he was very surprised at the tenacity Ewan was showing to hold onto the day. And the truth about 'Vee' was also a surprise.

"How about Jonathan Ross and Graham Norton instead? Whilst I'm here? Yeah? It makes sense! The damn film is just released here! Let me do some publicity here!"

"We don't have you booked on those shows! Ewan, I will not argue with you about it. You need to be in New York by tomorrow! End of story! Now get some goddamn clothing on. I'll send someone for your things after we get you in a taxi."

Rubbing his face like he was in agony, Ewan sulked.

As the stalemate in the other room hit a plateau, Jason crept his way to the open doorway to have a look at what Ewan was doing. Fully expecting him to be dressing obediently, he was not. He was still naked, still being obstinate while Adam stomped his foot, about to hit him.

Adam spun around to Jason and shouted, "This is your fucking fault!" he accused, pointing rudely. "I don't know who the fuck you are, or what you're doing here, but now I have a problem getting Ewan back to New York! Who the fuck are you?"

Ewan shouted in fury, "That's Dr. Jason Phillips! Don't you use that tone with him! He's got more bloody certificates and degrees than you could ever hope to achieve!"

"I don't give a fuck what his walls are papered with! Ewan, get dressed before I call in for some reinforcements and we dress you by force!"

"One day!" Ewan stood his ground. "I'll go back tomorrow!"

"Letterman's show is already booked!"

"Tell them I'll be a day later!"

43

"Tell Letterman you'll be late? Are you crazy?"

Throwing up his hands in complete frustration, Ewan would not budge.

"Love..." Jason moved to him slowly.

Ewan held up his hand to stop him. "Don't you go telling me about me obligations! You stay out of this! It's me bleedin' life, Jason! I do as I please!"

An ironic smile fell over Jason's lips. "You always have, love."

Catching it and trying not to flinch, Ewan shouted again at Adam, "I've told you! I'm not bloody going yet! I don't care if you call in the bloody SAS! The answer is no! And as of now, it's only one day! You keep pushing and it'll be a week! Yeah?"

"Oh, that's it." Adam grabbed his mobile phone and dialed frantically.

Jason wondered if he was indeed calling for back-up. When Jason glanced at Ewan, he was not intimidated. Ewan had finally spotted his briefs on the carpet, however, and tugged them on.

"Yeah, Jack? Adam. Look— I'm in Ewan's hotel room and he's being an ass. He's met some man who claims to be a doctor—"

Ewan bristled, balling up his fists. Moving to prevent violence, Jason touched his arm and shook his head.

"...been fucking him all night, now I can't get him to get dressed and in a cab!...yeah, hold on." He handed Ewan the phone.

Ewan grabbed it and twisted away from Adam.

Even with his back turned, Jason could hear the man shouting on the other end.

Withstanding the tirade, Ewan finally said, "Look, Jack—it's one bloody day! I don't give a fuck! Tell them I'll be there the next night!"

More screaming came over the line. Ewan had to hold the phone away from his ear.

"You keep that up, and I'll be here a month!" Ewan

warned.

Immediately, Jason knew Ewan was pushing it. He moved to touch his shoulders from behind. "Love—"

"What?" Ewan spun around, his eyes wild with rage.

"Go back for now. We'll make arrangements."

The tears welling in his eyes, Ewan shook his head no as Jack continued to roar in anger long distance. "No…no…" he whimpered.

"I've got lots to do to keep me busy. All working my way to you. Let me get back to Carlisle and start."

Jack's shouting still heard in the background, Ewan threw the phone to Adam, and embraced Jason, crying over his shoulder.

"Hey! Jack, it's me. I think we have it worked out. Yeah. A later flight, but we'll be there. Right." He hung the phone up and stared at the men as they rocked in each other's arms. Checking his watch continuously, Adam waited.

Jason leaned back and tried to smile into Ewan's face, wiping off Ewan's tears with his fingers. "Soon, love. I'll give you my number, my address, we'll call every day."

"Yeah…every day. But, you come to me!" Ewan warned, welling up with his tears. "You don't change your mind, even if you lose the estate, yeah?"

"I won't change my mind." Jason kissed his wet eyelashes.

"Oh, Jason…" Ewan wrapped around him and sobbed miserably. "I can't let you go now that I found you again. Oh, love. Please…please don't let me down again."

"No. I won't. No way." Jason held back his own tears, crushing him in his embrace.

Adam was tapping his foot, arms crossed, "Ewan!" he whined impatiently.

"Fuck off!" Ewan shouted through his tears.

"Shhh, baby…please." Jason cupped his face, kissing his cheeks, his forehead.

"Yeah…all right…" Ewan wiped his eyes with Jason's

robe lapel, then tried to think. "You write it all down for me. Yeah?" He nudged Jason to find a pen and paper. "And you!" Ewan pointed at Adam, "Make yourself bloody useful and write all me home info on a card, yeah?"

Shoving his mobile phone into his pocket, Adam grumbled, taking a business card out of his wallet and a pen out of his jacket.

Slowly gathering his clothing up, Ewan slipped on the trousers, holding the rest of his things in his arms.

Jason approached him, holding out his hand.

Opening his to receive the information, Ewan felt something else in his palm. The little brown mouse was sitting on the folded piece of paper. Wiping at a fresh tear, Ewan couldn't even speak, just nodded and wiped his eyes.

Jason walked him to the door with a very anxious Adam already opening Ewan's own room. Ewan turned to Jason and kissed him, about to burst into sobs of hysteria, and Jason knew it. Jason nudged him away and nodded for him to go and take care of business.

Forcing himself to part from Jason, Ewan disappeared into his own room to get ready quickly while Jason turned his back, trying to control his emotions.

Only moments later, Ewan was dressed in blue jeans and a cotton shirt and nodding to Adam that he was ready. When he came out of his room, Jason was there, at his doorway for the last good-bye.

Ewan flew to him, wrapping his arms around him and burst out crying.

Unable to hold back, Jason kissed his face, tears running down his cheeks, whispering, "Soon, love...I'll ring you the minute I get back home. All right?"

"Right...all right, love. I love you, Jason. I love you."

Holding his face in his hands, making sure he met his eyes, Jason smiled, "And I love you, Ewan, with all my heart."

Waiting until the elevator doors closed, Jason caught his last sight of those red-rimmed blue eyes, then locked himself in his room to wail in misery.

After the release of that pain, he was resigned to getting to LA within months.

Scuffing to the bathroom to shower and get tidied up, Jason spotted the gold wedding band in the sink. Slowly, in a haze, he lifted it and stuck it back on his finger, feeling the weight of it like an albatross around his throat.


Adam opened the taxi door for Ewan, then climbed in beside him in the back seat. Once he had spoken to the driver, he sighed tiredly and stared at Ewan's profile as his charge sank deep inside himself.

"He a real doctor?"

"Aye." Ewan rubbed his face and cleared his throat. "Worked at Carlisle General Hospital when I lived there. Met him when I got hit by a motor."

"You were hit by a car?"

"Aye. Broke me leg." Ewan rubbed his left shin as if he could still feel the ache. "He was in casualty. I took one look at those green eyes of his, and I never looked back. Yeah?"

"He's a very handsome man, Ewan. How old is he?"

"Guess." Ewan smiled wickedly.

Adam sat back. "Early thirties? Thirty-one? Two?"

Laughing about it, Ewan said, "Naa, he's thirty-eight. Bleedin' fit bloke. Oh, what a body on him...what a piece of crumpet he is..."

Smiling as he gazed out of the window, Adam said calmly, "You think you'll really get him to come over?"

"To the States?" Ewan asked. "Aye! He'll not let me down again!" he warned.

"Did he once?"

Ewan's eyes lost their focus. "Aye. Once."

"Well, he's a professional. A doctor. I would expect that, Ewan. He's not some flake."

"No...no, Adam, he's no flake. He's everything to me."

47

As a fresh tear rolled down Ewan's cheek, Adam rubbed his leg warmly. "You'll see him again, Ewan. Don't worry."

Wiping it quickly, Ewan nodded, "Aye. I'll make sure of that!"


"Checking out early, sir?"

"Yes." Jason set the key on the counter.

"I hope everything was satisfactory, sir."

"It was." Jason signed the credit card slip.

"Do come back again." The man handed him the receipt.

"I shall."

A valet drove his car up to the front of the hotel. Another employee placed his suitcase in the trunk for him. As he pulled out into the London traffic, Jason began devising a plan to get the money out of the estate before the divorce was settled. That way, his parents couldn't take everything back from him. He wasn't going to be shafted this time! No way! This time, he had a plan!

# Chapter Seven

Priscilla invited Jason's parents over in his absence. As they dined she asked, "More gravy, Paul?" offering him the ceramic boat.

"Yes, thank you, Priscilla," he smiled, taking it to pour over his white meat chicken breast.

"Charles does a lovely afternoon tea, doesn't he?" Priscilla smiled as she stuffed a brussel sprout into her mouth.

"It is lovely," Victoria agreed. "Do you cook at all, Priscilla?"

"No. Not really. I should learn, but Father has always had cooks in the house. So, why bother?" She lifted her stemmed glass.

Paul and Victoria exchanged glances at the comment, then changed the subject. "So," Paul began, "You say Jason is at a doctors' convention? In London?"

"Yes! He was very excited to go. I wanted to attend, but he said it was men only."

The Phillipses once again looked at each other skeptically.

"Do you and Jason get on well, dear?" Victoria sipped

her white wine.

"Oh, yes!" Priscilla answered quickly, "He's very affectionate and dotes on me constantly!"

"Has he rung you since he's been there?" Paul chewed the mashed swede and carrot mixture.

"Of course!" Priscilla laughed. "I tried to ring him earlier, but he was out. I wanted to let him know poor Willie had to be put down."

"Oh. We're so sorry, Priscilla." Victoria sat back to show her sympathy.

"He was an old boy and not able to improve, according to the vet. I've his body in the freezer, waiting till Jason returns so we can bury him properly on the estate."

Paul stopped eating and put his fork down. "The freezer, did you say?"

She giggled. "Not the one with our food in it! It's an extra one, out in the garage! It was used for game birds and the like!"

"Still, Priscilla," Victoria said, "Freezing a corgi…that's a bit odd."

"I knew Jason would want to be here for it. He adored that dog."

As Priscilla's eyes misted over with some internal sentiment, Victoria and Paul once again glimpsed each other's shocked expressions.

"If I recall, Priscilla," Paul tried to put it delicately, "Jason really didn't have much to do with Willie at all. He was Marge's pet."

"Oh, nonsense!" She laughed and poured more wine.


Seven and a half hours of traveling behind him, Jason pulled into his drive to find his parents' Land Rover parked out front.

Pausing, he considered the idea of leaving and waiting for them to go before entering his home. But he was so tired he just couldn't face the delay.

Hearing the door, Charles hurried to greet him. "Hello, sir."

"Charles." He nodded, setting his suitcase down.

"Did the meetings end early, sir?"

"They did, Charles. Are Mum and Dad here?"

"They are in the dining room. Are you hungry?"

"I am, but let me wash up first."

"Very good, sir." He bowed and took Jason's suitcase up the stairs.

A few moments later the group heard someone enter the room. They looked up to see Jason standing at the doorway.

"Son!" Paul went to stand as Jason waved him back to his seat.

Finding a spot at the table, he never even bothered to greet his wife, nor kiss her hello.

"How was it, dear?" Priscilla didn't react to the oversight.

"Exhausting. I'll have a bite and go to bed." As he spoke, Charles set a loaded plate in front of him and poured him wine. "Thanks."

"My pleasure, sir."

Jason ignored the company and ate quickly because he couldn't tolerate any of them. As a matter of fact he despised his parents for the role they played in breaking him and Ewan up. His feelings for his wife were well known as far as he was concerned. This was their sham marriage, not his.

In the awkward silence, Priscilla spoke up nervously, "Willie died."

Jason didn't look up from his plate. "'bout time. He was limping around here in pain constantly. Poor thing."

Victoria and Paul again exchanged worried looks.

"I…" Priscilla stammered.

Waiting for her to finish her sentence, Jason peered up over his plate. "You what?"

Checking back to see the other two holding their breath, Priscilla found her courage and said, "I've him in a freezer.

I thought you'd want to be there for his burial."

Raising his head, expressing complete disgust, he shouted, "You what?!"

"Jason…" Victoria chided.

"I…" Priscilla stammered again.

Before she got another word out, Jason stood up and shouted at them all, "You see?" he accused, "You see what you saddled me with?! She freezes bloody corgis!! Sick! Sick!" He twisted away from the table and stormed up to his bedroom.

The icy silence was much worse than the awkwardness of a moment earlier.

"I thought it was what he would have wanted—" Priscilla mumbled.

"Well, dear," Victoria whispered, "it is a bit out of the ordinary."

Slamming his door, Jason rubbed his face in frustration, then checked the time. He sat on his bed with the telephone and hit the buttons. When Ewan's answering service picked up, he left a message. "I've no idea what time it is there…uh, eight hours earlier? It's four in the evening here, oh, forget it, early. Are you back home yet? In New York? Still en route? I miss you, love. Don't forget me." Pausing to see if anything else came to mind, he hung up and rubbed his forehead tiredly.

Setting the phone aside, he entered his study, found a yellow pages directory and looked up the phone number of an auction house. As he carried the book to his bed, he wondered if they were open on the weekends. Seated once again on the mattress, he dialed, then waited. "Oh! Good, I didn't know if you kept Sunday hours."

"What can we do for you, sir?"

"Yes, well, I have some paintings I'd like to auction."

"What sort of paintings?"

"Uh, I've a George Stubbs, a Constable landscape…let

me think, oh, a Waterhouse sketch—"

"My word! You should be in touch with Sotheby's!"

"Well, I was hoping you could represent me. Act as my agent, with your own cut, of course."

"We'd be delighted! When would you like to bring them by?"

"Tomorrow. First thing."

"Excellent!"

Jason gave him his name and home information. "Look, could you not ring here? I've a sick wife and she needs rest. Let me contact you. Is that going to be a problem?"

"No, sir. No problem at all. I'll be looking forward to seeing you, Dr. Phillips."

"Right. Good day." He hung up the phone and smiled. The plan was already in motion.

Lying back, his hands behind his head, he closed his eyes and dreamed of Ewan.


Almost dozing, Jason opened his eyes to hear a light rap at his door. Thinking it was Priscilla, he shouted, "Not now, dear!"

"It's your father, Jason."

"It's not locked," he grumbled, but had no intention of entering into a deep discussion. He as so angry at him, he wished he could ban him from the house. "What do you want?" he snarled.

Paul closed the door behind him. "We're not idiots, Jason. We can see how the two of you get along."

"So?" Jason placed his hands behind his head again, not looking at him.

"It's not fair to the girl—"

"Not fair?" he roared, sitting up violently. "You dare tell me what's fair and not fair?"

Paul replied, "Look, your mother and I thought that once you married, got the estate, you would grow to love her and the life you have here."

Shaking his head in disbelief, Jason sneered, "You've gone completely mad. Grow to love her? I love Ewan! I have always loved him! And even though you have taken him away from me, I shall continue to love him!"

"Is that why you went to London? To see your actor?"

"He lives in the States now! Not England! Are you happy you made me so sick and miserable, Father?"

"Then you actually went to a convention?" He stepped in closer.

"Again you ask me questions! Like you have any right to the answers! Like you still have some sort of hold on me! Get out! I did your dirty deed! I'm not a child any longer! Though you have always treated me like one! You have me tied to a freak who puts dead pets on ice! Happy now, Father?"

"Jason..." He shook his head.

"What!" he screamed in absolute fury. "Leave me the hell alone! But, one day—when you come here and I'm hung from a rafter, blame yourself, Father! Blame yourself!"

"Jason!" Paul shouted. "Don't you dare talk of killing yourself!"

"Talk? I'm not just talking! I'm already dead inside! What the fuck difference does my damn body make?"

"If you feel that strongly, go to him! Go and find him!"

"Oh? You mean, get a divorce, take my estate and go? Or—"

"Well..." Paul lowered his head. "The conditions of Marge's will are very clear—"

"Get the fuck out of here!" Jason rose off the bed, seemingly out of his mind with anger. "Leave this house and never come back! You don't care one bloody bit about me! And I hate you as much as you hate me! So, stop coming here! When that insane woman extends an invitation, refuse!"

Paul's mouth was agape.

When the phone rang, Jason knew he had only one

more ring before Charles would pick it up. He lunged for it so quickly, Paul gasped at the abruptness.

"Hullo, lover!"

"Yes, hang on." Jason cupped the phone. "Get the fuck out," he snarled.

Flinching, Paul nodded his head subserviently and backed out, closing the door.

After his father had left, Jason exhaled a deep breath and said, "Hullo, Ewan."

"The wife there?" he sneered.

"No. Worse. My father."

"Oh." Ewan was disarmed immediately. "Bad timing?"

"No. Good timing. I wanted him to fuck off, and now he did."

"I got your message through my answer service. I miss you too, love. So badly I ache. Yeah?"

"Oh, baby…you have no idea." Jason sat back on the bed and allowed his muscles to unwind.

"Long drive home? I'm surprised you made it before me."

"Not by much. But you had to drive home after LAX."

"No, love. I'm in a hotel in New York for Letterman's Show. Remember? It feels so weird to talk to you, you know, you there, me here."

"Oh, yes. I forgot you have to be in New York. I began my preparations for leaving." Jason smiled.

"Oi? Told her you're divorcing her?" Ewan asked in excitement.

"Well, no. Not yet. But I shall. Very soon."

"What are you waiting for? I thought that was top on the list!"

"It is! Don't upset yourself. You just leave it to me."

"Oh, Christ…" Ewan moaned. "The wedge. It's always about the wedge! Jason, I've got enough for two!!"

"Please. Trust me." He paused, then whispered, "You naked?"

"No. I can be."

"Phone sex? Are we pathetic?" Jason loved the idea.

"Maybe. But, I'll do it anyway!" Ewan laughed.

"Oh, yes…" Jason began undressing.


When Paul descended the stairs to the dining room, the women were chatting about roses. As he entered, they stopped talking to smile pleasantly at him. Seeing his expression, Victoria's grin dropped as she said, "What's happened, Paul?"

"Nothing." He shook his head.

"Who was on the phone?" Priscilla munched on another cookie.

"I don't know." Sitting down again in his place, Paul nodded yes as Charles raised the kettle over his cup.

"Did Jason pick it up?" Priscilla checked with everyone at the table, then Charles.

"I tried, Mrs.," Charles defended himself, "But, after one ring, when it didn't ring again, I assumed the other party had hung up."

"No," Paul intervened, "Jason did get it."

"Did he say who it was?" Priscilla asked.

"No. I've no idea." Paul thanked Charles for the tea and mixed some sugar and milk into it.

"Huh. Funny that." Priscilla shrugged it off, and lifted a piece of toffee for consumption.

As Paul and Victoria finished their tea, some polite protocol of not leaving too early and insulting the hostess, Priscilla's curiosity grew. In the silence that had engulfed the little trio before the Phillips' departure, she rose up and went to the telephone at the desk in the hall.

Though the other two watched her go, they didn't question her motives, very curious themselves as to whom Jason had expected to phone.


Panting, getting his breathing back to normal, Jason

peeked down at his chest to see small puddles of semen on it.

"Oh, love," Ewan moaned, "It wasn't your touch though, was it?"

"Just hang in there, Ewan. Please. Don't go with another man. I know it's hard, but wait for me. It'll be quick, love."

"Yeah? Only if you tell the wench you're divorcing her!"

"I will. Please, trust me."

"I've got to go. Got to get ready for me stint on Letterman's Show."

"Right, good luck with that."

"Cheers, love."

"Bye. Love you—"

"Love you, too."

Jason hung up after hearing the other end go dead first. Lying back, setting the phone down on the nightstand, he hated the whole situation, no matter which way you looked at it. Hated it.

He had to get out there.


Her hand on the receiver, she inhaled for courage and lifted it quickly. Only a dial tone returned.

When she sat back down at the table, a little confused, Paul asked softly, "Who was it, dear?"

"No one was on the line. He must have hung up."

"Oh. Not to worry." Shoving out the chair, Paul stood, leaving his napkin behind and nodded for his wife to join him.

As they fastened their coats at the door, Victoria thanked her for the lovely meal.

Priscilla nodded graciously and waved to them as they drove off.

Inside the Land Rover, Paul exhaled anxiously, "It's worse than we imagined, Vicky. I think Jason has really lost his mind. He's talking about hanging himself!"

"Oh, no! Paul!" she gasped.


Closing the door and hearing Charles in the dining room clearing up the dishes, Priscilla climbed the staircase to Jason's room.

Listening at his door, hearing nothing within, she tried it gently and was very surprised it wasn't locked. He usually locked it. Pushing it back, the trace scent of male cologne in the air, she peered around the heavy oak door to the bed.

He had fallen asleep, sprawled out, naked, on top of the blankets. Pausing, seeing if the slight click of the knob would disturb him, she entered the room boldly, wanting a closer look at what she was missing.

Undressing quietly, the last article of clothing left behind, she stealthily moved back to the bed again. His broad ribcage rose and fell with his deep slumber. As the idea of lying near him, holding him to bring him in contact with her skin became almost a reality, she couldn't believe the sensations arising from inside her body.

Moving to the opposite end of the bed so as not to jar him awake, she crept over the enormous mattress to where he lay. Finally along side his perfect frame, where a wife was meant to be, she propped up her head to smile adoringly at him, imagining him waking, giving her a soft kiss, and folding her into his arms.


His exhaustion from the long drive and stress of the day laying heavily on him, Jason struggled miserably to wake when he felt something intruding on his slumber. A cold hand was touching his chest and abdomen.

Moaning in annoyance at being disturbed, he struggled to open his eyes from what was an almost drug-like sleep. When his pupils came to focus on that mousy face, smiling greedily at having gotten as far as she did, he cringed and sat up, rubbing his eyes to make sure he was awake and not in some nightmarish realm.

"What are you doing?" he groaned, inching back from her.

"Just want to cuddle…" She stuck out her bottom lip in an exaggerated child's pout.

"I don't want you in here! Cilla, I need to sleep!" Searching for something to cover himself up with modestly, he grabbed at the blanket beneath him in frustration, then just used his hand.

Undaunted, she shimmied closer, leaning over him. "You can sleep…I'll just lay with you."

"No! No!" Jason rolled and stumbled off the bed, both hands in front of his crotch. "Cilla, go to your own room! Just let me rest!"

Trying to position herself in a seductive pose, which for someone like her seemed very animated and ridiculous, she craned her finger to him and purred, "Come back…don't be shy with me! I'm your wife! I can see you naked!"

About to cry from the frustration, Jason moaned pathetically and opened his door, "Out."

She sat up and glared at him. "You mean I can't even lie next to you?"

"Please, get out." One hand on the door knob, the other over his crotch, Jason was so tired all he wanted to do was sleep.

He noticed that for the first time in months she was beginning to get emotional. Through her jerky breaths, she said, "I just want to be near you! I won't expect anything! But a wife should have these things! She should be able to lie in the same bed as her husband!"

"Please. Please get out." Jason was almost in tears from the injustice this whole sham marriage was to both of them.

Her crying increasing to loud sobs of pain, she climbed off the bed, gathered her clothing in her arms and raced out of his room, wailing loudly.

Locking the door behind him, he scuffed back to the

bed, pulled down the sheets and crawled under, trying to get back to sleep.


As she barreled down the hallway, she collided with Charles, who was on his way to tend something efficiently. When they hit, she cried on his shoulder as he patted her gently trying to quiet her down.

"What's wrong, Mrs.?"

"Charles! He hates me! He doesn't want me near him!" she wailed.

Gently, he urged her to her bedroom and sat her down.

Through her jerking breaths, she cried, "He thinks I'm horrible. He won't touch me!"

"You are a lovely lass. A very lovely lass." He tried to dab her tears.

Holding back her sobs, she opened her eyes to stare at him. Though he was old enough to nearly be her grandfather, she sighed seductively, "Oh, Charles..."

# Chapter Eight

"Good job, Ewan." Adam patted his back as he stepped off the stage to very loud applause.

"Aye. I didn't fall on me face. Yeah?" He was glistening with sweat as he caught his breath from the nerves. "I thought he'd do me in. But he was all right."

"I think it's because of your honesty about being gay, Ewan." Adam dabbed his face with a clean cloth, nudging him to go wash the stage make-up off before they left. "I think if you were in the closet, Letterman would have had a reason. But, you were very sweet out there. Very likable."

"Cheers!" Ewan laughed, then allowed the young woman to lead him to the back room to get cleaned up.

Once he was washed and more relaxed, he and Adam rode in a black limousine, back to his hotel.

"So, the tabloids have already figured out you've dumped Vincienzo—" Adam said while checking his mobile phone for messages.

"He was strangling me. Yeah? Besides, I've got me doc back. I don't need anyone." In the darkness, Ewan watched the streetlights passing as they drove down the Avenue of the Americas.

"No. We want to hook you up with someone else. The publicity is fantastic. All the major magazines want you on their cover, holding another man."

Laughing at the insanity, Ewan tilted his face over to him and said, "No. Yeah? I just told you no."

"I don't give a fuck what you think. Jack wants you associated with some big names."

"Oi!" Ewan grew upset quickly. "I'm not giving the impression I'm with someone! Yeah? If word got back to Jason, he'd be gutted!"

"Just tell him it's for the PR...hello?" He had already dialed someone's number and began chatting to them over the phone.

Ewan didn't care what he was doing and shouted, "No! You can only push me so far! Yeah? I put me foot down on being seen with some queen just to suit you!"

"Hold on a minute—" Adam cupped the tiny cell phone. "You do as you're told! If we say you are to be seen out with some other actor, then you will be! End of topic!" He went back to his call again.

"Fuck you!" Ewan shouted, "You can't run every part of me life! You can push me into promoting the movie! Yeah? That I understand! You can push me into schedules for filming! For photos! I get all that! But, don't you push me love life!"

"Yeah, he's still babbling, hang on," Adam growled and cupped the phone once more. "I'm not telling you who to screw! You don't have to stick your dick into anyone! It's all pretence! It's image! You have hardly any background, Ewan! You're only a one hit wonder right now! If word gets around at how impossible you are—"

"Oi!!" Ewan resented the accusation.

"—I'm just telling you! Reputations are made and broken in LA! If you do as you're told like a good little boy, you'll be rewarded! If you kick and scream at every suggestion, you'll be avoided like the fucking plague!" Adam felt the limousine stop. He peered out and realized they were parked in front of Ewan's hotel. "Now, get the fuck out and try to behave! Jack and I know what's best for your career! So, don't blow it!"

When Adam's ear was back on the phone, explaining to the person at the other end what a 'pain in the ass' Ewan was, Ewan got out and slammed the door before Adam climbed out. Adam was staying in the next room, keeping a better eye on him this time.

As the limo pulled away, Adam continuing to babble on the phone as he entered the lobby, Ewan looked up at this stately hotel tower, thought about its vacant room, and wanted to fly to England very badly.

Checking the time, seeing it was four in the afternoon, the minute he sat down on his bed, he picked up the phone and dialed the U.K. "Hullo, Mum? It's Ewan…"

Jason was showered and dressed very early. Creeping downstairs, he searched for some movement and found none. Taking several of the paintings off the walls, he stacked them near the door and found his keys.

Opening her eyes, Priscilla smiled sweetly at Charles who was still resting next to her in the bed. When she caressed his cheek gently, he woke and checked the time. "I've got to get up to see if the master of the house needs anything."

"Let him get it himself," she purred, cuddling closer.

"He'll be ever so cross with me. I dread to find out what he'd do if he knew, Mrs."

"He's been pushing me into an affair for months. Don't worry, Charles. I won't let him do anything to you." She kissed his cheek. "Can we make love again?"

He loaded the Mercedes with the paintings, then,

glancing back at the house, he climbed in and drove off.

"Oh, these are spectacular!" Faye adjusted her glasses as she found the signature on the bottom of a Duncan Grant original watercolor. "I'd like to get them photographed and make sure the museums see they are available. Wherever did you get them, doctor?"

"My Aunt, Margerie Witcomb. She was a great admirer and collector. This really is just the tip of the iceberg. The manor is filled with them."

"And you're sure you want to part with them?" She couldn't take her eyes off of the masterpiece.

"Quite sure. I think they should be where the public could admire them. Inside our stuffy estate, they aren't really appreciated properly."

"No. I see!" She moved on to the Sir Henry Raeburn oil painting. "Oh, this one should fetch half a million pounds."

Jason restrained the urge to shout in joy.

"I'd like a special auction of just your lot. How many more did you say you have?"

"About a dozen altogether." Jason nodded, keeping a serious expression.

"Lovely! Oh, I'd imagine you'll be a very wealthy man once these are sold, doctor."

"Well, that isn't a bad thing, is it?" He smiled ironically.

Laughing, she said, "No. Not a bad thing at all!"

"I do have one request."

"Anything, doctor." She finally stood straight and gave him her undivided attention.

"I'd like them photographed and enlarged to their original size. It's just for sentimental reasons, you understand. Auntie wanted the manor to look a certain way after she passed."

"I see. And they left gaps on the wall!" She laughed sweetly.

"Yes. Precisely. Could you see to it I have, well, replacements? You get my meaning?"

"I do. I'll get right on it, doctor. I should think you could have some doubles made rather more quickly than the sale."

"That would be splendid. I may not be able to attend the auction personally—"

"Oh, that's no problem!" She smiled. "Though, I would think the excitement a collection like this will generate will be hard to miss."

"I will try. But my wife is an invalid and I don't want to upset her."

"Oh, yes, of course. I remember a note stating not to call you."

"Yes. That's right. I'll be ringing you often, so don't worry about us not connecting."

"Very good, doctor." She leaned back over the paintings, glowing with excitement. "Oh, that Waterhouse is my favorite!"

"Is it?" He leaned to have a look. "I prefer Stubbs' horses!" he laughed, then said, "I'll bring the rest by this week."

"I can't wait!" She shook his hand.

When he left, he drove into town and parked on the high street. Before he stepped into a bank, he raised his head to the cold sunshine. The Red-Green Room Theater was within walking distance. How he wished his beautiful young Ewan was still there.

Shaking off the drafty wind, Jason waited in line at the largest bank in the area. When he came up to the window, he leaned down to ask, "Yes, uh, this bank, I hear it has branches in the United States."

"Yes, sir. It has locations in New York, Chicago, and California."

"Brilliant. I'd like to open a dollar account, please."

After completing the paperwork and applications, Jason stepped back outside and wandered down the pavement to kill some time preventing his inevitable return home. Deliberately setting out to walk past the theater, he paused to see what production was showing. It was another new play he'd never heard of. Curious if anyone was about, he shook the front door. When he found it locked, he stepped away, his attention down the road.

A moment later he heard it open behind him. When he spun around, he found a familiar face.

"Doc!" Marcus shouted.

"Hullo, Marcus!" Jason stepped back to greet him.

"What brings you to this part of town?"

"Just reliving some fond memories." He smiled, sticking his hands deep inside his jacket pockets.

"Aye. Our Ewan. I miss him something fierce."

"Can you sneak away for a cup?" Jason wanted to talk about Ewan with someone, desperately wanted to share him.

"Aye! Let me get me jacket!" Marcus ducked in quickly as Jason waited, watching the few pedestrians walk by.

Still sliding his blue fleece on, Marcus bounded down the steps to him, with a big delighted smile on his face.

Jason showed him into a café and asked him what he wanted. As Marcus found a seat, he shouted, "A cup of tea, please!"

Nodding, Jason ordered some tea and bought them both a sweet roll as well. When he carried the tray to the table, Marcus helped him unload the plates, then they got rid of the tray. Finally comfortable and sipping their hot brews, Marcus asked, "Have you heard from our Ewan? I've heard naught!"

"Aye. Just recently. Did you know he just had a premiere in London?"

"Aye! *Murphy's Hero*! Our little production!" Marcus shook his head. "Sold that for six figures according to our playwright! He's moved as well! Everyone's going."

"Yes. Well, there's not a lot in Carlisle for someone like that, is there?" Jason regretted his words when he found the impact on Marcus' face. "I mean, it's not Hollywood, love."

"Aye, I know...I know..." Marcus laughed softly. "I just thought when our Ewan made it big, he'd remember us here. Yeah? I thought he'd come back and spend some time with his mates."

"I thought so, too." Jason tore a piece off his roll and ate it.

"I notice a wedding ring on your finger, doc. You got married, yeah?"

Jason's face darkened as he looked down at it.

"Ewan knew you might. That news would break our Ewan's heart." Marcus frowned.

"He knows, Marcus." Jason sighed tiredly.

"Knows? Then ya did talk to him?" Marcus sat up in excitement.

"I went to the premiere in London. We ended up next door to each other in the hotel."

"No!" Marcus laughed loudly. "Did ya! Fancy that! Next door! What did he say? How is he doing?"

"He's very busy, Marcus. They have every minute of his life planned."

"Aye...I would think so." He finished his bun and licked the crumbs off his fingers.

"We wanted to spend some time together, but some minder, Adam, kept him on a very tight leash."

"Uh oh, our Ewan doesn't like that much!" Marcus laughed, shaking his head.

"No. Truly, Marcus, he hates it." Pausing, looking at Marcus' plate, Jason asked, "You want something else to eat?"

"No. I'm cushty. So, about this minder...he some nasty git?"

"Not really nasty. Just strict. All Ewan wanted was one day. But he was scheduled for some television promotions back in the States. So, that was denied."

"Oh, crikey!" Marcus kept laughing.

As they sat silently, imagining Ewan as he was, back a year ago, laughing, carefree, and with them, they grew more solemn.

"I miss him, Marcus." Jason inhaled a deep breath. "Oh,

I miss him dearly."

"Aye, me, too, mate. You'd have thought he'd at least visit his mum. She was so upset he didn't even arrange for her to go to the opening. Oh, she almost cried real tears, mate." Marcus finished his tea and moved the cup aside.

"Oh, dear." Jason shook his head. "He should have gotten Siobhan there. I never even thought about that, Marcus."

"You know what they say, once you're rich and famous, you turn into an arse."

At the offensive word, Jason peered around to see if anyone took notice, then he leaned over the table to talk softly. "No, love. It's not what's happened. He's still our Ewan. He's just under too much pressure for a young lad. It was a rocket rise to fame, and it's taking its toll on him."

"Ya think?" Marcus met his eyes. "You got that when you saw him?"

"I did. It seems the reality of the fame isn't what our Ewan once thought it would be like."

"How could that be? He's a mega-star. Bet he's got loads of wedge."

"At what cost, love?" Jason tilted his head gently. Thinking of his own situation, he said, "We all pay a dear price for greed and power. Make no mistake, Marcus, it's not all wonderful."

"Then he should come back!" Marcus shouted angrily. "If it's bullocks there, then he should come back here! We had a laugh. We did all right!"

"I want him back here, too. I would give anything to have done things differently a year ago." Jason stacked the empty plates, then noticed a boy picking them up for him. They paused as he cleaned the table, thanked him, then leaned close again. "I'd have him back, Marcus."

"Yeah. Too bad you're married. Was it a big one? In the cathedral?"

"It was in the cathedral, but it was very small. Just a few family members."

"She some stunner nurse?" Marcus grinned impishly.

"No. She's far from it."

"Wha-at?" Marcus leaned back in confusion. "I don't get you? And besides, was it hard being with a woman? You know, being gay? I can't imagine it, really. Do you fake it?"

Not wanting to dredge up all that bad feeling and gory detail, Jason's mouth formed a grim line when he said, "Let's just say we all made sacrifices for money."

Blinking his eyes at the comment, Marcus stared at Jason in surprise.

"Enough said on the topic." Jason made a move to get up.

Marcus joined him and removed his jacket from the back of the chair. "Will you talk to our Ewan again soon?"

"Aye. I've got his home number." Jason opened the café door for him to exit first.

"Do ya?" he shouted in excitement. "Could I have it, doc? I'd love to call our Ewan!"

"Of course. I'm sure he'd be well pleased to hear from you." Jason searched for a pen in his pockets.

"Doctor! Marcus!"

They spun around to see Siobhan, Ewan's mother, about to enter the café.

"Hello, Mrs. Gallagher." Jason kissed her cheeks and smiled sweetly.

"Hiya, Siobhan!" Marcus waved awkwardly.

"What a coincidence seeing you two together!"

"Yes. We just met up at the theater and were catching up on Ewan in the café." Jason stepped aside as people came and went from the shop.

Seeing it was a busy spot, they moved to huddle against the front window, out of the way.

"I just spoke to him!" she gushed.

"Did you?" Jason lit up.

"Brilliant!" Marcus stuffed his hands into his pockets and waved the corners of his jacket around like wings in excitement.

"Yes. Well, he was a bit lonely, coming back to that empty hotel. He's in New York for one day, then flies back to LA. He's homesick, you know. Misses his mum." She giggled.

Jason was smiling brightly. Being able to discuss Ewan after the months of silence about him was such a relief. "I know. He does think of us often."

"Said he saw you whilst he was in London!" Siobhan pointed to him. "Aye!" She nodded it was true. "The premiere!"

"Yes. I did go. I was hoping to see him." Jason blushed.

"Said you two were right next door in the hotel! Now, I ask you! Is that a bit of fate?" She nudged Jason playfully. "Oh, you two were meant to be together. I can't imagine why you're still here and he's still there."

"He's married!" Marcus shouted before Jason had a chance to stop him.

"What? Married?" Siobhan tilted her head in disbelief. "No— You're a gay bloke, aren't you?"

"Aye." Jason agreed, "Gay as they come, love."

"I don't understand." She appeared terribly hurt by it.

"It's complicated." He smiled gently. "But I've never stopped loving our Ewan."

"Nor he you!" she shouted in annoyance. "He talks of nothing else! Even before today— Had I seen you? Had I heard from you? Well, I told him in the beginning you rung, trying to find out where he was, then you disappeared."

Guilt surfaced like oil on top of a rain puddle. "Siobhan—" Jason tried to stop her growing tantrum.

"Now I hear you're married? Oh, doctor, that'll break our Ewan's heart."

"He knows, love," Jason assured her, making her search his eyes. "He knows."

"Oh, I hope the tart is happy! Having hooked a looker like you!" She was furious. "I hope she's happy!"

"Love, calm yourself." Jason reached out to touch her

arm as Marcus looked on in amazement. "It'll all work out. All right? You just don't worry yourself."

"Work out?" she shouted. "Work out? Whilst me Ewan's all alone, crying over you? Work out?"

Looking over his shoulder as people came and went, the last thing Jason wanted to do was show his hand. Not before he had gotten his money problem solved. "Trust me." He held her by the shoulders and made her look into his eyes.

When she finally relented and gave him that gaze, she connected to his eyes. Letting go, as did so many others who were taken by their embrace, she de-escalated her anger and released a long exhaled breath.

Then, impulsively, he wrapped his arms around her width to embrace her, leaning down to her tiny ear. "You don't worry about him, love. You just give us some time. Yeah?"

Comforted by his strength, warmth, and lovely scent, she nodded, resting her head on his chest for a moment.

"I've got to go." He set back from her gently, and smiled lovingly into her pudgy face. "You don't worry. Okay, love?"

"Okay, doctor. I won't." She smiled dreamily at him and watched him go.

"Bye, doc!" Marcus waved.

"Oh! That number." Jason patted his pockets for a pen.

"I can get it from Siobhan," Marcus shouted. "Don't know why I didn't before!"

"Aye. All right. See ya." Jason smiled sweetly and headed back to his car.

As he left, the other two waited until he vanished then Siobhan said, "He's got something up his sleeve, love."

"Aye. I think he has it in mind to get back to our Ewan."

"Aye!" Siobhan shivered excitedly. "Buy you a cuppa, love?"

"Aye!" Marcus replied enthusiastically.

Hoping he'd not been missed, Jason parked the car and entered the house looking for Charles and Priscilla. Seeing neither were about, he headed to the kitchen and started the kettle. Then, noticing something out in the back garden, he found Charles digging a hole, a large plastic bin bag with something in it sitting near, and Priscilla looking on silently.

"Oh, Christ." Jason wondered if the new inhabitants of the manor would mind a dead dog under their lawn. It was bad enough he was going to have to dig up Margerie's casket and have her body re-buried in a churchyard. Who in their right mind would want some stranger's monument on their own estate? The entire task sickened him, but he didn't know what else to do to make the estate saleable. Getting Margerie moved would be a top priority.

He would do it with respect, but, it had to be done.

The hole dug, Charles brushing off his hands, Priscilla rolled the stiff body into the ground and nodded for him to cover it up.

With efficiency, Charles had it made into a neat and tidy mound, awaiting a stone and possibly some flowers.

A fresh cup of tea under his nose, Jason watched the solemn ceremony, feeling strangely detached. When he was through, Charles once again, brushed off his hands, holding the shovel like a soldier's rifle.

When Priscilla leaned over and kissed the valet's lips, Jason gasped and spilled the tea. "What the bloody hell?"

Hooking the stately older man's elbow, Priscilla leaned her head on his shoulder to stare sadly at the little grave.

"Cilla and Charles?" Jason set the cup down and wiped at the spill with half his attention. "Oh, this is too good to be true!" He started laughing. "Oh, yes! She finally had an affair! Yes! Yes!" He danced around the house in joy, jumping and spinning for the first time since he had ever set foot in the place, even as a child, more than thirty years ago. "Woo! Woo!" He leapt into the air, punched his fists up and knew he was suddenly a free man.

Taking off their muddy Wellington boots at the back door, Priscilla and Charles stepped in, trying not to make a mess.

When they raised their heads, Jason was grinning like he was demonically possessed.

"Jason!" Priscilla gasped, not expecting him home so soon. "I— We—"

"Burying Willie. I know." He was about to laugh hysterically.

Charles bowed his head. "I'll get your meal prepared, sir," he said and left without making eye contact.

"I—" she shook her head, trying to string together words to make a logical sentence.

"Isn't it a lovely day?"

She gasped. "I shouldn't think the burying of a pet would make you that happy!"

"Oh. No. Poor little Willie. He was a good ol' boy. I do miss him. Rest in peace." Jason attempted to form a pout.

"Where did you go? You left very early." She moved passed him, going to the sink to wash her hands.

"I took some of our paintings into town to be cleaned. The dust and grime of centuries was on them. They looked terrible." Oh, it was so nice to be in control finally! He was so happy, he felt like kissing her!

Staring at her homely face, he reconsidered.

"I was wondering. Well, I noticed the gaps on the wall." She dried her hands and then faced him.

"Only temporary. They'll be cleaned and re-hung very soon." On a cloud of relief, Jason walked through the house to the front room, turning on the television, hoping for a glimpse of Ewan.

As he left her standing there, she tilted her head back to the kitchen where Charles was busy preparing their meal. An expression of worry washed over her face.

# Chapter Nine

The phone ringing woke Ewan from a deep sleep. He peeked at the clock, found it was two a.m. and groaned in agony. "What?"

"Ewan? It's Marcus!"

"You plonker! You know what time it is here?"

"Oh. No. What time?"

"It's two bleedin' a.m.!"

"Oh, it's ten here. I thought you'd be up. I wanted to call you before I missed you."

"There's an eight hour difference, yeah? Oh, never mind. How are you Marcus, love? Darren treating you well at the theater?"

"Aye! Got a good part! He's always fair to me. And he's never asked me to suck his cock."

Ewan cringed, rolled over and rubbed his face, yawning. "Good. I'm glad."

"Saw Jason!"

That woke him up. "Did you?"

"Aye. He was shaking the door of the Red-Green Room. Seeing if it was open, I reckon. I've no idea why. Missing you?"

"Aye." Ewan smiled dreamily.

"Well, I caught him before he left. We had a cuppa. Talked about you the whole time."

"Yeah? Cushty." Ewan smiled, stretching out in the big bed.

"Oh, he misses ya, mate. Had no idea he got married, though! What's the idea of that?"

"Oh, it's a long story. It's not love, Marcus, it's money."

"Oh. Well, your mum showed up just as we was leavin'. She was very upset when I told her he was married."

"You're such a plonker…" Ewan sighed, rubbing his face.

"Well, Jason, he holds her close, see? He tells her not to worry, to trust him. Well, put your mum into a right swoon!"

"Aye?" Ewan laughed heartily at that image.

"Aye! Oh, she just loves him, Ewan. I can see she wants you two together."

"We will be. We will be." Ewan thoroughly enjoyed the story.

"So? Tell me what's happening in Hollywood? When's your next film?"

"I dunno…my agent, Jack, he's looking into some projects. I've no idea yet."

"You did good by the ol' Carlisle playwright. Heard the bloke got six figures for that *Murphy's Hero* play."

"Aye. They loved it. Ate it up. I think he's out here now. Someone told me."

"I heard that as well. Lucky bloke."

"You want to visit? I can send you a ticket."

"I would! Cheers! But, I'm set up with the new play. Maybe after. And I have to get a passport."

"You don't have a bloody passport?"

"Naaa…never went anywhere."

"Tell me more about Jason. What else did he say?" Ewan curled into the pillows.

"Not a lot. Just that he misses ya. I can tell he's still madly in love with ya. And it's not because of the fame! He knew you before!"

"Aye. He did." Ewan crushed the blankets and smiled at the warm glow created by talking about his lover.

"Look, this is costing me a mint. Can ya ring me back?"

"How about tomorrow, yeah? I need some sleep and I've got some appointments in the morn."

"Aye. You just don't forget your mates, yeah?"

"No, love. I won't. Ta."

"Ta."

Hanging up, smiling at the image of Jason and Marcus in a café chatting about him, Ewan curled into the blankets and sighed, "Come to me, doctor. Come to your Ewan."

Whistling as he removed more paintings off the walls, Jason felt truly vindicated. When he was ready, he'd point the accusing finger at the two of them, ask for a divorce, and take everything the pre-nuptial agreement stated was his—everything but Priscilla's own assets, which he didn't want.

Finding Charles dusting something directly outside her room, Priscilla checked down the hall quickly, found it was clear, slammed the man-servant into a wall and planted her lips on his, kissing him passionately.

Dropping his feather duster, Charles returned the passion, embracing her tightly.

Squinting at the lovely sunrays, Jason carried the paintings out to the car, gently setting them in the boot and back seat. It was the lot. All the paintings of substantial value. If they didn't amount to a few million pounds he'd be very surprised. There were some pieces of furniture next on his list, but only after the fake paintings arrived. He didn't want to make it look too obvious.

As he finished up he walked up the front steps to close the door. Priscilla was just coming down them, noticing him outdoors. "Oh? Are you going out?"

"Yes!" He smiled brightly. "A few more paintings to get cleaned. I shan't be long."

"Oh! Take your time!" She waved as he climbed into his car.

Knowing exactly what she was thinking, he shouted, "Be back at two-ish, so Charles can get dinner ready."

"Righto!" She waved. The moment Jason pulled out, she raced to find Charles and dragged him to her bedroom.


Bringing the paintings into the auction house, two by two, Jason smiled at Faye who waved excitedly. "Doctor!"

"Hullo, Faye." He set the paintings down. "A few more in the motor, and that's the lot for now. I have some furniture I'll bring, once these are sold."

"Spring cleaning?" She laughed, checking out the new additions.

"Well, to be honest," he lied, "the wife's health is terrible. She needs some hot sun. So, I have been considering moving us to Spain. The extra money will help with her long term care."

"Aren't you the dearest man?" she sighed.

"Oh, not really." He shook his head, smirking.

"You'll be very happy to know..." She rushed to get some paperwork and then scooted back. "...the British Museum is highly interested. They may want to make some offers before the auction."

"Is that wise?" He paused, setting his hands on his hips.

"Well, it's a sure thing. Auctions are fickle, doctor."

"I'll have to see what they are offering, won't I?"

"Oh, it'll be a fair market value. They won't undersell them, I assure you."

"Great." He nodded, then headed back to the car for the last few.


Adam stood at his front door, the mobile phone to his ear. Addressing the man standing with him first, he said, "He's been a fucking pain in the ass, Jack. Ever since this doctor-jerk has come into his life. I swear, he used to be so fucking pliable. Now I have to scream at him to get him to do anything." Back to the phone again, he said, "Yes? Hello?"

Chewing the end of his cigar in anger, Jack didn't want to hear Ewan was doing anything but being grateful. Pounding the door once more, he twisted his girth to Adam and said, "Give me the fucking key."

A moment before he had opened it, the door swung back from the other side. Ewan was there, his long hair wild from the night's rest, a robe around his tall frame.

When the door opened, the other two shoved in as if Ewan would see who it was and slam it shut.

"Jack…" Ewan greeted him quietly.

Adam knew the man intimidated Ewan on sight. As Adam stared at Jack, he studied that heavy-set, darkly tanned pocked, rutty skin, as if he had terrible acne as a teen, bushy thick eyebrows, black with some white wiry hairs sticking out from them, and a thin goatee, groomed by his private hairdresser attempting to elongate his round fat face. His hair was jet black, tight waves made it appear lumpy; a cap of bumps and holes on his dome.

He reeked of smoke and expensive cologne. What would have been fragrant in small doses was overwhelming as an after-bath splash. The gold curb-link chain around his neck had all but disappeared into a thick skin fold.

But what Ewan hated the most about him, was his power over him. Jack had been the one. The one to formulate his break through into films. Short-tempered, demanding, and extremely abusive, you did what Jack

Turner wanted, or he hung you out to dry.

Taking his time, Jack entered Ewan's house and had a gander into the clean light rooms. Tossing his hat on a white leather couch, he puffed his cigar smoke out in a mushroom-cloud plume, then finally looked at Ewan while Adam continued his phone conversation in another room.

"What the hell's going on with you?"

"Me?" Ewan pointed to his own chest, as if there could be someone else responsible.

"Yeah, you!" Jack poked his lit cigar at him. "As far as you're concerned, Adam is me! He shouldn't have to call me to get you in line!"

"Jack—"

Reaching out, digging his hand into Ewan's thick dark hair, Jack pulled him closer. "Listen to me, pretty-boy, I made you, I can un-make you."

Ewan cringed.

"Now, who is this doctor?" Jack didn't release his hold, massaging Ewan's head through his hair.

"He's a mate of mine. From Carlisle. Me lover." Leaning back, it was as if sniffing Jack's cigar breath made Ewan queasy

Finally finished with his call, Adam stepped into the room and found Jack touching Ewan. Adam paused, cringing at the sight. "I know you over a year and I never heard of a doctor-lover." Jack set the dead end of his cigar in a ceramic dish on a table, then moved back to Ewan once more, like a predator.

Wrapping his robe around him tightly, Ewan said, "Aye. I thought we were through. I'd lost him. But, he's still in love with me."

"So? You think just because some doctor loves you, you can neglect your responsibilities? Give Adam a hard time?" His stubby ring-covered fingers opened Ewan's robe, untying the belt.

"Jack…" Ewan stepped back

Adam turned around, leaving the doorway, making

himself scarce, a pinched expression on his face.

"I don't care who you screw." Jack's voice sounded as if someone were choking him. Years of smoking had made it as raspy as sandpaper on rubber.

When that pudgy palm moved under his robe around his naked waist, Ewan tensed up and turned his face aside.

"...you just don't let it get in the way of your commitments." Rubbing the velvety skin of Ewan's back, his eyes took in that nakedness exposed from the parting of his robe.

"I need some time off. I've not had a day in the last year. I just wanted some time off." Ewan kept his face away from Jack's leering.

"You want a day?" Jack laughed, the sound of some mucous slime caught in his throat.

"I want more than a day. I would like a week." Ewan turned back to look. Adam thought it was as if Jack were some nasty letch, ogling school children as he fingered himself.

"More than a day?" That rattling laughter was heard again. "The young Brit wants more than a day...?"

It was as if Ewan knew what was coming, the nudge downward. Payoff and be rewarded. Adam knew he couldn't do it. Ewan backed out of Jack's reach, closing his robe, and mumbled, "Let me shower and get dressed."

And before Jack could shout, argue or grope, Ewan had left his sight.

Waiting, when the conversation stopped, Adam stepped into the room. Seeing Jack lifting his cigar, he sighed with relief that Ewan was gone and the groping had ceased.

"The kid wants a day off." Jack adjusted his tie.

"Yeah, I gathered. We've been pushing him non-stop since we met him, Jack. What's one day? He's got no commitments today. Why don't we let him take it off?"

"Yeah, all right." He patted his pockets, looking for his lighter. "But only for the day, he's back on track by the end of tonight. I have two producers lined up for him to meet tomorrow. Make sure he's taken in for a manicure and a trim. His hair is getting very long."

"Right." Removing his electronic pocket notebook, Adam added the details to his list.


Showered and dressed, Ewan located his wallet, his keys...and his passport.

Grabbing his black leather, shin-length coat, he hopped down the stairs and found the men discussing him in the foyer.

Seeing him dressed and groomed, Jack smiled wickedly and made for him. Both his hands holding Ewan's clean-shaven face, he gurgled, "You're fantastic...absolutely gorgeous."

"Cheers, Jack." Ewan tilted his face back, away from those nicotine-stained hands.

"All right. You've got your free day." Jack grinned as if he were telling Ewan he won an Academy Award. "Adam's got you penciled in for a manicure and trim tomorrow. I've two producers you are to meet with. Both with huge blockbusters in the works. Right?" He dug his hand into Ewan's clean, damp hair.

"Right, Jack." Ewan's expression never changed.

"Now, you be a good boy. Don't go getting yourself into any trouble or it'll be your last free day." Moving his hand to Ewan's bottom, he squeezed it tight.

Withstanding the groping as well as he could, Ewan's eyes met Adam's.

Adam stared back with the same dull gaze.

"Yes..." Jack sucked in some of the saliva he had created from drooling over his protégé. "All right. Go enjoy your day." Stepping back, he appeared to be the sole distributor of time, grandly gesturing to the front door and the flight to freedom.

As he passed, Ewan kept his stare on Adam, glaring at him. He was too afraid to show Jack his anger and frustration. Adam was an easier target.

When Ewan passed, leaving the house for them to secure, Adam tilted his head at him strangely.

Hopping into his gold Jaguar, Ewan started the engine, shifted into gear, and made a beeline to LAX airport.

Locking the door after setting the alarm, Adam walked back to Jack's Lexus. "Do you think it was wise?" Adam asked, "Allowing him to go like that?"

Climbing into the passenger side, Jack grunted as he adjusted his girth in the leather seat. "What harm can one day do? If he fucks it up, it'll be the last day off he'll ever get."

Turning on the ignition, Adam shook his head and let loose a very deep sigh.

# Chapter Ten

Awkwardly carrying the copies of his paintings back into the manor, Jason tilted his head towards the staircase, wondering if he had given his wife and his elderly valet enough time to get in their shag. A bit disgusted with the image of the two of them writhing in bed, Jason shook off that nasty thought and continued to bring in the photographs of his masterpieces.

All the paintings re-hung in their correct places, Jason hoped no one was sharp enough to look closely at them. Even the frames were duplicated. It was really quite amazing. Though from a distance they looked perfect, close up, one could immediately tell they were not originals. "Hello, sir."

Jason spun over his shoulder to see his valet. "Hello, Charles."

"Back from their cleaning, sir?"

"Yes." Jason adjusted the frame to hang straight.

"They look lovely, sir." Charles didn't bother to inspect them and looked away sheepishly.

"Thank you, Charles." Jason faced him, crossing his arms over his chest. "I assume there were no problems whilst I was away."

"Sir?" Charles smoothed back his gray hair anxiously.

"Everything all right, Charles?" Jason did his best not to laugh at the old man's nervousness.

"Yes. Right as rain, sir. Are you hungry?"

"Famished!" Jason let him off the hook.

A half hour later, Priscilla came bouncing down the stair, her black hair pinned up in its bun, her dowdy clothing in place, a slight blush to her cheeks from her rushing. "Oh! The paintings are back!"

Jason heard her voice in the hall from where he was, sipping a cup of sweet tea in the kitchen as Charles saw to their meal.

As she came in, breathless, she found him there, leaning against the counter, the cup covering his smirk. "Hello, dear." She tried to smile, then made an effort and leaned up to kiss his rough cheek.

He tipped down to allow it, then continued drinking his tea.

"Were you happy with the cleaning job?" she asked, pouring a cup for herself.

"Very." He smiled, wryly.

"Good." She appeared frazzled, fidgeting, fretting, spinning to find a correct place to stand, as Charles went on with the task of cooking, not meeting anyone's eye.

"I've invited Father for dinner tonight. I hope you don't mind."

Jason did. He was an even bigger pompous ass than Margerie was. "Mind if I don't join you?"

"Jason! Yes! Why on earth?" She set her cup down in the saucer loudly.

"Because I can't stand him," he put bluntly. "He belittles me, looks down his nose at me, and makes me very upset." He set the cup in the sink, then moved to leave them.

*For Love and Money*

"He doesn't mean to! Since Mum died, he's been very lonely!"

Before he exited, Jason paused, then turned over his shoulder to reply smugly, "Maybe he should have an affair."

Charles froze mid-chopping as Priscilla bit her lip.

Seeing the comical reaction, Jason laughed his way down the hall. "Call me when the meal is ready."

Closing himself into his study, he once again opened the directory and searched for a service. Finding an appropriate listing, he dialed the phone. "Yes, hello, my name is Dr. Jason Phillips and I was wondering if there was a real estate agent available I could speak to."


Having slept most of the way on the plane, Ewan stirred from the comfort of his first class accommodation and found the air hostess coming around with a tray of coffee.

"Morning, Mr. Gallagher." She blushed and batted her lashes at him.

Yawning, covering his mouth, Ewan squinted tiredly at her. "Morning."

"Coffee? Tea?"

"Coffee, please." He shoved the blanket off his lap and unfolded his tray table.

"I loved *Murphy's Hero*!"

"Cheers." He smiled, nodding, taking the cup from her.

"I know it's tacky, but, can I have your autograph?" She looked over her shoulder to make sure no one else was listening.

"Of course." He checked his shirt, looking for a pen he knew he did not have.

She pulled one out of her apron quickly, along with a pad. He tried to wake up a bit, then scribbled something appropriate, handing it back to her.

"Thank you!" She held onto it tightly.

"Yeah. Ta...no problem." He lifted his cup and sipped

85

it, then shoved open the plastic window cover to see how close they were to landing in Scotland. LA to Chicago, then on to Edinburgh, almost ten hours in the air. He was shattered.

Having no luggage, frightened of Jack seeing him carry anything out of the house that would indicate a trip, he didn't even have a toothbrush apart from the tiny travel bag the airlines supplied. It didn't matter. All that mattered was he was away. Eventually, when he went back, it would be hell on earth. But not now. Now he had to think of Carlisle and the life he left behind that long year ago.

"I've a peculiar problem," Jason relaxed on his bed as he spoke, "I've a grave on my estate. My aunt was buried here."

"I see. What did you want to do?"

"I want to move it. After all, if it was me buying the estate, I wouldn't want someone else's grave site on it. It's a bit tack, don't you think?"

The agent laughed softly. "It isn't a selling point, doctor."

"Exactly. You've just verified my own thoughts."

"But how do you feel about moving her?"

"I think if I find a church plot, near the cathedral perhaps, that would be acceptable."

"The cathedral?" He laughed, "No one's been buried there for years."

"They'll take her. Believe me, make the right 'contribution' and they'll take her."

"It's a bit of an expensive way to go. Maybe we can look into a suitable alternative."

"Well, I just want to do right by her. That's all. Maybe Carlisle Cemetery, then."

"Let me look into it. Meanwhile, I'll get some comparables done up and come by to get some photographs—"

For Love and Money

"No!" Jason shouted.

"No?"

"No. Uh, my wife's an invalid, and if she found anyone lurking around the place, it would upset her. May I take the pictures?"

"All right, doctor. Do your best."

"Right."


Ewan passed through customs and immigration smoothly. With no baggage to collect, he was outside the airport looking for a taxi stand.

Hardly inconspicuous in his long, black, flashy leather coat and tight black slacks, Ewan dreaded anyone recognizing him, but knew with the stares he was already getting, it was inevitable. The last thing he wanted was for the tabloids to get wind he was back in the UK before his agent even knew it.

"Oi!" Ewan waved, then whistled loudly for the cab. When it pulled up, he climbed in quickly. "Carlisle, please."

The man nodded, giving Ewan a once over in his rear view mirror. "No bags?"

"No. I travel light, yeah?" Ewan tilted to gaze out of the back window, not up to idle chitchat.

"I know you." The cab driver pointed to his rear view mirror. "You're Ewan Gallagher."

"No, mate, I'm his twin, Patrick. Yeah? But I'll tell Ewan you were askin' for him."

Giving Ewan a suspicious look, the driver ignored him the rest of the way to his home town.


It was five p.m. and Siobhan was getting ready to go to work at the pub, putting make-up on her pleasantly plump face. She puckered her lips for her lip-gloss and leaned across the sink to the mirror. A noise down at the front door startled her. At the sound of the door actually opening, she grew afraid. "Oi! Who's there!" she shouted aggressively. Moving down the staircase, peering around the lower floor, she caught sight first of a long leather coat and black boots.

"I know judo!" she warned, "You best be getting out before you get hurt!"

A big boyish grin greeted her. "Hullo, Mum."

"Ewan!" she gasped, jumping down the last few steps to throw her arms around him.

He hugged her tight, rocking her in his arms. "Oi! Judo?"

As she set back from him she giggled like a little girl. "You gave me a fright! Yeah? What did you want me to say?" She stepped back from him and took in his entire image. "Oh, look at you. A whole year and I've not seen ya except on the telly."

"I know, Mum. I should have had you attend the premiere. Could you forgive me?"

Pushing back all his long hair from his face, she smiled adoringly at him. "Of course. Are you hungry? I'm just on me way to work, but I can phone Max and tell him I'll be late."

"No. You go. I'll be here tomorrow when you're home. When are you off?"

"If I can, I'll get us some time. How long you here for?"

"I don't know." Ewan felt a pang of guilt, then ignored it.

"Why didn't you tell me you were coming?" She stroked the soft supple leather at his sleeves.

"I wanted to surprise you." He smiled shyly. "Still have me key."

As he held it up she laughed at him. "Oh, lad, you are full of surprises! Wait till Marcus sees you! Oh, he's been asking about you every time I see him."

"Aye. He finally called. Woke me at 2 a.m. last night! The plonker! Or was it the night before? I can't think straight after that flight."

"Oh, you must be shattered. Poor baby." She brushed

the hair back from his forehead.

"I am. But I need to see someone."

"Our handsome doctor?" she whispered.

"Aye..."

"He's married, love." Siobhan saddened, rubbing his black leather arms again.

"Aye. I know, Mum. He had to. To get his aunt's estate. Long story. Mum, Jas is used to the finer things in life, yeah? He's always had money and he's the type that would really go mad without it. He's worked hard as a doctor, but that time he spent in Carlisle General almost killed him. Mum, he was working long shifts and had no life. He was in misery...he needs the lifestyle he grew up in. Do you understand?"

"Oh! I see now. Yes, he would have been spoilt as a lad. I see." Nodding, she checked her watch. "Oh, love! I hate to leave ya!"

"No. You go. I'll be walking down to the Red-Green Room looking for me mates."

"Okay, ta...I'll see you after shift? You won't disappear on me?"

"If I get to see Jason, I'll be out. If not, I'll be in me bed. Yeah? But no matter what, we'll get some time together. I promise."

She jumped on him and hugged him again. "I'm so proud of ya'. So proud."

"You always were me biggest fan, Mum."


On stage, going through his lines, Marcus gestured grandly, "And who do you think should do it, madam?"

"Not you, surely!" the petite actress answered.

Ewan closed the door behind him, walking down the aisle of the auditorium quietly. The scent, the sight, it was so invitingly familiar, he never knew how much he missed it until he had gone.

"Of course me!" Marcus shouted, then turned to look

over the vacant seats for his next line. When he found a male standing there, all in black, a leather coat past his knees, tight slacks, boots, and long flowing hair, he blinked in awe.

Darren, script in hand, shouted his next line, as if Marcus had forgotten it.

When Marcus still did not say it, Darren began screaming at him.

"Why don't you close your mouth and give your bleedin' arse a chance?"

Spinning around to that familiar voice, Darren gasped when he found Ewan's wicked smile behind him. "Oh, holy Christ! Ewan!"

Marcus leapt off the stage along with the entire cast and crew to hug and kiss him.

"Ewan!" Marcus shouted in excitement. "Ewan! What are you doing here? I didn't know you were visiting!"

"Neither did I, mate. It was just a spur of the moment thing, yeah?" He smiled adoringly at him.

"Does Jason know you're here?"

"No. Not yet. He's next on me list." Ewan winked at him.

"Oh, he'll be well pleased."

Tapping his foot impatiently, Darren didn't utter a word. Finally, after hearing all the excitement Ewan generated, he asked, "Will you stay and see the performance?"

Ewan looked around at the hopeful stares. "Ah, I don't know. When's it opening?"

"Day after tomorrow!" Marcus shouted enthusiastically.

"Aye. I'll try." Ewan nodded, wondering how long he could stretch this little escapade before killing his career.

"Best seats in the house," Darren offered, trying to entice him.

"Aye. Thanks, Darren." Ewan nodded graciously. "I'm holding your rehearsal up." Ewan waved at them all.

"Will you be around?" Marcus asked.

"Aye. I won't leave without seeing you." Ewan grabbed his hand and squeezed it.

"You better not!" Marcus warned.

Bowing, backing up, Ewan waved at everyone, one thing on his mind...Dr. Jason Phillips.

Turning on the lights as the interior darkened, Jason sat in the den, reading the real estate section of the newspaper, trying to estimate what he could get for the place. Flipping the black and white pages, he next investigated cemetery plots.

Ewan had the cab drop him off at the top of the lane. He paid him, then stood looking at the manor house for the first time in his life. The property was almost an acre back from the street. Islands of trees dotted the massive grounds. In the distance, Ewan was stunned to see a small herd of deer grazing.

The manor house was a massive brick structure built originally in the late 1800's and redone numerous times by even more numerous owners. Two stories, thirteen rooms, it was an obvious statement of wealth and power.

A four-car garage/coach house was detached from it, set back and to the left of the house. Hundreds of rose bushes adorned a pathway that crossed the front entrance, which was grand and graced with two massive white columns.

For the first time since he met Jason, Ewan realized why he clung so tightly to this estate. It was very impressive and worth at least five to ten million pounds in the present sky-rocketing housing market.

His focus entirely on the newspaper's small print, Jason heard an odd sound. Raising his head to the direction, he paused, then heard it once more.

Folding up the paper and setting it aside, he moved to the front window and peered out.

There, standing in his front garden was a man in black leather tossing stones at his window.

"Ewan!" Jason gasped, peeked behind him quickly, then darted out of the house.

Tearing across the gap between them, wrapping his arms around Ewan's waist and lifting him up to spin in the air, Jason could not believe his eyes. The moment he set Ewan back on his feet, Jason gripped Ewan's hand and hurried him to the garage to be able to speak privately.

"What on earth?" Jason panted in excitement.

"I had to get away, Jason. I had to come see you." Ewan touched his hair, his rough jaw, not taking his eyes off of him.

The way it was said, the tentativeness of it, Jason knew. Remembering Adam and the traumatic scenes in the London hotel, he knew. "You ran away."

"Aye. It was getting on top of me, love. You've no idea." Ewan shivered involuntarily.

Wrapping around him again, pulling him close in the cold, their breaths making small puffy clouds of vapor, Jason knew it would eventually take its toll. "Oh, baby. Please, don't worry. I'm getting us in line for millions. You don't have to do anything you don't want to do."

Setting back to look into his eyes, Ewan smiled sweetly. "Jason, this house…"

"Yes. You see? You see why I did it now?"

"I had no idea…"

"I've got all the artwork at the auction house presently," Jason whispered in excitement.

"How did you manage that?" Ewan ran his hands over Jason's chest and shoulders to warm him.

"She's a bloody tart. I told her I had them cleaned, then replaced them with copies."

Ewan laughed softly.

"The furniture is next. Then I have to move Margerie's grave. It's on the bloody estate. I'll think of something to tell the twit."

"Tell her you're getting a divorce." Ewan met his eyes again.

"Not yet. Ewan, I've got it all planned. And you know what the best part is?" Jason grinned like a child.

"What?" Ewan began pressing his hips into Jason's playfully.

"She's having a bleedin' affair! With my valet!"

"What?" Ewan gasped.

"My pensioner valet! The two of them sneak off every time I'm out. I'm so tickled about it, I can bust!"

"Criminy!" Ewan laughed, then lowered his voice.

"Lover…" Jason squeezed him close, answering his rubbing hips with his own. "She's just fucked herself. As soon as I get the money out from inside the estate, I'm going to put it on the market and tell my parents of her affair. They're sunk, love. They've got no choice but to give it to me."

"You sure?" Ewan kept up rubbing their hard cocks together.

Distracted by it, Jason grabbed Ewan's bottom and arched his back, making Ewan press against him hotly, then he moved him to lean on the fender of the Mercedes and humped him in excitement. "I'm sure…" Digging under Ewan's hair, he licked at his neck, finding his way to his jaw line, then his mouth.

On contact with those lips, Ewan groaned in agony. Going crazy, twirling his tongue around Jason's mouth until Jason was writhing, Ewan reached down and cupped that wonderful cock of his, squeezing it lovingly in his palm.

About to go wild, Jason opened the back door of his Mercedes and shoved Ewan down onto the leather seat. Pushing the long black coat wide, he opened Ewan's slacks and began kissing his stomach and pelvis hungrily.

Ewan purred in pleasure.

Dragging those tight pants down his thighs, Jason wanted one thing, Ewan's cock. When he finally exposed it, he opened his lips and devoured him.

As that hot mouth enveloped him, Ewan shivered and gasped.

The deed was very daring and risqué. Jason couldn't believe he was in his garage giving his actor-lover head. It was all inconceivable, wasn't it?

Ewan gave in, coming and grunting at the intensity as Jason continued, trying to prolong it for him. The moment he recovered, Ewan sat up and reached for Jason. "Give it here…"

Wasting no time, Jason opened his fly and yanked down his pants.

In the awkward confines of the back seat, Ewan managed to crawl over to Jason as he knelt up. His own slacks still at his knees, Jason reached over Ewan's back to stroke those exposed buttocks. "Christ, I am so in love with you!" Jason hissed as his cock was sucked by this incredible superstar.

In pleasure, Ewan sucked deeper, closing his eyes and whimpered in delight.


Pricilla's father's limousine pulled in front of the manor. The driver opened the back door for him and bowed politely as the well-dressed, stately man stepped out.

"Tend that bird dropping on the hood, James, would you?" Mr. Prescott murmured as he climbed the steps carefully with his walking stick.

"Yes, sir." The chauffeur tipped his cap. When his employer had disappeared into the house, the driver took another look at the spot in the sparse light of the drive, shook his head angrily since he had just washed it, and walked to the garage to hunt for a rag and some wax.

When he found the door open, he peered in. An odd noise met his ears. Squinting into the dimness, he noticed a set of exposed cheeks poking out of the back seat of the Mercedes. Covering his mouth before he breathed a word in surprise, James could make out Dr. Phillips' profile and the obvious long lean legs of another male.

Backing out, catching his breath, the chauffeur stood still in the dimness.

Panting, recovering, Jason sat back as Ewan did the same. "Christ," Ewan laughed, "It was cold in here only a moment ago! Yeah?"

"Now I'm boiling!" Jason laughed with him. Backing out of the car, he stood on the concrete and fastened his pants. As Ewan tried to join him, Jason helped pry him out so he could stand, his leather jacket hanging around him once more.

"Look at this coat." Jason touched the leather, shaking his head.

"It's all the rage in LA I do like it, makes me feel very wicked."

"Come here, you wicked boy," Jason purred, grabbing his face for more kisses.

When a noise of a scuffed heel met their alert senses, they parted and exchanged panicked looks. Jason put his finger to his lips and stepped out of the garage to check on it as Ewan zipped his pants. Seeing his father-in-law's chauffeur fretting by the limousine, Jason felt sick instantly.

Ducking back in the garage, he whispered, "Christ, Priscilla's flamin' father is here. His chauffeur is right outside."

"What should I do?" Ewan brushed his hair back from his face and tucked in his shirt.

"Come here." Jason held his hand and boldly exited the garage with him, right passed the chauffeur.

When James found them coming out and walking toward him, he stood up off the car and widened his eyes in amazement.

"James..." Jason nudged Ewan to keep walking past him. "I know how this looks to you."

"Sir?"

"Please. Keep it to yourself." Jason tucked a small wad of cash in his palm.

Tipping his cap, James nodded, "Yes, sir. I understand, sir."

"Good man." He waited for another reassuring smile, then met Ewan who was standing by the door.

"Are we done in?" Ewan whispered.

"No. You'd be amazed how discreet these servants can be. He won't let on."

"Does he know who I am?" Ewan whispered in fear.

"I doubt he recognized you. Now, hang back just a moment." Jason opened his front door and peered in. When he found it clear, he waved for Ewan to come in. Shoving him to the stair, he said, "Second door on your left. Lock it. I'll knock lightly three times. Meanwhile, get some rest. I know you've just flown in, right?"

"Aye. You're a love." Ewan peered around, then tiptoed up the stairs.

Making sure he was presentable, Jason followed the dull hum of voices to the dining room.

"There you are!" Priscilla shouted, laughing. "Father's here!"

"I see that." Reaching out his hand to greet him, he said, "Hello, Crispin."

"Jason. Sit down, sit down. Charles is just serving."

Though originally he had no intention of joining them, he thought it may be a way to put off any suspicions.

Priscilla asked, "Where were you? We checked everywhere."

"Paying my respects at Auntie's grave. It's a year to the day she died."

"Is it?" Priscilla gasped. "Oh, I'm sorry, Jason."

"I'll just wash my hands and join you presently."


Ewan ducked into the room and locked the door. Pausing before he entered, he studied it in the dim ambient light. A very masculine bedroom, autumn colors, wood flooring and an oak bed frame came into focus. Stepping lightly, wary of the creaking boards, Ewan found an attached bathroom and study.

He removed his long coat and draped it over the chair at a desk, then remembered something and searched the pocket. Wrapped in tissue paper was a tiny item. Worried it may have been damaged from such a long distance in a very precarious spot, Ewan unfolded the paper to see the tiny face of a porcelain brown mouse. Smiling at it lovingly, as if it had become the mascot of their entire relationship, he set it down on the desk, resting on a stack of paperwork, too dim to read in the sparse light.

Taking off his boots to avoid any noise, he then crept back to the bathroom and washed up, remembering at the last minute not to flush the toilet.


Standing at the sink in the kitchen, Jason thought his options through; dinner with his cheating, homely wife and her condescending father, or a romp in bed with his lover. The only problem was, he was hungry and could well imagine Ewan was as well.

As Charles began to arrange a plate of food for him, Jason moved behind him. "More of the chicken. That's it. And another helping of the steamed vegetables."

Charles did as he was told silently. Jason slipped a knife and fork into his pocket, a bottle of wine and a corkscrew under his arm, and topped the plate with two rolls. "I'll be eating in my bedroom. I don't wish to be disturbed. Tell Priscilla and Crispin I am very distraught about Auntie's passing and make my apologies. Can you do that, Charles?"

"Of course, sir." He bowed obediently.

Taking the back stair, Jason climbed it carefully, trying not to lose any food from the heaped plate.

"Oh, Daddy, of course I'm happy. Jason is a dream. He treats me like gold—"

"Excuse me, Mrs." Charles cleared his throat.

"Yes, Charles?" She batted her lashes at him flirtatiously.

"Doctor Phillips has asked me to pass on his apologies. He said that he is distraught at the passing of his aunt and wishes to be left on his own."

"Oh! How sweet!" Priscilla sighed. "You see, Daddy? He's a perfect husband. Very sensitive. Right, Charles?"

"Right, Mrs.," he mumbled, then excused himself quickly.

Crispin hadn't stopped stuffing food into his mouth. When he paused to swallow, he dabbed his napkin on his lip and muttered, "Just as well. I find his solemn presence intolerable. The man never speaks a word unless you badger him. What an odd fellow."

"He's just shy, Daddy."


Struggling to be able to knock with such an armload, he did manage three taps. A moment later the door cracked open and Ewan peeked out. Seeing it was Jason with food, he opened it, then closed and locked it behind him. "Oh, love!" Ewan whispered, "Cheers! I'm starved!"

"I thought you might be." He tried to set the plate down, then said, "Give us a hand, would you?"

Ewan took the wine bottle and corkscrew from out from under his arm, then pushed the telephone aside so Jason could set the plate down. He emptied his pockets of the fork and knife, then tried to hand them to Ewan.

Nodding he noticed them, Ewan stuck the bottle between his legs and twisted the screw into the cork.

"No glasses. Ran out of hands." Jason turned on one of the lamps on the nightstand.

Popping the cork out, Ewan set the opener aside and lifted the bottle to Jason. "Cheers."

Jason took it and swigged some down. Wiping his chin he laughed. "I feel as if I'm back at med-school."

Ewan smiled at him, lifting the fork and knife to cut into the chicken breast. "Come here and let's get this down, yeah?"

Jason nodded, and then knelt on the floor beside him. Passing the bottle, sharing the meal, they ate quietly, sating their hunger.

When the plate was down to scraps, they finally set the silverware aside and focused on the wine.

"She have a clue what's going on?" Ewan sat cross-legged on the bed.

"No. She's a twit. You have to believe me. Worse than Kelly." He drank from the bottle and handed it over remembering the nurse he dated while he was working at Carlisle General Hospital.

"Crikey," Ewan sighed. "I've not laid eyes on her. I am a wee bit curious, love."

Jason cringed. "You'll get sick to your stomach."

"That bad?"

"Oh, not half!" Jason laughed, then lowered his voice. "Flamin' mouse."

"I thought you liked mice!" Ewan referred to his collection of tiny porcelain figurines, grinning at him.

"Aye. Of the furry rodent variety!" Jason made a face of repugnance and shook his head. "Never mind, she fits that description as well." Taking back the bottle, he whispered, "Can you kip overnight?"

"Aye…" Ewan grinned wickedly. "Was my intention. I just didn't know the bloody house would be big enough to get away with it!"

"You didn't believe me when I told you I had to have this estate."

Ewan raised his hand to Jason's mouth to stop his comments. "Don't go there anymore, Jas. It's done."

"Right. Sorry, love." Jason caught his hand and kissed his knuckles.

"How will you get me out in the morn?" Ewan stretched out his stiff legs as Jason continued the light finger-kisses.

"Let's worry about it later. I don't think it'll be a problem." Still holding Ewan's hand, Jason set the wine bottle aside, and then stretched out along side him.

"Before we shag, I'd love a shower. You think it's possible?" Ewan wrapped around him tightly.

"Anything, my love." Jason kissed his lips, then climbed off the bed, reaching out to haul Ewan to his feet.

Flipping on the light, Jason faced Ewan and smiled at him adoringly. "I never thought I would ever see you in my own rooms. Oh, make no mistake, you've been here in fantasy, but I never thought you'd be here in reality." He began to open the buttons of Ewan's shirt.

"Me neither, love. When I think of the full circle I've made, coming back here—"

Jason dropped Ewan's shirt, then ran his hands over his flawless skin.

"...and...and the sacrifices—"

Jason kissed his nipple, licking his skin, sliding his hands downwards inside Ewan's slacks.

"...the..." Ewan swallowed a shiver of excitement, "...price I've paid..."

Opening his zipper, dragging the slacks down his thighs, Jason let out a deep masculine groan at the sight.

"...to...to be here...to have gotten on a plane—"

On his knees, rubbing his jaw against those soft, dangling testicles, his eyes closed, loving the feel, the scent.

"...risking all...just...just for this...for you..." Ewan's head fell back as Jason's scratchy five o'clock shadow tickled his thighs.

His right hand cupping Ewan's wonderful bottom, his face still nuzzling that fantastic anatomy, Jason used his free hand to undress himself, not wanting to stop what he was doing.

"...for me entire career...simply to be in your arms again..."

They were finally both naked once more. Though the shower awaited, Jason knew he had time. Time to savor this treat. This male delicacy.

"...Jason....yeah? You hear what I am saying?"

He hadn't heard a word. Moving his hands over his long lean legs, his tongue teasing the tip of his hard cock, his eyes closed in a swoon.

"...Jason?" It was softer, lacking the strength to get his attention.

Snapping out of it for the moment, Jason looked up at those light blue eyes to whisper, "Shower...sorry." Getting to his feet, Jason reached into the large stall and started the water, testing the temperature.

Ewan was silent behind him.

Allowing him to step in first, Jason followed, sliding the glass door closed. As they wet down, Jason found the soap and began washing Ewan's body.

Relaxing under the hot water, Ewan closed his eyes and smiled at this simple pleasure.

But to Jason, it was far from simple. It was merely foreplay. Gently turning him around, Jason made a good rich lather and covered Ewan's back and bottom thoroughly, then he covered his own cock.

Leaning on the tiles, the heat lulling him to a state of complete relaxation, Ewan's eyes sprang open at the sensation of being penetrated. Spreading his stance, bracing himself, he gazed down at Jason's long wet legs as they widened behind him.

Like silk, sliding in, slippery and smooth, Jason held Ewan's narrow waist and moved inside him gently, loving the tightness, the feel of him as he entered.

Purring, his deep basso voice echoing in the ceramic tiled room, Jason whispered, "I love fucking you...oh, my lovely male, you are perfect...perfect."

And answering his love-sick call, Ewan responded, "Fuck your toyboy, doctor, fuck him good..."

"Naughty...naughty..." Jason laughed demonically

behind him, shoving his cock deeper inside until he was lightheaded from it.

That hot pulsing echoed through Ewan's body as Jason tensed up, gasped and shivered with the climax.

Wrapped around his back to prevent from toppling over, Jason caught his breath.

"I take it there's no lube, yeah?" Ewan whispered.

"Not unless I hunt some petroleum jelly down, and I've no idea where to start looking." Jason pulled out, watching as he did.

"Yeah. Soap it is, then." He swapped places with Jason in the tight space of the upright shower stall. Nudging him to bend over at the hips, Ewan then found the soap.

Leaning his head on the tiles, Jason closed his eyes and tried to relax his mind so he could savor the fantastic loving.

The minute they were both completely covered in bubbles, Ewan pushed in, gasping in ecstasy. "Oh, Jason, love...so tight...so bloody tight..."

Bracing himself as the thrusting grew, Jason hissed, "Come for me, toyboy...come for your lover."

Instantly, Ewan came, pushing his hips deeper into Jason and shivering from his toes up.

After he pulled out, Jason turned around and drew him near. Under the tap they kissed, slowly, leisurely, like they hadn't a care in the world.

Charles served them tea in the sitting room. Waiting until he had left, Crispin lifted his cup and said, "Do you think you should check on Jason? Just how distraught was he at the death of Margerie?"

Her ankles crossed daintily, her long cotton frock covered in lace and tiny flowers, Priscilla shook her head, holding her cup and saucer on her lap. "Oh, no. He likes his time alone, Daddy. I daren't bother him. He stays up reading medical journals. He told me he wants to keep abreast of the new changes. He's ever so clever, Daddy."

She sipped her tea, and continued, "I know he adored Margerie. She told me he visited her every week. Well, she never had a son. You know he was the next best thing."

"Speaking of a son." He raised his eyebrows at her.

"I'm working on it," she chirped timidly.

"We've such an enormous estate, Cilla, it needs some heir to pass it on to."

"Yes. Of course, Daddy." She blushed. "Not to worry. Jason and I will eventually have a child. Not to worry," she said as a shiver of panic seized her

Under the duvet, Ewan in his arms, Jason stroked his long damp hair lazily, completely sexually satisfied. "You still awake?"

"Aye," Ewan whispered softly, his body resting comfortably on top of Jason's.

"I remember that minder, what was his name? Adam? When we were in London... Ewan, what did you do to get here?"

Inhaling a deep breath, Ewan caressed Jason's chest, stroking the hair there softly.

When he didn't get an answer, Jason asked, "Do they know you left California?"

"No."

Jason had a feeling. He nudged Ewan to be able to see his face when they spoke.

Groggily, Ewan shifted over, leaning first on his elbows, then crushing a pillow under his chin to see Jason's face. "They wouldn't give me a bloody day off, love," Ewan began, "A whole year...not one day."

Petting the long mane back from Ewan's light eyes, Jason stroked his rough jaw lovingly, allowing Ewan to explain without prodding.

"And Jack..." Ewan shivered, grimacing, "He's such a flamin' pervo."

"He the one?"

"Aye. He is."

"How did you two meet up? You never told me what happened once you set down in LA"

Anger flashed quickly across Ewan's handsome face, then some look of resolve followed. "You'd paid for the hotel. Yeah? Half board? I had about two hundred quid of me own money. I changed it up to almost four hundred dollars." Jason nodded silently. "Then I sold both yours and my return tickets for a few hundred more."

"Aye. All right." Jason acknowledged he understood.

"I sent your passport back the minute I found a post office. It dawned on me, even if you did try and catch another flight out, I had it."

"Yes. I got it whilst I was still living at the other house."

"Should do! I sent it there in only two days!" Ewan snarled.

"Yes. Right." Jason decided to keep quiet once more.

"Well, you never showed. Yeah? I tried to call your place, but, all I got was just the damn answer phone. It was very wrong of you to not call back, but, I don't want to bring up all the bad feelings again, love." Ewan pouted sadly, resting his hand on Jason's chest, then continued. "I tried to get in with an agency. I read the directory and knocked on a few doors to nothing. The money was stretching, but I needed to do something to make a bit more. I figured I'd give myself a month of trying, then I'd have no choice but to come back."

Jason held Ewan's hand, kissed it, then replaced it on his ribcage again.

"I'm out wandering, which I did daily as you can imagine. I see this cardboard sign on the pavement. *Topless models wanted for car wash promotion.*" He paused, seeing if there was a reaction. Jason was trying his best not to interrupt. "So, I knock. Well, the bloke was so amazed at my cheek, he hired me for the day. You know, Jas, all I have to do is open me gob and when that accent comes out, these Yanks are so taken by it, they don't know if I'm a bloody stupid northerner or from the smoke!"

Smiling at Ewan's nickname for London, Jason allowed him to continue this unbelievable story.

"So, I show up. It's a scorching hot day, luckily. There in the office are about half a dozen birds, all the same plastic manikins you'd expect. Turns out, it wasn't really topless. Not for them, just for me. They had tiny string bikinis on top. You know me, I wasn't bothered either way. Yeah? So, this bloke, he hands me these trousers. White cotton. Tells me anything I wear under them will be seen through it. I get the hint. I changed into the things. Nice slacks, really. Light weight, cool. I'm happy as you like." Ewan leaned up off the pillow, resting on his elbows to watch Jason's face as he explained the story. "We go out onto the lot, hoses, buckets, soap, and sponges all over the place. It was to promote some auto dealership. The birds are flagging down cars, jiggling their tits at them. As you can imagine, a line formed quickly, love. At first we were all business, trying to get the damn cars cleaned. Then, after the first dozen or so, we gets punchy…you know, silly. The birds, well they think they're funny, yeah? I get the damn wet sponge on me arse…pretty soon we're all throwing soapy sponges and hosing everyone. The customers are loving it, the girls are a soapy mess, and the few women car owners are eyeing me up." Ewan chuckled as Jason's mouth cracked a smile. "It was a bleedin' panic, love. I never laughed so hard. Then one of the busty birds comes up to me, slithers on me, yeah? Then she looks down at me crotch and says, 'Are you gay?' Yeah? Just like that! You know me, love. I said, 'Aye, gay as they come, love!' Then I asks her, 'How the hell do you know?' She steps back and eyes me again. I look down and Jesus, Jason! Me pants are sticking and see-through! She can plainly see I've no hard-on. And well, I reckon any bloke that's straight would have been creamin' his knickers, yeah?"

A bout of laughter began to well inside Jason. He did

his best to stifle it.

"It was clear I was the entertainment of the day for the ladies, both for the customers and the bikini birds. And gay blokes too, I'd reckon. Hey, I didn't mind. The more motors we brought in, the more wedge. So, we're back to business again. The birds made bloody sure I was soaked from the waist down! Loving teasing the poor gay bloke."

A chuckle escaped Jason before he could prevent it. He covered it with his hand and nodded to go on.

"Yeah. Well, it's getting later, the end of the day is coming. We were knackered, I have to tell ya. This big Lexus comes in. Top of the line model, yeah? Driving it is this big fat greasy looking bloke. Beside him was that Adam fella you met. Yeah?"

"Ah!" Jason immediately got it.

"Yeah!" Ewan nodded. "That was it. Jack Turner is the agent's name. Queer as shite and in the flamin' closet. Gets his jollies from having newbies suck him, yeah? Well, do I know this? No. He steps out of the car while we carry on washing it. I see him and Adam whispering, staring right at me crotch, yeah? Well, I'm thinking rich pooftahs. Nothing more."

The smile vanished from Jason's lips. This part of the story he was not amused by.

"Then Adam approaches me, passes all the birds right up and is handing me a business card. I thought the birds would have me! I mean, that was the reason we were all there. Not to wash bloody cars! Right off Hollywood Boulevard! Scantily clad models. Yeah? You figure it out. It was why I did it." Ewan was tempted by Jason's chest hair again, petting it lightly. "I see the word 'agent' on the bloody card. I jerked me head up and find that ugly git grinning at me, a cigar poking out of his fat gob. Adam holds me by the arm, brings me over to 'im. The perv never took his eyes off me balls. Aye, now, Jason, I don't expect someone to not look. I mean, I was dressed like the birds. Deliberately showing me body. I knew that. But, a discreet

106

glance was all I got from most. They knew I knew they were looking, but it was civil. Polite, yeah?"

Jason rubbed his forehead, hating this part of the tale before the punch line even appeared.

"Well, it wasn't polite, it was over the top. For the first time all day I wanted to cover meself up. I'd not felt intimidated even after a hundred people got their look." Ewan inhaled and said, "He extends his hand and asks me name. Oh, Jason the minute he hears me accent he creams his knickers. 'I want you to come to my office', he says, 'First thing tomorrow! I'm going to make you a star!' I look at his bling, his jewelry, see he's got some serious gold chains and the like on. Back at his Lexus, maybe a sixty thousand dollar motor? And his assistant, Adam, very good looking, well dressed, a mobile at his ear, then behind me, at all the bloody angry leers from the birds. Well, was it my lucky break?"

Jason rested his arm at his side, paying close attention to every word Ewan was saying, picturing the day exactly.

"I thought it was, love." Ewan sighed, cupping Jason's melancholy face. "The birds? Never said another word to me. They hated me from then on. Well, I thought it had to be legit. Next morning, got me best clothing on and took a cab to his office. Oh, love, very posh! Faces of stars I recognized all over the bloody walls! The place dripped of money. I'm shown in to his office. Adam's there, ready to take all me details, filling out contracts. They knew. They knew I was a nothing and they had what I wanted. I wasn't the first, I won't be their last." Moving his leg higher on Jason's body, Ewan gently laid his thigh on top of Jason's genitals. "I thought it was all cushty, Jason…the contracts, the big office. There I am imagining me mum, Marcus, you, all so proud of me." He smiled, his eyes misting over. "Then…Adam leaves us. I'm about to sign on the dotted line, yeah? when Jack snatches the pen from me fingers. I stood straight, feeling very confused. He says just what bloody Darren said, 'How bad do you want it?' You remember what I told you? When Darren asked if I wanted the part in that play over a year ago? Remember, Jas? But, I told him to fuck off...remember?"

Jason nodded, then felt Ewan's body shiver.

"I got sick all over. Oh, I knew what that line meant. I'd heard it before from another fat ugly git who couldn't get laid unless he paid, yeah? This bloke was a monster. Ugly as they come, Jason. Ugly as they come." Ewan cringed. "He sees me hesitate. Shows me an audition list. Asks me if I'd like to be starring along with George Clooney and Tom Cruise in their next film. Oi! I thought he was joking, but he wasn't! It was there in his hand. My chance. I told him I wanted that chance. Then just like bloody Darren, but infinitely worse, he opens his flamin' trousers. If you knew how sick I felt, Jason. If you knew..." He paused, swallowing the black water that rose in his throat.

"Don't tell me anymore. I don't need to know what happened next." Jason was so angry he was about to fly to LA and buy a shotgun.

"Aye. You already know. Within a month I'm starring in a small role with those very men. He did come through. It wasn't a hollow promise. I showed him *Murphy's Hero*. He asked if I'd like to be the star. Christ, Jas, it was happening so quickly me head was spinning. Aye! I said, I would! Again, he opens his bloody zipper."

Lowering his lashes, Ewan tried to get through it as Jason's chest was beginning to rise and fall rapidly as his fury grew.

"I stayed away from him after that. He'd already found another bloke to abuse, according to Adam. I was last week's trash. But there I was. Starring in me first big movie. It was the worst mixture of pride and disgust I'd ever felt in me life. I keep askin' meself, would I have been discovered otherwise? Would I have made it without—without doing the thing I did? I know the answer. No. I would not have made it. I would have been washing cars on Hollywood Boulevard, or waiting tables. Yeah? I know. But he gave me a name. He made me something I couldn't have been. Though I will never be grateful, I do feel, well, chosen. But I can't stand him, Jason! When he gropes me, I get physically sick! The day I asked for some time off—yesterday?" Ewan rubbed his face. "He catches me just awake. Opens me bloody robe up as he talks to me. And what do I do? Nothing! Allow it! I'm so intimidated by him, I do nothing!"

"Shhh…" Jason could tell he was growing upset and his volume had increased. Cuddling him, hoping no one was near the hall and doorway, he kissed his face in an attempt at calming him.

Ewan took a few deep breaths, then spoke softly. "It was then I decided. I just grabbed me passport and left. I know when I return the wrath of Mr. Turner will be brutal. He'll kick me out. I'm through with being on his client list. He had two movies I was to audition for. Not now, love. Not now."

"You don't need him! Ewan, we have choices!" Jason tried to keep his voice down as well. "You could stay here, go there, get a new agent or represent yourself! Everyone knows your name now."

"No. No, love. It doesn't work that way. You get branded with a reputation and labeled a pariah. I'm not the only one it's happened to, Jas. On the street they call it getting 'the couch' treatment. I can't do a thing about it. It's his word against mine. And if I do say something, if I do try and stop it, what does that make me look like, love? A slut. A flamin' slapper. I'm stuck with it. Like it as not. Yeah? You see? No one will have me. If he drops me, I'm done in Hollywood."

Squeezing him, holding him tight, Jason whispered, "Is that so bad? Do you need to continue now that you've proven yourself?"

"Proven meself?" Ewan sat up and shook his head at him in disbelief. "Proven what? That I can suck a fat git's cock and get a part? Proven what?"

"Hush, all right…" Jason tried to calm him again. "We'll talk more about it. I just don't want that man near you!" Jason growled. "Right now I want to kill the fucker! You are not to go near him again!"

"Aye…aye…I know." Ewan lay his head back down on Jason's chest, cuddling.

"Baby…" Jason purred, "Let's sleep on it. Okay? It's too late and we're too tired."

"Aye. I'm over-tired."

"Exactly. Close your eyes and try and rest, love. We'll figure it all out. You'll see." Jason kissed his hair.

"Aye…as long as you are with me. I'll be all right." Ewan closed his eyes and let go a deep sigh.

Rubbing him gently, wanting him to sleep, Jason wrapped around him protectively. Never would anyone take advantage of him again. Never!


"Good-night, Daddy." Priscilla walked him to the door.

"Night, Cilla. You be a good girl."

"I will. I'll ring you soon." She waved as James opened the car for him, waited until the limousine had vanished, then smiled in excitement and rushed to find Charles.

He was loading the dishwasher, just finishing up. Feeling her arms surround his waist, he smiled sweetly. "Has your father gone, Cilla?"

"Yes, Charles. And I want to go to bed." She kissed his neck.

"We need be very careful, Mrs. I don't want the doctor finding out."

"Don't worry!" Grabbing his hand she dragged him up the staircase. As they passed Jason's suite of rooms, they heard a low murmur of voices.

Priscilla paused to listen.

"What is it, Mrs.?" Charles whispered.

"His voice. He's talking."

"On the phone perhaps?"

"This late?" She raised Charles' wrist to check the time on his watch. It was nearing nine p.m.

Charles shrugged.

"Oh, well, never mind." She resumed escorting him to her bedroom.

# Chapter Eleven

A light rap woke Jason out of his deep slumber. Coming aware, he found Ewan still out of it next to him and another tapping sound from the door. "Yes?"

"Would you be needing breakfast or coffee, sir?"

"Ahhh, later. I've decided to have a lay-in, Charles."

"Very good, sir."

The clock on his nightstand read 8:15.

Hearing the noise, Ewan stirred, rolling over and trying to open his eyes. Smiling up at Jason, he whispered, "Morning, love."

"Oh, I do love this arrangement. You, here in my bed again. I remember it well."

"Aye. Me as well. It was a lovely bit of bliss." He stretched, finding Jason's legs under the covers.

"And I want it back." Jason curled around him, nuzzling his neck under his hair.

"Oh, doctor, you say all the right things to me!" Ewan batted his eyes coquettishly.

Loving the tease, Jason wrapped around him, dragging him on top. When he felt that hard morning cock he spread his thighs for it. "You have to hit the loo?" Jason whispered.

"No. I'm all right."

"Mmmm…" Jason clamped his thighs shut, trapping Ewan's cock between them, and started kissing his neck and rough jaw.

Loving the tightness, Ewan began pumping his hips. "Lovely…lovely …" He closed his eyes, raising up for a better angle.

Jason watched his expressions change from passive, to interested, to on-fire, to climax.

Gasping, arching his back, Ewan came creating a sticky hot wetness between Jason's legs. Completely taken by this young male, Jason embraced him, bringing him back down, chest to chest, to sniff and cuddle.

And sated like never before, Ewan whispered into his ear, "I love you, love you, love you…"

A deep rumbling laughter erupted from Jason's chest. Mimicking Ewan's comment of a moment before, he said, "Oh, Mr. Gallagher, you say all the right things!"

Ewan sat up, grinned impishly, then squirmed his way down Jason's body to get his mouth around his hard-on.

Closing his eyes, wanting this to be permanent, wanting them to live at a beautiful home near a sandy beach together forever in peace and luxury, Jason knew he had a long road ahead to achieve that goal. But, for now, he needed to push all the distracting thoughts out of his head, for a more carnal diversion took priority at the moment.


Sipping coffee as Charles made her breakfast, Priscilla peered up to see Jason standing at the doorway. "Oh! Good morning, dear!"

Jason nodded, tight-lipped, and poured a cup of coffee for himself. "I'm off early. Be gone all day."

"Oh? Doing what?" Trying not to act excited, she put on a serious expression.

"Errands. Shall I ring you when I'm on my way back? To give you notice?"

Charles froze mid-way buttering toast, as Priscilla choked on her coffee.

Though Jason knew very well what they were all talking about, he added, "So Charles can prepare dinner."

Priscilla shook her head vigorously. "Yes! Good thinking, Jason. Yes."

"Right." Without saying good-bye, Jason left the room.

With a silly grin on her face, Priscilla turned to look at Charles' expression of concern.


Ewan was standing on top of the landing. When Jason nodded to him, he came down quickly and was handed the coffee to take with him. They left through the front of the house without looking back.

Standing, her coffee cup in her hand, Priscilla wanted to make sure Jason had actually left the house before playing with Charles. She moved stealthily to the front windows and peered out. The Mercedes was backing out of the garage. It appeared two people were in it. Squinting to get a better look, she caught just a glimpse of long dark hair. "What? Who is that woman?" As the car vanished down the lane she began shouting, "Charles! Charles!"

Rushing when he heard her call, he came in to see her pale face. "What's happened?"

"I thought I just saw a woman in Jason's car!"

"A woman?" Charles tilted his head in disbelief.

"Yes! She had very long dark hair! Just now! I swear to you!"

Breathing out a sigh, Charles shook his head and replied, "Cilla, dear, your imagination is playing tricks on you. I fear it's only your guilty conscience that has perceived it. That is all. Doctor Phillips would never bring another woman to the manor. And if you think logically about it, when could she have come? You see? Use your head, Cilla."

"No...no, you're right, Charles. I must have been

imagining it."

"Yes. You must have." Making a move to continue what he was doing, she followed like a puppy dog and asked in excitement, "What shall we do today?"

"Jason! Love!" Siobhan opened the door to the flat when she heard someone trying to put the key in. "You and our Ewan finally met up again!"

"Aye." Jason kissed her cheek affectionately.

"Put the kettle on, Mother!" Ewan shouted enthusiastically, taking off his long coat.

"Yes! A cup of tea! Oh, it is a bit nippy out there!" She rubbed her hands together briskly and made for the kitchen.

"Give us your coat, love." Ewan reached out to help Jason take off his jacket, then hung them both up by the door.

"Ewan, love…" Siobhan set out three mugs. "I got a very frantic call from a Mr. Lewis."

Ewan cringed.

"He asked if I had seen you. I didn't know what to say, love." She dropped a tea bag in each.

"Mr. Lewis?" Jason asked.

"Adam," Ewan answered.

"Ah…" Jason nodded.

"What did you tell him, Mum?" Ewan leaned against the wall in the tiny kitchen as she poured boiling water into each mismatched mug.

"I said I hadn't heard from you. Oh, I could tell by his tone and temper I shouldn't say you were here! What did you do, Ewan? Did you leave without telling them?" Setting the kettle down, she turned to look at him, shaking her head. "You've a good thing in Hollywood. You shouldn't upset anyone."

"I missed me lover." Ewan opened the top of the sugar bowl and dipped his spoon in. "They wouldn't give me time off, Mum. What was I to do?"

"No time to come home? No holiday?" She set the mugs on the table for them both to prepare the way they like it. "There's milk in the refrigerator, Jason."

Spinning around to it, he opened it and took out the carton.

"No, Mum. Not even a day! I was losing me mind!" Ewan stirred the sugar into the cup, then nodded yes to Jason's offer to pour his milk for him. "I had to get back to see 'im. You know how I feel about 'im."

"Aye! I do!" she shouted in irritation. "But, you've got a proper job to do, and he's got a wife!"

Jason flinched at the comment, averting her eyes as he stirred his cup.

"Not in the proper way! He's never even shagged her!"

"Ewan…" Jason didn't want his personal laundry hung out to dry.

"Well, that's besides the point!" Siobhan raised her tea and blew off the steam. "I want to know if you've risked your career for this— this escapade!"

The pout formed quickly on Ewan's lips. "If I'd've known I was in for a bullocking, I wouldn't have bothered to stop by."

"Oh, stop acting like a child." She snorted. "Now, you get on the phone and ring Mr. Lewis! This instant!"

"I can't. It's eight hours behind, Mum. It'd be one in the morning." Ewan bit his lip in anxiety.

"I don't understand you." She exhaled in irritation. "All your life you've wanted to be a star. And now that you are, you ruin it!"

"Mum!"

Siobhan turned to a silent Jason. "You tell him! You tell him he's ruining his career over a married man!"

Again Jason flinched, not answering her, not looking at anything but his tea.

Ewan puffed up in anger. "Shut up!" he screamed. "You don't know what you're talking about! Yeah? You just keep your oar out and let us get on with it! If you don't like us

116

around, we'd be happy to avoid you! Is that what you want? Or do you want to at least act sympathetic to two blokes who are madly in love and have some obstacles to get over. Yeah? Which is it?"

Suddenly, the wind out of her righteous sails, Siobhan deflated and sighed, "No. You're right, love. I know what you two mean to each other. I knew it from the start. How you ever got into this kind of jam I don't know. If you ask me, you should have been together a year back. Not like this. Not an ocean between you."

Both men stood silently absorbing the comments. An 'ocean between them'. Is that really where they were? And as to how they had come that far, well it was as clear as the queen's face on a ten pound note.

Jason was the first to succumb to the painful reality. He left the room, wandering to the lounge, gazing at some photos of Ewan as a child.

Ewan shivered visibly when he did. Setting his empty mug in the sink, he exhaled and then addressed his mother, "We know we have some very big problems, Mum. But it doesn't help, you pushing it into our face."

Siobhan avoided his eyes. "I just want what's best for you, love."

"Aye. I know. And what's best for me is Jason. Full stop."

"You're giving up on acting then?" she whispered.

Once again, faced with the same dilemma, Ewan said, "No. I couldn't do that and be complete as a man."


In the photo Ewan was thirteen. He was standing with a group of young lads all in their soccer uniforms. Even at that age, he stood out. His pretty features made the rest seem flat and dull. Jason imagined knowing him then. Except he would have been almost thirty. A thirty year old male admiring a thirteen year old boy. How sick is that?

"Jason?"

His half full mug in his hand, 'Newcastle United' written on the side of it, he turned lazily to face his twenty-one year old lover. A thirty-seven year old with a twenty-one year old. He had to ask himself, *How sick is that?* yet again.

Tilting his head curiously, Ewan drew near. "Lover—don't let what she says affect you. Yeah? Please?"

Jason lifted the frame off the mantel. "How old were you?"

"Oi?" Ewan appeared confused, then looked at the photo. "I was in school, eh...I dunno. Twelve? Thirteen? Why?"

"I would have been twenty-nine, thirty."

"So?" Ewan set it back and tried to see the significance.

Jason rubbed his free hand over his eyes and face tiredly.

"Oi!" Ewan growled, "Age never entered in before! Don't you throw another bleedin' issue at us! I think we have enough to deal with, yeah?"

"I'm ruining a promising young man's acting career—"

Gutted, Ewan snatched the cup from Jason's hand, set it on the coffee table and then gripped him by the lapels of his cotton shirt, dragging him close. "Don't you do this! Don't you move away from being on my side! You have to stick with me! You can't change your mind!"

Siobhan heard her son's voice rise in anger. Moving to the edge of the hall, she lowered her head to listen.

Jason didn't know what the right thing to do was anymore. Life was such a complicated mess.

Ewan shook him violently. "I love ya! You listening to me, Dr. Jason Phillips!? From the first time I set me eyes on you in the casualty room, I loved ya! No matter what this bloody world throws at me I will still love ya! You can drag me away kicking and screaming, yeah? But, you'll still be in me! You are me very soul! I lost you once and I died! Do you hear me? I died!" He choked up. "You stop being defeated! We'll get there! By hell or high water! We'll get back together!"

Siobhan dabbed at a tear before it fell.

"Jason!" Ewan gasped in exasperation. "Look at me, love! Look at me and tell me you think what we have isn't worth fighting for!"

Forcing himself to raise his dark lashes, Jason met that brilliant sky blue stare. Ewan's pupils were dilated from his panic and the dim light, but there was a ring of the most amazing color surrounding that black hole.

The moment Jason connected to his eyes, Ewan jumped on him, wrapping his arms around his neck and sucking on his mouth.

As that eager tongue made its way in, a tear of emotion ran down Jason's face. Kissing him passionately, never wanting to let him go, Jason rocked him in his arms, fully aware that being together was the only acceptable solution. And he would do whatever it took.

Creeping to the edge of the wall, Siobhan found them in a deep swoon. She smiled sadly, hoping against all the odds, they could somehow live happily ever after.


First thing in the morning Adam made some more phone calls. "Yes, this is Adam Lewis, I was talking to a detective about—yes...you did? Where? Oh, for Pete's sake. Thanks. Right. I'll take care of it." He hung up and dialed frantically. "Jack?"

"What?"

"His Jag was just located at LAX."

"No great surprise."

"What do you want me to do?"

"Go get it. Bring it back to his house so nothing happens to it."

"Then?"

"Then nothing. We wait."

"You know he went to England to be with that doctor."

"Another big surprise." He coughed as he laughed,

choking up phlegm.

"You going to can him?"

"Naaa, wouldn't be the first time a star has gone a bit AWOL. Besides, he's become a commodity. Let him have his fling. He'll figure out he needs this place. We'll make a show of it when he gets back. Make him think he was on the brink."

Adam was very surprised Jack was taking it so calmly, but then again, he'd been in the business for almost thirty years. He'd dealt with much worse. At least Ewan was drug free and not dependant on alcohol. "Any idea what that time frame is? I've got several producers hanging."

"Tell them his grandmother died. That he went back suddenly for the funeral. Make something up. Say English custom dictates he sit around for a while. I don't know. Use your imagination. Make 'em wait. They know Ewan's worth it."

"If you say so. You want my opinion?"

"No."

When the line disconnected, Adam stared at his phone in irritation. "Whatever." Getting back on the line with a towing company to go and retrieve Ewan's car, Adam mumbled, "You are one lucky boy, Ewan Gallagher. Jack must see huge dollar signs when he stares at you."


Needing to get away from Siobhan's prying presence, they strolled into the city center to the local café. Jason bought them both a cup and then sat down.

Ewan was avoiding the odd stares from the residents. They knew he looked familiar and they had the expressions of people trying to guess where they knew him from.

"We have to figure out some kind of plan." Jason warmed his hands on the white cup.

"I know. Half the problem is not knowing what the hell we're both doing." Ewan glared at a man who was staring at him rudely until he turned away.

"Right. So, what do you suggest? Are you going to stay here for a while?"

Ewan thought for a moment, then said, "I would. If you were living in that manor house alone. There'd be no question to me staying a bit."

Jason frowned. "But I don't live alone there. Will you stop at your mum's?"

"Oh, no. I can't be put up there. No." Ewan shook his head.

"Want me to look into getting you a flat?"

"That's a bit permanent. Look, Jas, I do have to get back to LA I've a house there, a car, a..." He paused then said, "A job."

"I know. But if and when you go back, will it be to wrap things up there? Sell your house, car, and pack in the job, to come here?"

"Here?" Ewan choked, then looked around at the staring faces again in annoyance. "Jason, you yourself said you hate it here! The bloody weather! Yeah? Remember? California is lovely! The beaches, the sand. I don't want to leave it permanently."

"No. Of course not."

"So, you have to come out."

"Yes. That's right. I have to come out there." Jason sipped his cup. "I have to come out..." he repeated mostly to confirm it to himself.

"Yeah. So, when can you come out?" Ewan leaned across the table to him.

"When...when..." Jason tried to get through the quagmire in his head. "Sell the paintings, move Auntie Margerie, sell the estate—"

"Get a bloody divorce!" Ewan snarled.

"Yes...I'll get Margerie dug up this week."

Ewan cringed. "Sounds 'orrible."

"It is. Make no mistake." Jason looked around first, then said, "What choice do I have? Would you buy that gorgeous estate with a bloody grave site on it?"

121

"I don't know."

"I wouldn't! Stupid wench. She was so bloody cocky she thought no one else would ever want to sell the place."

"All right, don't get all wound up, yeah? Just tell me when you can come out!"

Jason hated the fact that it may be months. A year? It was an awful thought.

When he didn't respond, Ewan threw up his hands in frustration. "Here we go again! I'm getting on that plane alone and you're staying behind! Jason, we've been through this already! Yeah? I can't do it again!"

"What do you want me to do?" Jason tried to keep their voices down, but they were both becoming emotional.

"Want to know?" Ewan spoke like a dare. When Jason nodded his head he said, "Come back with me! Tell the wench you're leaving her. Phone a solicitor, give him me number to reach you. Then have him take care of all the details, the divorce, the estate…yeah?"

"Oh, I don't know, Ewan." Jason wanted control. How do you control something from another country?

Ewan leaned back and crossed his arms over his chest. "You don't fucking love me. You love your flamin' money."

Jason looked around once more in paranoia, then leaned across the tiny round table to whisper, "You know that's bullocks. I could say the same. If you loved me, then don't go back until I get this shite done with!"

They had reached another stalemate.

Angry with each other, they sipped the coffee in silence, each trying to decide how to reach a compromise.

Finally Jason sighed, "You said once a long time ago, we both wish the other would just say, 'Yes, dear. Yes, dear.' That was very prophetic, Ewan, yet also the basis for our attraction. I don't want some weak poof I can manipulate. I want an equal. Someone with strength and will. Yes, and someone who is stubborn, maybe, as well. We are so much alike it frightens me."

Ewan's eyes grew large as he listened. Jason had sixteen years more life experience than he. When he spoke, Ewan always paid careful attention.

"I do have an idea. Tell me what you think of it."

Sitting up anxiously, Ewan nodded, "Yeah, go on."

"I'll come back with you—" Jason found that uncorked enthusiasm and was quick to add the disclaimer, "Temporarily. If for nothing else—to stop that nasty piece of work—Jack Turner—from touching you again. I want a word with him personally. I'll not have him taking liberties with my man."

Ewan grinned excitedly. "Yeah? Go on!"

"I'll come out, see how you're getting on. Make sure things are settled. Okay? Then yes, I'll ring a solicitor, get things going. Ask for that divorce, let my parents know she has been unfaithful…the works."

"Yeah?" Ewan replied. "How long will you stay?"

Knowing Priscilla no longer resented his absence, and as a matter of course, desired it, he said, "Start with a fortnight?"

"Yes!" Ewan laughed, then reached out to hold Jason's hand as it rested on the table. "I'm so glad. Oh, Jason, I want to bring you back with me. I need you with me, love. I need you there."

"I'll be there. I will." Jason impulsively brought Ewan's hand to his lips to kiss, not noticing the nasty sneers of the few who spied it.

# Chapter Twelve

"Going where?" Priscilla stood near as Jason packed a suitcase.

"A doctor's convention. In California."

"And you just found out about it now?"

"Yes. Whilst I was out, I stopped at the hospital to meet with my old colleagues. Dr. Kraus told me I shouldn't miss it." Walking to the bath, he loaded his shaving kit with his essentials.

It was a mixture of suspicion and delight. She liked the idea of not having to hide her affection for Charles, but seeing Jason pack, thinking she noticed a woman in the car with him earlier was all a bit suspect. "Are you having an affair?" she blurted, before thinking things through.

The rage on Jason's face terrified her. As he rose to full height, appearing very powerful and menacing, he roared, "How dare you!"

Instantly regretting her words on so many levels, she immediately began backtracking, stammering, "I'm sorry! I forgot you're impotent!"

"Priscilla!" he shouted in fury.

"It was a stupid thing to say!" she fretted, babbling,

"How could you have sex with anyone else? You don't have a proper sexually functioning—"

"Cilla!" he cut off her humiliating accusations. "Don't you ever talk to me about having an affair!" he warned, moving toward her step by step, backing her up. "You may think I'm unaware of the goings on in this manor, but you're sadly mistaken!"

"Jason!" She cringed at the implications. "I didn't! I never!"

"I don't give a rat's ass what you do!" he roared, "But don't you ever treat me like I am an idiot!"

"No...I didn't mean— I only meant, I don't think—" Incoherent syllables followed as she fidgeted with her hands.

With his hatred billowing out like steam, he continued throwing things into the bag.

Lost for words, she finally stood back as he carried the suitcase to the hall. "Have fun!" she chirped.

Glaring at her, Jason stormed down the stairs. Charles was there waiting for him at the door with his jacket.

Setting the case down, he allowed the old man to help him with it, then stood tall over him to say, "I'm leaving the manor in your hands, Charles."

"Yes, sir." Charles nodded in understanding.

"Once I arrive, I'll ring you with a number where I can be reached in emergency."

"Yes, sir."

Priscilla stepped down the stairs quietly, listening.

"Meanwhile, whilst I'm gone, I've given instructions to a funeral home to have Margerie's body moved."

Charles blinked and held back his, 'yes, sir' as Priscilla's gasp was heard.

"I want her to have a proper religious plot. I hate her under the cold earth alone. It sickens me. It always had. She loved the church, so I want her near one."

Finally, swallowing down his shock, Charles said, "Yes, sir."

125

"You make sure it's done properly. I've even sent a note to the vicar so he can advise them. It's all sorted. When the plot is removed and relocated, I've arranged a gardener to clean up the area. If there are any problems you notify me when I call. Do you understand, Charles?"

The force, the power in which Jason was delivering his instructions frightened the elderly valet. Underlying that vocal strength was knowledge. It was enough to put the fear of god in him. "Don't you worry, sir. Everything shall be taken care of."

"I know I can count on you, Charles." Jason met the old man's eyes. Before he left, he glared at his wife. "Don't go calling my parents and getting them involved in this burial move. If you do, then I'll have a word with them myself about something concerning you. Do I make myself clear?"

Swallowing in a gulp, Priscilla nodded.

"I'll be back in two weeks." Jason lifted his bag. "Don't disappoint me or you'll both regret it."

Watching his broad back move down the stair to his car, Charles looked back at Priscilla in fear. "Did you tell him?"

"No! I swear!" She rushed down to stand beside him as the Mercedes receded into the distance.

Closing the door, Charles loosened his collar to be able to breathe. "We had better do all he says, Cilla. I don't want the doctor to have me head."

"No, Charles! We'll make sure everything he wants done is done, spit spot." Then, knowing she had a full two weeks of freedom, she grinned and wrapped around the old man's neck. "But—for now!" She giggled wildly and dragged him up the staircase.

Stopping at Siobhan's flat, Jason parked out front and knocked on the door. When Marcus answered, he smiled sweetly into his kind features.

"Doc!"

"Hullo, Marcus. What brings you here?" Jason stepped

in, looking for Ewan, who was easy to find in the tiny two-bedroom townhouse. He and Siobhan were in the lounge. Siobhan was showing Ewan the scrap book she had started with all his clippings.

Marcus waited as he stepped in to greet them, then said, "Just having a cuppa with me mate and his mum. You taking our Ewan back to Tinseltown?"

"Aye." Jason smiled and winked at him. "He needs looking after."

"Not half!" Marcus laughed wildly.

"You ready, love?" Ewan rose up off the couch.

"I am." He nodded, smiling, trying not to reflect the bad temper he had only a short while ago.

Standing for her hug good-bye, Siobhan reached out to her son emotionally. "Oh, love. When will I see you again?"

"Don't know, Mum. I'll ring you." Ewan squeezed her tight.

When they parted, Siobhan reached out to Jason. He smiled and wrapped around her plumpness affectionately. "You take care of our Ewan, yeah?"

"I will. You can count on it, love." Jason kissed her cheek.

"See ya, mate." Marcus reached out to shake Ewan's hand.

Ewan smiled and embraced him instead. "You will. Maybe I'll send you tickets soon, to come for a holiday."

"Yeah. After the show closes. Wish you would be there for a performance."

"Me, too, yeah? But not this time. Got to get back." Ewan parted from him and smiled into his sad face.

Jason shook Marcus' hand when he extended it. Marcus shouted, "You take care of me mate!"

"Oi!" Jason laughed, "I remember the last lecture you gave me when he moved in!"

Ewan turned to look back at them, an amused smile on his lips.

"I did! Double that now!" Marcus pointed at him.

"Yes, Marcus," Jason gave him the same answer he did the first time.

Sliding on his long coat, Ewan peered around. "I didn't come with much, so I leave with the same." He laughed sadly.

"Travel light." Jason tried to keep it upbeat.

After kissing his mother once more, Ewan stepped outside the flat to Jason's car. "I'll ring you!" he promised. "And you start looking for a nice detached home, yeah? I can't have me mum in a two bed semi!"

"Aye. All right, love!" She wiped at a tear and held onto Marcus as they stood together at the doorway.

Waving, trying not to prolong the sad good-bye, Jason started the car and pulled away from the curb.

Seeing Ewan composing himself, dabbing at his eyes, Jason smiled and squeezed his knee. "You all right, love?"

"Aye. Just always miss me mum."

"She is a love. Not like mine. I don't miss either of my parents. Could give a shite if I ever see them again."

As Jason focused on the road once more, Ewan replied, "I'm sorry, love."

Turning back to him to give him a reassuring smile, Jason said, "That's why you mean so much to me, Ewan. You're all I've got."

"You can count on me, love." Ewan squeezed his hand tightly. "You can count on me."


After a short jaunt up to Edinburgh, Jason was anxious that the tasks he left behind for others to tend would most likely end up a disaster, but, trying to pretend this was the holiday they had missed over a year ago, he put on a brave face, resigned to see it through.

Having no problems at the airport, Jason was beginning to believe things might go smoothly. It wasn't until they arrived at the other end that his plan fell apart.

Through customs and immigration, Jason's attention

was drawn to identifying which conveyer belt held his bag. As he wandered to the reader boards to discover the flight information, he heard a scream behind him and twisted in panic to see some girls recognize Ewan and run straight towards him.

"Oh, shit!" Ewan grabbed Jason to use as a shield.

"Bloody hell!" Jason couldn't believe his eyes as a small mob of teenagers attempted to maul his lover.

Pens and pads got shoved under his nose, cameras flashed, and enough chaos was generated that the armed airport security guards became aware and began strutting over to find out what was going on.

Using his body to protect Ewan, Jason tried to calm the crowd down while Ewan signed autographs and smiled, though he was exhausted and just wanted to be horizontal.

"What's the problem here?" one of the soldiers asked, his rifle in his hand.

"No problems here, mate!" Jason panicked, holding up his hands defensively.

"There is!" Ewan insisted. "Get these people back! I'm getting claustrophobic! Yeah?"

The young man in army fatigues laughed, and said, "You're Ewan Gallagher!"

"Aye! It's me!"

The man checked around. "Where are your bodyguards?"

"Not here at the moment! Do us a favor?" Ewan winked at the man.

Immediately, the two armed men began pushing back the crowd. "All right! Back off! Give him some space!"

Jason was in shock. He'd no idea this would happen.

As more officials were alerted by radio, a small band stood around Ewan until Jason got his bag. "Cheers!" Ewan thanked them all gratefully.

"My pleasure, Mr. Gallagher!" The young soldier smiled at him. "I admire your courage in coming out."

"Aye." Ewan smiled knowingly at him. "It's better

having it behind you, yeah?"

Leaning to Ewan's ear, the young clean-cut man said, "I'd like to be behind you—"

Choking at his cheek, Ewan nodded, "Not in front of me lover!" and laughed in hilarity.

Jason was so overwhelmed, he had trouble doing anything but walking, trying to avoid the flashing cameras and odd armed escort.

"Where's your car?" one soldier asked.

Ewan removed his wallet and found the ticket. "Second floor, row A."

Taking the elevator, two guards still at their side, Ewan went to where he left it. Checking the area again, he shouted, "It's been nicked!"

"Great," Jason sighed.

"Gold Jaguar! I left it here!" Ewan ran his hands through his hair. "Oh, bollocks. I need a phone."

He was escorted to a pay phone by the elevator. As the guards kept onlookers both curious and manic, back, Ewan rang Adam. "Oi! Me bloody car's been nicked!"

"No. It hasn't. We didn't know how long it would be there. I had it towed to your house, Ewan."

"Oh. Cheers." Ewan cupped the phone to tell Jason, "Not nicked," then he went back to the conversation. "Come get me."

"I'll send a limo. You all right?"

"Aye. Am I dead?"

"I was supposed to give you a good ass-kicking, but, in reality, no. Christ, only two days? That's your big escape?"

"Oi!" Ewan pouted. "I was thinking of you! Thought Jack would have you!"

"No. Thank fuck, I'm not Jack's type."

"That's not what I meant—"

"I know what you meant. Go to the arrivals area. The limo should be there in about ten minutes or so."

"Cheers, you're a mate." As he hung up, he was smiling.

Jason was still jumpy. Overtired, jet-lagged, and surrounded by U.S. army soldiers was not a good way to start their trip.

"We have a limo on the way, love." Ewan caressed Jason's weary cheek.

"Good. How long?"

"Ten minutes." He held his hand. "Okay, lads, to the arrival and pick-up point!" Ewan was enjoying the attention.

Marching once again to the terminal to more crowds and more shrieking females, Jason thought he was going to lose his mind.

The limousine pulled up shortly after they stepped outside into the morning light. As Jason climbed in tiredly, his baggage being loaded in the trunk, Ewan shook hands with the two young soldiers, thanking them.

"My pleasure, Mr. Gallagher!" One waved, smiling. "I can't wait to tell my sister I met you! She's a big fan!"

"Give us a pen." Ewan reached to the chauffeur. When he produced one, Ewan wrote his name on a British twenty pound note. "What's sis's name?"

The young man laughed. "Susan."

"Aye…" Completing his gift, Ewan handed it to him. "Thanks again, mate."

Jason leaned down to watch the odd spectacle. His lover was a big star here. It was something he knew, but still hadn't grasped.

After Ewan had settled down and waved to the small crowd of adoring fans, he grinned back at Jason for his reaction.

"I'm gob-smacked."

"It's brilliant!"

"I don't know what to say." Jason enjoyed that boyish glow in his cheeks.

"How about, I love ya?"

"Oh, yes…I love ya, love ya, love ya!" Jason wrestled him down onto the back seat as the chauffeur raised his eyebrows in the rear view mirror.

When they arrived at Ewan's home in Beverly Hills, Jason gaped at the posh landscaping and the large white structure with the terra cotta roof. "Christ! Look at this cactus!" He paused to admire a saguaro that towered over his head.

Ewan smiled, then looked up to see Adam standing at his doorstep, waiting for him. The grin dropped from Ewan's face. "Jack here?"

"Inside." Adam's ear was stuck to his mobile again as he split his attention between two conversations.

"Shit. How upset is he?" Ewan whispered.

"Like I said. He wants to make a show of it." Pausing to admire Jason, he reached out his hand. "We meet again, doctor."

"Adam." Jason took it, not feeling particularly friendly.

Ewan touched Jason's sleeve. "Jack's inside."

Hearing that news, Jason immediately tried to shove passed the two men to get at him.

Jumping on his back, Ewan prevented it while Adam stood in his way. "I don't advise a showdown, doctor."

"Let me kill him!" Jason was seething.

"Jason! Calm down! At least let me see how much trouble I'm in before you make more!" Ewan trapped Jason's hands behind his back.

Twisting to get free, Jason snarled at Adam, "He dares to even lay a finger on my lover and I'll break it off. He may hold Ewan's contract, but he doesn't hold mine!"

Smiling at the chivalrous attitude, Adam took a better look at him. "Oh, do come in, doctor." Adam backed up, smirking, gesturing for him to get inside.

Shaking out of Ewan's grip, Jason stepped into the house to find the fiend.

The driver set Jason's bag in the house, then left.

A nasty aroma of cigar smoke was looming like a

noxious cloud. All three men followed their sense of smell to the living room.

Splayed out in his expensive designer suit, a freshly opened bottle of scotch in front of him, a half full glass, and a smoldering cigar end in an ashtray on the coffee table, Jack never looked up at them, flipping channels on Ewan's big screen TV.

While Adam stood back smugly, his arms crossed over his chest, Jason paused, as if he were trying to assess the size and prowess of this man from behind as Ewan cleared his throat and walked front and center.

"Move. You're blocking my view," Jack grumbled.

Ewan shifted one step to the left. "I...I'm sorry I just picked up and left."

When those dark lifeless eyes found Ewan's frightened blue ones, Adam could see Ewan shiver even though he had reassurances from him it was all an act.

Closing the set behind him, Jack leisurely sipped his drink, then set it down. "You think you can just do as you like? Just leave the fucking country? Even though you signed a contract with me?"

Still unnoticed behind him, Jason clenched his fists, obviously waiting for this bastard to step out of line.

"I just had to get away. Yeah?" Ewan shook the long hair back from his eyes.

"No!" Jack rose up menacingly. "No, you don't do as you please! You hear me?"

Adam watched Jason carefully. He knew Jack had no idea he was in the room.

"I'm sorry. All right, Jack? Only a couple of days. Yeah? I'm back. No harm done." Ewan trembled.

Moving like a snake across the room, Jack stood before his young star. "Never again. The next time you play a trick like that will be your last. Not only will you be finished with me and my agency, but you'll never work in this town again, you hear me?"

"Aye! Loud and clear!" Ewan laughed uneasily.

"Good." Jack softened. "Good boy," he purred, reaching up to touch Ewan's hair.

Sprung like a panther, Jason shoved that arm away before it made contact and snarled, "Get your bloody hands off my man."

Eyes lit up with delight, Adam covered his impish laughter, moving to get a good view of Jack's shocked expression.

"Who the fuck are you!?" Jack shouted.

"Someone you should be afraid of. I should kill you, you bloody—"

"Jason—" Ewan wrapped his hands around Jason's muscular biceps. Clearing his throat, Ewan said, "Jack, this is me doctor-lover. Dr. Jason Phillips."

Blinking his eyes in surprise, Jack took a step back to take him in. He shouted, "Perfect! Oh, look at you! Ewan, I couldn't have picked a more handsome fellow!"

Tilting his head as if he was confused at the strange change in attitude, it seemed as if Jason tried to shift his own gears.

Adam was completely let down at the lack of a battle.

The bizarre behavior had Ewan tilting his head as well. "Oi?"

"Adam!" Jack swiveled his girth around and came up a bit short with surprise at finding him right there, eavesdropping. "I want these two photographed while they're out and about. Take them shopping on Sunset Boulevard. One holding hands, one kissing. Make it like it's tabloid press. You know, blurred, through a fucking tree. Then get it to the rags ASAP!"

"All right." Adam blinked at him in surprise, and then found his pocket notebook.

"You're gorgeous!" Jack reached out as if he meant to touch Jason's face until he connected with the homicidal look in his eye. "Just what Ewan needed to boost his profile!" Jack made a pretense of trying to look like he was actually meaning to run his hands through his own hair. "How old are you?"

"Why?" Jason snarled.

"He's thirty-seven." Ewan knew Jack's strategy.

"Oh! A boy-toy! Yes!" Jack suddenly seemed to be too busy to stay put. He grabbed his cigar and mobile phone. Before he left he turned back to Ewan. "You're lucky you squirmed out of it this time. Not twice, Ewan."

Adam was mimicking him silently behind his back. When Ewan noticed, he tried not to smile. "Right."

"Hair cut and manicure!" Jack reminded, pointing his finger in the air as he left.

"Right," Ewan shouted after.

"Then see Adam. You're booked, Ewan, booked!"

As his voice faded out the front door, Ewan sighed and lowered his head.

Jason's expression hadn't changed. It seemed as if he just needed one punch to satisfy him.

Sighing tiredly, Adam was checking his electronic notepad as his mobile phone rang. "Get some rest. First thing tomorrow, hair and nails, then later that afternoon, movie producer's office. I'll send a car for both."

"Thanks, Adam." Ewan walked with him to the door.

"Oh." Adam stopped and tried to see Jason from over Ewan's head. "Sorry you missed the opportunity. Now that he's seen you, and your size, you won't get another."

"Good." Jason's lip snarled over his clenched teeth.

Hesitating, Adam gave Jason another good once over. "Good taste, Ewan, my boy. Very good taste."

"Aye. I know." Ewan blushed , seeing him out.

# Chapter Thirteen

Jason was the type of man who preferred the quiet life. Sedate, shy by nature, he became a doctor because it seemed noble and the money was good. But being a physician, he did have to contact many strangers on very intimate levels. Still, it never prepared him for this.

At sunrise, the phone rang; Adam reminding Ewan of his appointments.

No time for Jason to prepare them a decent breakfast, Ewan sipped his cup of drip coffee, leaning against the sink and assuring him they'd catch some food on the road.

The doorbell summoned him to the driver waiting outside. Grabbing his mobile phone, his wallet and a baseball hat and sunglasses for disguise, Ewan clutched Jason's hand and rushed him out.

A private salon was first on their list. Jason kept silent. Though Ewan seemed to be thriving, living it large, Jason was the voyeur in this spectacle. The brisk pace, the hiding from the public, the constant jingle of the cell phone, Jason didn't think he could stand it for a fortnight, let alone a lifetime. All he wanted was a quiet life; a mansion on an expansive tract of land, and peace and solitude. Not unlike his home in Carlisle, but without Priscilla and on a hot sandy beach.

Jason stood in the background as a smock was wrapped around Ewan's shoulders. At the same time his hair was tended, another chair was set next to him to clip and polish his fingernails.

"Oi!" Ewan laughed at him. "What's with the look of misery?"

It woke Jason up from his daydream. He smiled sweetly and said, "Just a bit jet-lagged."

"Yeah. Me, too. It'll pass."

The man behind him straightened his head back out in the mirror, trimming just the ends of Ewan's trademark long hair. "What do you think of me lover?" Ewan grinned, tilting back to Jason.

The hairdresser gave Jason a peek in the mirror, then smiled wickedly.

Ewan grinned. "Aye...he's some lovely bit of stuff, yeah?"

"Maybe he'd like a trim," the young man asked, his own mop multicolored and shaggy.

"Ohh, you'd like to get your hands on him, yeah?" Ewan laughed again, then peeked up at Jason.

Seeing the two of them glancing at him and laughing, Jason figured it out quickly. "Oi! I hope I'm not the butt of your joke!"

"Naa, Jas!" Ewan smiled brightly. "He just wants to give you a trim as an excuse to touch you."

"Hey!" The hairdresser whacked Ewan playfully. "Careful or I'll cut your ear off!" He snipped his scissors in warning.

Moving closer to the mirror, Jason touched his hair, checking it out. "Could use a trim. I don't usually like it over the ears."

"I like it long!" Ewan objected.

"I'm a doctor, not a superstar." Jason shook his head, then caught the eye of the woman buffing Ewan's nails.

137

"A doctor, huh?" She smiled flirtatiously at him.

"Yes..." He blushed modestly.

"Oh, Mr. Gallagher, you go for gold, don't you?" She clicked her gum and went back to her task.

"Aye..." Ewan smiled proudly.


Two hair cuts and manicures later, the men were rushed into the car and moving to another meeting. The raisin muffins they consumed while in the salon weren't sitting well with Jason. He preferred a poached egg with some toast and jam.

Though they were passing several promising areas that Jason would have loved to explore, never having been to the west coast of America before, all he caught were quick glimpses out the tinted window.

As he leaned to have a look at everything he wasn't seeing, he spotted Adam standing in front of a building, the phone to his ear.

The car stopped and Ewan's door was opened.

"What do you want me to do?" Jason asked.

"Come! Oh, Jason, come with me!" Ewan reached out for him.

All they received from Adam was a nod. He was busy on the line to another client. Opening the doors for them as he entered the air conditioned lobby, Adam paused, wrapping up the call. When he flipped it off and stuffed it into his pocket, he inhaled and said, "His name is Dennis Foreman. You met briefly at the premiere. I already know he wants you." He pushed the buttons of the elevator.

"What's the film about?" Ewan tucked in his shirt.

"Oh, Christ," Adam rubbed his forehead trying to remember. "Uh, some love triangle thing with you in the middle. You've got a woman hot for you and a friend you've known since college who just came out and comes on to you."

Ewan stifled a laugh and glanced at Jason.

He covered his smile and shook his head at the silly plot.

Whisked down the corridor, Ewan could only glimpse back at Jason who was purposely not moving with them, not wanting to get in the way. Ewan kept reaching back his hand to him.

Finally at the door of the office, Jason caught up, but only gave Ewan's hand a quick squeeze before letting it go. Last thing he wanted was for Ewan to appear to need a security blanket. Bad enough he was present.

Always in control, Adam met the receptionist and then paced as the other two took a seat. Answering his mobile phone twice in ten minutes, when they were finally called to the office, Adam popped it back into his pocket quickly.

"Should I go in?" Jason held Adam back as Ewan strutted through the door pretending to be confident.

"Sure. Don't worry about it." Adam nodded and allowed Jason to go first.

A thin man, much younger than Jason expected, rose to his feet and reached over the desk to shake Ewan's hand. "Glad to see you again, Ewan."

"And you! Cheers!" Ewan shook his hand briskly and then stuffed his nervous fingers into the tight pockets of his slacks.

Adam nodded to Jason. "This is Dr. Jason Phillips. He's Ewan's partner."

"Jason." The young man reached for him next.

"Mr. Foreman." Jason nodded politely.

"Dennis, please." He gestured to the chairs. There were two. Adam nudged Jason into one and then walked to the door to listen to the phone messages he'd just missed.

After they had settled, Dennis leaned on the desk, a big smile on his face. "You know the plot?"

"Aye…"

"Obviously you have no objections to male sex scenes." Dennis smiled at Jason.

Jason shifted uncomfortably, then couldn't prevent

139

himself from asking, "Is it x-rated?"

Ewan laughed as Dennis shook his head. "No, doctor. It's PG-13. That's recommended for over thirteen years of age. The sex is only implied, and there is slight nudity and kissing."

Feeling like an idiot, promising himself to keep his mouth shut, Jason nodded silently.

With his attention back on Ewan, Dennis said, "I'd like you to read the script through." He had a copy of it on his desk which he nudged to him. "I want you to play Mark Richfield. He's the man in the middle."

"Is he English?" Ewan took the heavy manuscript onto his lap.

"Well, originally he had an English mother and an American father, but it's okay that you have an accent, Ewan. We can work it into the film very easily, and the audience will find it very endearing."

"Aye...good." Ewan nodded his head in relief.

"Great." Dennis leaned back contentedly. "Have a gander through it, tell me what you think, then we'll decide if it's right for you."

"Right." Ewan rose up, holding the manuscript under his arm as he reached to shake Dennis' hand.

Jason got to his feet quickly, not wanting to waste anyone's time.

Finished with the phone messages, Adam had heard most of the meeting, and waited for Ewan, opening the door. "I'll call you," he shouted to Dennis who nodded and waved at him.

Walking silently through the lobby, Ewan waited until they were in the elevator to look at the script in his hand. Opening the protective cover, he read the title. "Oi! Listen to this! *'A Man's Best Friend'*! What am I, in love with a bloody dog?"

Adam laughed under his breath. "Oh, I doubt you'll be paired with a dog, Ewan. The female role has been offered to Cameron Diaz, and the male lover will most likely be played by Ben Affleck or someone similar."

Jason let a chuckle slip out, then stifled it.

"Bloody hell…" Ewan sighed in amazement.

"One more stop." Adam gestured for them to go out into the sunlight to the waiting limousine.

With Adam leading the way in his BMW, Ewan flipped through the script while Jason tried to absorb the overload.

The same routine, another posh glass office building, Adam met them at the entrance and they rode upwards in the lift.

An even younger producer met him this time. Jason felt like a dinosaur at thirty-seven. Passing a mirror in the corridor, he peered at himself and wondered how old he looked compared to all the child protégés around him. Insecurity creeping in, he hoped no one mistook him for Ewan's father. If they did, he'd get violent.

"Ewan, so good you made it." The young man even had slight acne on his chin. Jason was completely flabbergasted that the industry was turning into a very young boy's game.

"…you play a motorcycle hood. Robin Grant. He falls in love with a senator and gets framed for his murder."

"Oi?" Ewan's face lit up. "I like it!"

"Can you ride a motorcycle?"

"Of course!" Ewan laughed.

Trying to appear discreet, Jason peered over at him. That was news to him.

"Here's the script, read it overnight and let me know what you think." Another heavy manuscript was passed over the desk.

"Cheers." Ewan forced a smile through his anxiety.

Shaking his hand, following behind Adam who was talking on the phone again, Ewan waited until they were outside to breathe a word.

"Oi, who they got to play the senator?"

Distracted, Adam held up his finger to make Ewan wait, then hung up and asked him to repeat the question. Ewan did.

"Uh…" Adam wracked his overfilled grey cells. "Either Harrison Ford or Viggo Mortensen."

Ewan's jaw dropped.

Jason read his expression and burst out laughing.

Trying to decipher his notes from his electronic pad, Adam once again split his attention in two. "What?"

"Bloody hell…" Ewan breathed in amazement.

"I should be very jealous!" Jason could not stop laughing.

"What?" Adam finally gave them his full attention.

"Viggo…" Ewan sighed, like a prayer.

Jason winked at Adam, and Adam got the hint. "I see. Someone you admire?"

"Oh, yes!" Ewan shivered in delight.

"You behave!" Jason warned, still trying to be playful.

"He's straight, Jas!" Ewan laughed. "Not to worry, love!"

"And if he wasn't?" Jason raised his eyebrows.

Ewan hugged him, grinning wickedly. "You know I'd never go out on you."

Seeing them snuggling, Adam remembered and shouted, "Pictures! Shit! Look, I have to get someone to photograph you." Instantly he flipped out his electronic notebook.

Though Jason kept his arms around Ewan as Ewan rested his head on his shoulder to take a mini-break, he said, "Look, Adam, I can't have you taking photos of me and Ewan together."

"Why not? Hello? Yes, I need you to do some pictures for some magazines."

Ewan pouted his lip and gazed into Jason's face. "Why not?"

"Ewan! If they get back to the UK, I'm knackered!"

Pushing back, Ewan grabbed Jason's left hand with his free one, the other was still clamped to the second manuscript. There, where his wedding band used to be, was a slight indent and lighter color where the sun couldn't get through. The band had been removed.

"Yes!" Jason shouted as Ewan figured out why. "Not yet!"

"When did you take it off?"

"Take what off?" Adam was still only half listening. "Yes, about an hour on North Rodeo Drive. I'll meet you at Versace's."

"When we arrived at LAX. I can't stand the thing." Jason rubbed his face, the exhaustion of the time change beginning to catch up again.

"But—you heard Jack—" Ewan pressed up against him again. "He wants me paired off, yeah? You don't want him finding some male tart, do you?"

"No. You already have one."

"Jason!" Ewan shouted in anger.

"Right. After a bite of lunch, some photos," Adam said, then waved the limo away once he had retrieved the first manuscript from the interior. "My car's this way."

"No!"

"Yes!"

"No!"

The debate was continuing. Adam chirped the alarm and door locks opened, then tilted back to them to finally. "Someone want to tell me about it?"

"Jason doesn't want to be photographed."

"Why?"

"He's…well, he's bloody married."

"Married?" he gasped. "Why the fuck are you married?"

"Good question." Jason rubbed his hands through his hair. He just wanted a nap, that was all he wanted.

"Where's your wife?"

He had no intentions of going into any of this. "Look—"

Adam relented. "Okay, whatever. Let's get you lunch. Never mind."

While he was seated in the back of Adam's BMW,

Ewan put the cap and sunglasses on.

"Does that work?" Jason thought he looked adorable.

"Most of the time. By the time they figure out it's me, I'm history. Yeah?"

"Oh, and since when do you know how to ride a motorcycle?" Jason's eyebrows raised skeptically.

Ewan blushed, catching Adam's eyes in the rear view mirror. "Well, how hard can it be?"

"Christ..." Adam shook his head. "Now I have to schedule you lessons."

"Sorry, mate."

Adam parked on the street and stuffed coins in the meter. It was after noon and the sun was almost directly overhead and warm.

"Go upstairs to the Fish House and get us a table, I'll be right there." Adam shoved them into the dim cool interior of a restaurant lobby, then flipped out his phone.

Obediently, the other two nodded and climbed the staircase.

Shutting his phone quickly, Adam sprinted down the street to meet the photographer. "Shane!" He waved and got the man's attention.

"Adam! Where's the celeb?" The camera was hanging around his neck.

"At the Fish House. Listen, slight change of plans. Keep out of sight. We have a live one! Married-older-male-doctor-partner! Don't you love it?! I couldn't make this shit up!"

"Married?" Shane laughed. "Oh, the rags will love that! Name?" He took out a pen from his pocket.

"Dr. Jason Phillips," Adam announced proudly.

"American?"

"No. British. From Carlisle. Check there for info on the wife."

"No problem. Carlisle? Where the hell is that?" He stuck his pen back in his pocket.

"No clue." Adam twisted back to look at the restaurant.

"Gotta dash. Ring me!" He touched his ear and sprinted across the street.


Seated in a back corner of the conservative room with the polished wooden flooring, Ewan took off his hat and glasses, then temporarily hid behind the menu.

Though Jason was starving, his exhaustion was giving him a headache. "Ewan."

"Yes, love?" Ewan lowered the menu, but hadn't looked at Jason yet, still deciding on a meal.

"After this—some much needed kip?"

Finally meeting his tired gaze, Ewan answered, "Yeah, of course, love. Sorry. I know you're having a tough time with the time change."

"Aren't you?"

"Outside, I'm fakin' it. Inside, I'm knackered. After this, back to the house. Yeah?"

Smiling, Jason squeezed Ewan's knee under the table. "Yeah."

They looked up when Adam appeared. "Did you order?" He sat down and set his phone next to him to keep an eye on it.

"Not yet. Service is a bit, you know—" Ewan rolled his eyes.

Immediately Adam twisted around. "Yo!" he shouted, waving a waiter over.

"That's one way to do it." Jason felt a bit embarrassed.

"Yanks." Ewan shrugged.

"We're in a rush, could you write down our order and then get it out here quick?" Jason knew Adam tried not to sound too harsh, but with his sharp style and immaculate appearance, it made its impact.

"Mr. Gallagher doesn't have all day," he added, impressing upon him the weight of the megastar in his presence.

"Sorry." The man found his pad. "You know what you

want?"

After they ordered their seafood salads and bottled water, Adam got busy on the phone as Ewan and Jason ate the bread hungrily.

"What's the plan later?" Jason whispered softly.

"Reading!"

"You really have to read both scripts?"

"I can cheat. Yeah? Skim them. But I have to get the gist. I have to know what I'm in for before I accept the contract."

"Doesn't Mr. Mobile-man do that?" Jason nodded to Adam, who heard, made a face at him and went back to his call.

"Not really. The decision is mine, love. He has a good idea before he gets the manuscript what the plot is, but it's up to me to make the final decision. They obviously will advise me strongly, either way."

Jason buttered the last piece of whole wheat bread and then cut it in two, setting half on Ewan's plate. "I could read one."

"Oh, cheers! That would be a big help, Jas." He lifted the tiny piece of bread and popped the entire thing in his mouth, smiling as he chewed.

"Eventually I'll need to get a run in, etcetera. I have to work out or I'll go batty."

When the waiter brought their salads, Adam ended his call and set the phone down once more as if it were a spoon and he would eat with it.

"There's a treadmill at me house. And some weights. I had it set up, but I'm too busy, or too knackered to do anything on it. But, you help yourself. Oh, there's also a pool out back in the garden."

"A pool?" Jason stuck his fork into a piece of romaine lettuce.

"Aye." Ewan began shoveling food to sate his appetite.

"Cushty!" Jason laughed.

"Cushty?" Adam mocked playfully.

"Oi!" Ewan defended, "You leave me lover alone, yeah?" Then he winked at him.

Within the hour they had devoured every scrap of food on the table. Setting the cap on his head and his sunglasses on his nose, Ewan nodded he was ready. Adam opened the door, spotted the photographer hovering in the shade, and nodded to him, making some space between him and the couple quickly.

Squinting in the glare, Jason wished he had more energy. "I'd love to do a bit of shopping. The exchange rate is almost two to one. I could really do with some new clothing to bring back."

"Bring back?" Ewan acted insulted. "You're not going anywhere, doctor!" He wrapped his arm around Jason's waist and squeezed him close.

"Oh, yes…" The photographer laughed. "Kiss…kiss…" he prompted to himself.

Adam paused at his car and smiled at them. "You two make such a good pair."

"Aye, we do that!" Ewan giggled, rubbing up against Jason's side comically.

"Really," Adam encouraged, "You make such a handsome couple."

"Oh, yer getting me going!" Ewan squirmed in excitement. "No rest for the wicked!" He laughed demonically.

His cheeks blushing with embarrassment, Jason tried to laugh, lowering his lashes at the compliment and his lover's revving engine.

Adam hissed seductively, "Ewan, Jason should be a model. Look at those green eyes." Glimpsing down at Ewan's crotch to see if he had an erection, he stood back to get out of the photo.

"Oh, yes…" Ewan moaned. "One lovely bit of stuff me doc is. Come here, you."

And though he was mortified to have anyone see it, Jason allowed Ewan a peck on the lips.

"Bingo!" The photographer laughed, giving Adam a discreet wave, then vanishing.

Grinning in satisfaction, Adam opened the car door finally. "Right. Home."

"Home for a nap!" Jason agreed, climbing in.

"Home for a shag!" Ewan corrected wickedly.

# Chapter Fourteen

"Don't forget the paper, Paul." Victoria pushed the shopping trolley down the aisle.

"Oh, right!" Paul stepped over to the extensive selection of periodicals and magazines. Going for the *Daily Mail*, he paused, leaned over to have a read of the front page of the *SUN* and went ashen.

Passing the fruit displays, she grabbed some bananas and then twisted back to have a look for him. Seeing he was still at the newspaper stand she shouted, "Paul!" When he didn't respond, she grumbled in irritation and pushed the cart back to where he was standing. "Just stick it in the cart! Don't read it here!"

"Vicky!" he breathed, sick and worn looking. "Look at the front of the *SUN*."

"The *SUN*?" She reached for it, giving him a bewildered look. Flapping it to get it to stand straight, she couldn't help but see the photograph first. "Jason!"

"Jason."

"Where was this taken?" She squinted without her reading glasses.

"Says Hollywood. Did you know he was out of town?"

"No! Priscilla never mentioned it! Is that the actor? The one he used to date?" Again she struggled to see.

Since Paul could read with his glasses already on his nose, he took it back. "Says, 'Ewan Gallagher caught red-handed, or should we say, tongued, with his new squeeze—handsome, married, Dr. Jason Phillips.'"

"Augh!" Victoria cried, then looked around her in paranoia. "Sod the shopping! Buy that and let's get out of here!" She grabbed her husband's arm and dragged him to the check-out as he searched his pockets for change.

Priscilla gazed out of the back window at the drizzle as the casket was loaded onto a truck. The vicar was there, his bible in his hand trying to pray and make a terrible situation better. It was an awful sight.

"You think he's doing the right thing, Charles?" she mused out loud.

Peering over her shoulder, he watched as the casket was covered by a tarp and carried away to the cemetery. "No. I think Lady Witcomb would be sick about it. If you ask me, Jason has something up his sleeve."

She spun around, fear in her eyes. "What?"

"I think he means to sell the estate. Why else move the grave?" Sitting down at the table behind her, Charles appeared very weary for his sixty years.

"Sell? He can't sell! We live here! How can he sell when we live here?"

"Sit down, dear." Charles patted the chair near him. "I have a story to tell you."

"A story?" She sat down and tilted her head at him. "What story, Charles?"

"Before you were married. One day an odd thing happened."

"What?"

"Well, Margerie was fading. Mr. And Mrs. Phillips stopped by to be with her."

"What's so odd about that?"

"Well, there was some debate about the will. Jason came over. He seemed very surprised to see his parents were here. Well, they hadn't spoken to Margerie in over a decade."

"No! Why?"

"I'm not quite certain. But, that's another tale. The odd part was, when Jason came down, after his parents had all but stormed out, he stopped to ask me some unusual questions."

"Really?"

"Yes. Like, who did I think got the estate when Margerie died? And when I said he did, of course, he asked me, 'Do you have a problem with that?' Well, I was dumbfounded."

"Why would he ask you that?" She rubbed her chin.

"Well, for weeks I wondered. Then, a very odd thing occurred to me."

"What, Charles?" She widened her twenty-five year old eyes.

"Maybe there was some question about whether he was deserving."

"No!" she gasped.

"Perhaps Margerie made some conditions to his inheriting it, that—" he paused making sure she was following, "...that quite possibly the estate would pass to someone else if he didn't comply."

"What conditions? To whom?"

"Well, that he marry. It was very sudden, Cilla, that you and he were wed. He never brought a woman over for Margerie to meet, but she often referred to 'the trollop' so I knew he was indeed seeing someone."

"Trollop?"

"Obviously someone Margerie and his parents disapproved of."

"The woman I saw in the car?" she asked.

"Well, I'm still not convinced he'd be so bold."

151

"Who, then, was to inherit the estate if not Jason?"

Charles hesitated, and then he finally said, "Well, me, Cilla. To me."

"You?" she choked and sat back.

"Yes! Why else would Jason have made those odd remarks? It stands to reason, Cilla."

"You?" She tried to grasp it. "But—then I'm completely confused. Why is he digging up Margerie?"

"Again, just a guess—" he clarified, "I would imagine, if he's broken the terms of the will, and you indeed spotted a woman here, then maybe he's trying to prepare it for sale, so he can get the money before the affair is found out."

"Oh, my Lord!" She rubbed her forehead until it crinkled.

"My dear, I'm afraid by our own indiscretions, we may have given the doctor his way out of the terms of the will."

"No!"

"Perhaps. It's just a theory."

Sitting back to think it out, she finally said, "Oh, never mind. Charles, even if he does sell and leave me, I still have you and I still have Daddy's millions."

"You don't care?" He was stunned.

"No. He's not been a proper husband to me." Leaning towards him to whisper though they were completely alone, she hissed, "He's impotent! He can't make love to me!"

"Impotent?" Charles' eyes widened.

"Yes! You see, that's why the idea of an affair is quite strange! If he can't have sex, then why cheat? He shows no interest at all. He won't even let me see him naked! I have to catch him coming out of the shower to even get a glimpse! It's most peculiar, Charles."

"My dear! I'm gob-smacked!"

Nodding, she continued, "That's why I love you! You are always willing! And quite capable in that department!" She blinked her lashes at him adoringly.

"Let me get this straight." Charles sat up in the chair. "You don't mind if he divorces you? Takes this estate from you?"

"Oh, well, it is my home. I do mind if I had to pack up and move to a new one. But, he's a burden on me, Charles. I feel ugly and unwanted with him. With you I feel desirable and loved! And Daddy will make sure we have a nice house."

"Oh, Cilla, no…your father would be beside himself with fury to know we are together. An old man like me? Nothing but a servant for the last forty years."

"Nonsense!" But, she shivered in fear at the possibility of her father's wrath.

"There is a chance he will be very upset, and for that reason we need to safeguard ourselves."

"How, Charles?" She reached over the table to hold his hands.

"If Jason is planning on divorcing you and selling the estate, we need to get to it first. I suggest you call his parents and tell them of your suspicions. Remember his warning about not letting them know about moving Margerie's grave? Well…"

"Ohhh! I see!"

"If he has violated some terms of the contract, then perhaps the will states an alternative heir. Perhaps me."

"Yes! Yes, if you can inherit the estate, then we wouldn't have to worry if Daddy is upset!"

"Precisely."

"Oh, Charles, you're ever so clever!"

"I'm just looking out for your well being, Cilla."

As they leaned over the table to kiss, the doorbell rang. Sitting back in panic, they gaped at each other. "Who on earth could that be?" she breathed.


"Knock again, Paul!" Victoria ordered, the newspaper in her fist.

"I am, Vicky! It's a very big house! Give Charles a moment!"

When the door opened, they pushed in. "Where's Priscilla!" Victoria shouted.

"In the lounge—" before Charles could finish his sentence they had shoved passed him.

Jason was doing laps in the pool as Ewan sat under an umbrella at a small table. A sweating pitcher of lemonade, two tall glasses; one opened and one closed manuscript in front of him.

Finishing his work-out, Jason stood at the deep end catching his breath, wiping the water off his face. He heard Ewan chuckle. "Is it funny?"

"Aye! Brilliant!" Ewan kept reading.

With both hands on the cement ledge, Jason did a press-up and climbed out of the pool.

As his shadow cast over Ewan, Ewan shielded his eyes and squinted up at him. "All done?"

"Yes. For now. You don't own a punching bag, do you?" Jason grabbed a towel and wiped his face.

"I'll get one. Let me ring Adam."

"No need, I heard."

They both raised their heads to see him, dressed in a swimsuit and t-shirt, walking out of the back sliding doors and over to them.

"You want it in the work-out room, or out here?" He took the phone out of his pocket.

"I dunno. Jas?" Ewan shielded his eyes again to look at him.

Unprepared for so quick a reaction to his request, Jason shrugged. "Either."

"Right."

As he dialed the phone, Jason shook his head at Ewan, expressing how amazed he was.

Ewan smiled. "Get used to it."

Laying the towel on the chair and then sitting on it, Jason dragged the second manuscript over, opening it to where he had left off last night.

Flipping the phone closed with a click, Adam said, "Done," and sat down with them. When he found only two glasses available for the lemonade, he shouted at the house, "Can you bring an extra glass out?"

"Who's here?" Ewan tore his eyes away from his reading.

"Jack. He's mixing a martini."

Jason bristled instantly at the news. Adam watched his reaction. "Will you promise me you'll punch him this time?" he whispered.

"Yes!" Jason answered eagerly.

"Oi!" Ewan shouted, "Don't wind him up, yeah?"

Adam sighed and leaned his chin on his palm to look over the script. "So? You like it?"

"I do! Brilliant!"

"Which are you reading?" He tilted to be able to see it.

"*Man's Best Friend*. The dialogue is hilarious. I love the part when Jack Larsen first finds Mark naked in bed after shagging that slapper. It's brilliant!"

Pausing, staring at him in confusion, Adam said, "Again? In English?"

"Oi!" Ewan laughed, "I am speaking English! It's you lot that's bastardized the Queen's language!"

"Err…" Jason interrupted, "Isn't that German?"

"What?" Ewan squinted at him.

"German?" Adam was confused.

Waiting, seeing his joke about the Queen actually being German was lost on them both, he shook his head. "Never mind."

Hearing the sliding doors, the three men peered over at the house to see Jack coming out with a decanter of martini's and a glass with an olive in it.

"Where's my glass?" Adam shouted.

"Get it your-fucking-self! I can't carry it all!"

Standing up in a huff, Adam went into the house again.

Watching the fat bastard walk to their table, Jason could

155

not prevent his sneer. Still covered with gaudy jewelry, his hair glistening from some greasy gel, black sunglasses over his puffy eyes, his goatee freshly dyed and jet back, wearing shorts that came passed his knees and a short-sleeved button-down shirt with wild Hawaiian flowers on it, he set his glass and pitcher down, then smiled at his handsome star.

Ewan was watching him as well. Jason couldn't tell what thoughts were passing through his head. His perfect physique was covered by a tiny black bikini and a white terrycloth robe. Looking down at his own body, Jason had the sudden urge to wrap a towel around him, avoiding the ogling gaze that was sure to come.

"Hello, boys...lovely day?" Jack sat his girth down and poured the martini through a strainer over his olive.

"Aye." Ewan nodded, still staring at his actions like he was mesmerized.

Jason didn't answer, then tilted over his shoulder to find Adam coming out with a glass of ice, saying, "We should order some food." He sat down in the last unoccupied chair at the table.

"All right," Ewan agreed easily.

"What do you want?" Adam flipped out his trusty phone. "I'm dying for sushi."

Checking with Jason first, Ewan asked, "You like sushi, love?"

"Yes. All right." Jason nodded agreeably.

"Good." Adam had already decided anyway.

"What do you think of the scripts, Ewan?" Jack sat back to sip his drink leisurely.

"Brilliant. I love it."

"Great. I was figuring on the response."

"You already have the contracts?" Ewan laughed.

"In the house." He pointed over his shoulder to it, then looked back at Jason. "You're quiet today, doctor. Did Ewan's humping libido keep you up all night?"

Adam's eyes immediately turned to Jason's expression

of rage, his mind blanking suddenly half-way through his order. "Ahh? Where was I? Oh, right, two dozen pieces of sashimi…"

Holding his breath, Ewan was trying unsuccessfully to get Jason's eye to tell him not to react.

"You are a vulgar, crass man, Mr. Turner," Jason growled, "I don't like you. I don't like your very presence here or near Ewan."

"Jason…" Ewan whispered, trying to get him to calm down.

Laughing, appearing as if he was loving the reaction of this prim British gentleman, Jack resumed sipping his drink, then answered, "You don't have to like me, doctor. I don't give a fuck if you hate me. Makes no friggen' difference to me. Your lovely young boy here is bound to me. I've got more of a contract with him than you ever could."

As Jason twitched, getting close to battle ready, Adam kept his eye on the action, continuing to order mounds of food.

"Please stop." Ewan sighed uncomfortably.

Jack set his glass down and spun to face Jason head on. "But, you've already got a contract with someone else, don't you, doctor? A woman? Priscilla Farnsworth-Prescott-*Phillips*?"

Both Ewan and Jason were shocked. Jason knew even Ewan didn't know the woman's name.

"Yes, how long?" Adam asked over the phone, "If I pay you extra, could you get it here in twenty?"

"You keep out of my personal life!" Jason pointed a warning finger into his face.

"Where's your ring?" Jack looked for it innocently on Jason's clenched fists. "Took it off? You think that nullifies the contract?"

"Jack—" Ewan sighed, "Enough, yeah? Why do you have to keep pushing at him? Leave me Jason alone."

Finally disconnecting the line, Adam flipped the phone shut, stood, took off his t-shirt and dove into the pool.

157

Staring at that smug expression, those capped white teeth gleaming at him from under the dyed black mustache, Jason wanted so much to justify hitting him. But, though he hated what he was spouting, he knew he was right. Shoving back from the table, Jason rose up and joined Adam in the pool.

Jack poured more martini into his glass and patted his pocket for a cigar, smiling to himself.

"Why do you have to wind him up?" Ewan leaned to whisper, "He knows it's wrong. He already feels bad. Yeah? There you go, getting him on the 'ump."

Changing the subject, Jack stroked back Ewan's hair from his eyes. "You were telling me about the script."

Withdrawing from his touch, looking back to see if Jason had witnessed it, Ewan found him talking to Adam at the other end of the pool at the moment, and brought his attention back to the manuscript.

"You had your opportunity," Adam laughed. "You disappointed me."

"I know, I know…but the bloody arse will probably have me nicked." Jason dipped under the water to slick back his hair.

"Probably," Adam agreed, then admired Jason's chest and arms. "You are one fit fucker. How do you do it?"

"I work out constantly." Jason wiped the water from his face.

"Doing what?"

"Running mostly. But swimming, biking—"

"Punching a bag." Adam smiled.

"Aye. Punching a bag. It gets the stress level down."

"I'd imagine." Adam smiled sweetly. "Was being a doctor stressful?"

"Yes. It was killing me." Jason dipped down and churned the water with his strong arms.

"How can you afford to leave it? I assume you're not

just on holiday here."

"No. I did leave it. I inherited an estate about a year ago." He rose up again and leaned on the ledge near him, glancing back at Ewan who was discussing the storyline with Jack.

"Independently wealthy…" Adam smiled flirtatiously. "How very appealing."

"Aye," Jason sighed tiredly, "I hate to admit it, but without money, life means fuck all."

"Greedy, ambitious…" Adam purred, "Just my kind of man."

Thinking about the comment, Jason made eye contact with him before he spoke, "I'm Ewan's lover. That's all."

"But he'll be very busy soon. The moment he begins filming, you'll never see him." Adam touched the tip of his finger on Jason's arm, running it downward to where the water met it at his elbow.

"I know he'll be busy. I'll just have to manage." Jason made sure Adam understood, though he was immensely flattered.

"Maybe it's that accent of yours. I do have a thing for it." He became bolder, running his entire hand up Jason's arm to his biceps, where he paused to squeeze that large round bulge.

"…so, I do like it. I don't think there's anything too risqué, Jack. It's quite moderate."

Jack had stopped paying attention to him suddenly, his vision at the far end of the pool; Adam making a play for the handsome doctor.

When Ewan realized he'd lost his gaze, he stopped babbling and twisted over his shoulder to see what he was looking at. "Oi!" Ewan rose up angrily, pushing back the chair. "What the fuck are you two playing at!?" He stormed over to them.

Jason and Adam hadn't moved. They just watched as

Ewan advanced, shouting at them.

"What's all this, Ewan?" Jason shielded his eyes from the glare behind him.

Avoiding Adam's smirk of superiority, Ewan yelled, "He's trying to pull you! You daft?" He pointed to Adam's hand, which was slow to relinquish its hold.

"Pull him?" Adam choked in a laugh, finally letting go of Jason's arm. "What the hell does that mean? Jerk him off?"

"No," Jason explained calmly, "Chat me up. Flirt."

"Oh." Adam squinted up at Ewan. "Yes! I am! He's gorgeous! So, get lost!"

Jason laughed. He thought the idea of anyone fighting over him hilarious.

Infuriated, Ewan threw off his robe and jumped in, splashing the other two. He waded over to Jason and wrapped around him possessively, physically moving him away from Adam.

"You keep away from me lover, yeah?" Ewan warned.

"You're not serious!" Jason laughed. "Ewan, Adam was not chatting me up!"

"Speak for yourself, doctor." Adam laughed demonically and made his way to the ladder.

Chuckling at Ewan's pout and glare, Jason shook his head in amazement. "Don't you worry, love." Jason kissed his cheek.

Watching Adam walk over to him, Jack smiled in delight as Adam grabbed a towel and dried himself off. "You're a fucking riot."

"Hey, doesn't hurt to try." Adam rubbed it through his hair.

"Any luck?" Jack asked.

"If Ewan wasn't here. Maybe. He did seem a bit intrigued." Adam caught someone shouting and waving from over the fence. "Food's here. I'll be back."

After he left, Jack kept his smile, then found Ewan and Jason snuggling up in the pool. His expression changed instantly.

With Ewan's arms around his neck, his legs wrapped around his waist, Jason carried Ewan around the pool slowly.

"You made me very jealous. You don't mean to, do you?"

"No. You're being silly, Ewan." Jason pecked him on the lips.

"You just want me, yeah?" Ewan shivered. "I don't like the idea of you meeting someone else while you're here. There were so many appealing men in Los Angeles, Jas, temptation lurks everywhere."

"I promise you, I will never go out on you."

"You did, though, Jas, you did. You got bloody married!"

"Don't throw that in my face again, Ewan!"

"Yeah. All right...all right." Ewan relented, then noticed their hips were attached nicely under the water. "Give us a kiss."

Backing so he could lean against the side of the pool, Jason smiled, "Gladly," and closed his eyes as he leaned close.

When Adam returned with the bags of food, he stopped to see the two in a deep swoon at the other end. Jack had been watching, getting himself into a lather over it.

Setting the sushi on the table, Adam got Jack's attention instantly. Then he nodded to the pool. "True love. Makes me sick."

"Won't last." Jack began opening the bags to graze.

"Hey, lovebirds!" Adam shouted, "Food's here!"

They acknowledged him, then continued kissing for a moment longer.

"I'd shag you now, Mr. Gallagher, if I could." Jason jammed his bikini-covered hardness up against Ewan roughly.

"And I'd let you shag me, Dr. Phillips..." Ewan licked at his rough jaw in excitement.

"We should eat. I am a bit peckish."

"Aye. Lunch, then shag."

"Cushty." Jason smiled.

As the two men climbed out and walked back to their meal, Adam and Jack stopped eating to watch.

"Two fucking hard-ons," Adam mumbled to him.

"Christ, look at the size of Jason's..." Jack muttered back.

"Oi! What are you looking at!" Ewan slanted his eyes at them. "You just look at your own plate, ya gits!"

Jason blushed horribly and tried to cover up as he walked.

"Doctor." Adam nudged his chair out for him to have a seat, smiling devilishly at him.

As he approached, Jason grabbed a towel and wrapped it around his hips, then sat down.

"Hung like a horse!" Jack laughed and then coughed in a crackle of phlegm.

"Oi!" Ewan took a seat and tried to smack both sets of ogling leers playfully. "He's spoken for, yeah?"

"No harm in looking, is there, Ewan?" Adam stuffed a piece of sushi in his mouth and winked at Jason flirtatiously.

Pretending this was not unusual or humiliating, Jason found some food to load his plate, grabbing a pair of chopsticks in the process.

Finally, smiling affectionately, Ewan moaned, "Oh, the cock on him, yeah? Oh, what a lovely cock."

"Ewan!" Jason choked on his rice ball.

The other two burst out laughing as Ewan winked at his lover.

# Chapter Fifteen

"We rushed over the first moment we spotted it, Priscilla."
Victoria handed her the newspaper. "Where is he?"

"Oh, my god!" She gave it to Charles quickly, who
grabbed it and stared at the photo in shock. "He's in
California right now! He left last Sunday. He said it was for
a doctors' convention."

Hearing the same patent excuse, Paul took off his
glasses and rubbed his eyes. "There seems to be quite a few
of those lately."

"Yes! I thought so as well!" Priscilla agreed innocently.
"But he does like to keep up with the medical news—"

"Priscilla!" Victoria shouted at her ignorance. "He's not
going to any conventions! He's in love with a young male
actor! This actor!" She pounded the photo with her index
finger.

"A male—" Priscilla gulped audibly. "In love with a
male actor? My Jason? No. This was just a kiss hello. Look.
It's a friendly peck." She showed it to Victoria again to
verify. "He's a very kind man. I'm quite sure you're all
mistaken."

Charles' deep sigh was heard behind her. She spun

around to see his face. "Charles?"

"You remember what I mentioned earlier?"

"No. What, Charles?" Typically she didn't recall a thing.

Glimpsing back at Victoria and Paul, Charles was hesitant to reveal what his suspicions were.

"If you have an opinion, Charles, feel free," Paul prodded him.

"Well, sir, it isn't my place to meddle in family affairs."

"You're family!" Priscilla shouted before she thought it through.

"He is?" Victoria blinked her eyes in surprise.

Growing increasingly uncomfortable, Charles bowed his head. "Shall I make some tea?"

"No. Charles." Paul went after him before he vanished. "You've been living here since Marge first came into the estate. We value your opinion."

Charles was dragged back to the lounge reluctantly, certainly feeling as if he had already said too much.

"He had Margerie's grave dug up and moved," Priscilla said casually, and fixed a loose strand of her hair.

"Wha-at?" Paul and Victoria shouted, then rushed through the house to gape at it from the rear window.

Using the opportunity to talk privately, Charles said, "Before, Cilla— Remember I mentioned something Jason must have done to anger everyone, so that he could not inherit the estate?"

"Oh! That!" She waved at him as if he were being silly.

"Yes! Well, the reason he was cut out originally from the will was that he is a homosexual!"

"No, Charles, he's an impotent!" she corrected.

Rubbing his face in frustration, Charles was beginning to think she was a complete idiot.

"Oh, my word! Paul! He's moved Margerie!" Victoria gasped at the gaping hole it had left in the landscaping. "What on earth is he doing?"

"Moving her? Selling the estate." Paul sighed, leaning

up against the glass, his warm breath clouding it. "He's got something planned. Maybe he thought enough time had gone by and we would not hold him to the contract."

"But it was so bold! Digging her up! Going to California to be with this—this actor!" she cringed. "He's gone mad, Paul! Our son the doctor has completely gone mad!"

"No, Vicky, not mad. He's just sick of the charade. And...quite frankly, he's lonely."

"Lonely! Oh, Paul, don't you go getting soft! Priscilla's a lovely girl! She's devoted to our Jason! She comes from a nice family! No! There's no excuse for this behavior! I want you to contact our solicitor first thing in the morning and go over the conditions we set out for him in order to inherit the estate! Margerie would be furious! Moved her grave! Oh! If that doesn't end all!"

"You hated Marge," Paul reminded her.

"That's neither here nor there! I want Jason to be married to a woman, become a father! Not photographed in some sleazy tabloid in a homosexual affair! It's unacceptable behavior! No! He is to return everything at once!"

"And give it to whom? Willie the corgi is dead!" Paul tried to keep his voice down.

"Then it goes to Charles!" Victoria shouted. "Charles was next on the list! You get busy and see to it Jason doesn't keep a pence of this estate!"

"Victoria, calm yourself! Listen to what you are saying!"

"I've made up my mind!" She twisted away in a huff and went back to the lounge.

In the light of the lamp on the table, Charles and Priscilla leaned close to read the article written to accompany the cover photo.

"It says he's involved with that actor, Ewan Gallagher. I've never heard of him, Charles."

"Neither have I, Cilla. But, it says he's from Carlisle

originally."

"Jason met him in the A&E." Victoria overheard their comments.

They spun around, guilt written all over their faces from their posture, but Victoria didn't react.

"Jason was his doctor. I'm sorry, Priscilla, that this has all been kept secret from you. But I'm sure you understand why."

"Is that why I was picked to marry him? Just so he could get the estate?"

"Yes, dear." Victoria peeked at Paul, who was hiding in a corner, trying not to become involved.

"So even though he's impotent, you still think he's seeing this actor?"

"Impotent?" Paul piped up.

"Yes. Didn't you know?" Priscilla nodded her head it was true. "Oh, yes. He can't make love. He told me it's a horrible problem. He's never even touched me. When I accidentally see him naked, he shies away and hides! Poor man."

Victoria and Paul exchanged glances of disbelief. It was Charles' turn to hide. "I'll make us a pot of tea." He left quickly.

"For Christ's sake." Paul rubbed his face tiredly. "Impotent."

"Oh, yes." Priscilla nodded her head again to prove it.

"You mean…" Victoria choked as her throat closed, "You and Jason have never consummated your marriage? In over a year?"

"Why, no. He can't have sex. I've just told you why." She laughed at their stupidity.

"He'll get it annulled," Paul fretted. "That's his plan. An annulment."

"He can't do that!" Victoria shouted, "It's been too long!"

"Never consummated the marriage. I'm not sure about that, Vicky."

"Nope. Impotent." Priscilla repeated proudly.

"Ahh...ahh..." Jason thrust into Ewan deeply, the orgasm rushing up his spine.

"That's it, love, that's it..." Ewan urged him on, sweat coating them both.

A deep masculine grunt emerged from Jason's lips as he came, his eyes sealed tight, his hips shuddering.

The moment he had, Ewan wrapped his arms and legs around him and urged him down on top of his chest.

Jason pulled out gently and rested, panting to catch his breath.

"What a shag you are, yeah?" Ewan kissed and licked at his dewy face. "Oh, my doctor, you are so hot in bed...so hot."

"Me?" Jason laughed tiredly, "I'm your puppet! You're the one with all the wild moves."

"No...it's you..." Ewan squirmed under him, mingling their sweat. "Get me hard again...I want another."

Jason started laughing, he was so exhausted from his *one* he was ready to sleep.

Nudging him over, Ewan began working himself to harden up. "You do it, you do it..."

Nodding he would, Jason leaned on his side and propped up his head in his hand. Taking over for Ewan, he massaged him and brought him back up again.

"Yeah...that's it, love..."

"If you scrub up, I'll give you a blow-job."

Before he had even finished his sentence, Ewan had popped out of the bed and bounded to the bathroom.

Stunned, frozen where he was, Jason wished he had that energy. Well, at twenty-one he did. At thirty-seven it had waned a bit.

A second later, Ewan dove back on the bed. "Scrubbed like a surgeon."

Jason just shook his head at him, smiling. "You'll wear

me out."

"Oh, bullocks. You're a perfect match for me. Yeah? Now stick me helmet in your gob."

"Okay, Mr. Romantic!" Jason started lowering down.

"You need romance? Yeah? You want red roses and some sweets?" Ewan teased.

"No, skip the sweets. Watchin' me waistline." Jason winked.

"All right, no sweets. Get busy." He raised his hips off the bed.

"Randy? After you just shagged me senseless?" Jason ran his hand over him, he was hard as stone.

"Watching you come, it made me crazy! Yeah? So, I'm randy again. Stop gobbing off and get to sucking me helmet!"

Maneuvering himself between Ewan's thighs, Jason licked and teased him, not giving him what he craved easily.

Ewan squirmed in delight, moaning and shivering with the game.


"Priscilla," Paul tired to be delicate, "Jason is not impotent."

"Oh, yes he is."

"No, dear. He's just gay. He doesn't get sexually stimulated from women."

As Charles set the tea tray down, he watched her expression carefully.

"Not stimulated by women?" Priscilla tried to get the meaning. "So, even another woman wouldn't make him excited?"

"Right." Paul spoke slowly, making sure she was comprehending it. "But, men, on the other hand, make him excited."

"Men?" She touched her lip. "Are you certain? Men?"

Victoria threw the newspaper at her and shouted in exasperation, "He's kissing a bloke here, Priscilla! See?

168

Kissing a bloke!"

As Priscilla attempted to grasp the concept, Paul continued, "He's not impotent, dear, he just told you he was so you wouldn't expect sex from him."

"You mean, he lied?"

"Did Margerie know you were this thick when she paired you off with my son!?" Victoria shouted in anger.

"Vicky!" Paul scolded her.

"Well, it's not that complicated to understand, Paul!" She waved her hands expressively. "He likes men! Full stop!"

"I need to lay down." Priscilla rose up unsteadily.

Charles rushed to help her. "Come along, dear."

Victoria and Paul watched as the old valet helped her up the stairs.

When they were gone, Paul shook his head at his wife. "You didn't have to be so insensitive. The poor thing has been through hell."

"Do you blame our son?" She gestured to the stair. "Look at what he was saddled with! I would have gone off women as well!"

"Vicky! You're not helping the situation!"

"He should have married Kelly. He'd have been happy with Kelly." She shook her head.

"Let's go home. I'm exhausted." Paul reached out to her.

"What are you going to do with that thing?" She pointed to the newspaper.

"Leave it. Maybe it'll help it sink in."

Finally sated, they cuddled together in the big king-sized bed. A ceiling fan above it kept a gentle breeze blowing to cool off their overheated skin.

"Oh, love, you are too perfect." Ewan kissed his sleepy face.

"Not perfect, knackered."

169

"Yeah. Knackered."

"You have to wake up early for anything?"

"Aye."

"Bullocks," Jason groaned. "I want a lay-in. I want to relax. I want us to sight-see."

"I'm sorry, love." Ewan kissed his face again.

"Do those blokes come over like they did earlier often?"

"Aye. They do. I think they like it here."

"It's strange."

"No. Not really, love. I know Jack. He thinks he needs to watch over me. See, he and Adam, they knew I was on me own when I first met them. On me own and in a strange country. So, they looked after me."

"What about 'Vee'," Jason grumbled.

"No. He wasn't living here. And he wasn't a minder. He was a publicity stunt."

"You and Adam ever shag?" Jason's eyes were closed, his body completely at rest.

"Adam? Me?" Ewan laughed. "No! Why? You fancy him, don't you?"

"No! I don't fancy him," Jason mumbled, totally exhausted.

"Then why did you ask?"

"'Cause he's a handsome bloke, and he's always here."

"You think he's handsome?"

"Aye."

"Not me. Too groomed. I don't know. There's something about him I don't find exciting."

"I'm shagged out." Jason was falling asleep.

"You promise me, even if he's sniffing around, you'll not go with him," Ewan warned.

"G'night, Mr. Gallagher." Jason curled into the pillows.

"Night, love." Ewan kissed his cheek and closed his eyes.

# Chapter Sixteen

Jason was just finishing loading the dishwasher after he had cooked them both some breakfast. It was almost eight a.m. and they knew they had a full day ahead.

Sitting at the kitchen table, the sunlight pouring in through the two walls of windows, Ewan was reading the last few pages of the manuscript.

"Morning, men." Adam strut in, the phone on his ear, then sniffed. "Did someone cook breakfast?"

Wiping his hands on a dish rag, Jason laughed at him. "Yes. You just missed it."

"Damn! You can cook, too?" Adam immediately went back to the call, "Yes? Hello— Adam Lewis here—"

When Jason sat down with Ewan, Ewan rolled his eyes at Adam's chronic use of the mobile phone.

"You want more coffee?" Jason asked, seeing his cup was empty.

"No, love. You don't have to wait on me. Really."

"I'm not bothered. It makes me feel useful."

Clicking the phone closed, Adam announced, "All right, Mr. Gallagher, motorcycle lessons in an hour, then elocution lessons at noon, acting coach at two, and..."

Checking the pocket notebook quickly, he added, "Dinner with Mr. Foreman at seven. I want you to meet with him over a meal to discuss the contract."

"Right," Ewan sighed, closing the last scene of the script.

"Crikey!" Jason laughed. "What a loaded day!"

"Me own fault. Have to learn how to ride a motorbike now, don't I?" Ewan stood, setting his empty mug in the sink, then stretched his back muscles.

"I reckon I'll just hang around here, then." Jason got to his feet and handed Ewan his cup to set in the sink as well.

Ewan pouted his bottom lip sadly. "You don't want to come?"

"Come? Watch you learn how to ride a motorbike?" Jason chuckled softly.

"You don't worry about Jason." Adam went for Ewan's arm and tugged him to get moving. "Go run a brush through your mop and let's go."

As he scuffed to do just that, he mumbled, "Bullocks," under his breath.

Smiling, Adam turned back to Jason and said, "What sights did you want to see when you came here?"

Crossing his arms over his chest and leaning back on the counter, Jason smiled in amusement. "I don't know. I suppose the usual."

"Have you ever seen the California coastline?"

"Only from the air." Jason smiled.

"Then you don't know what you're missing. Leave it to me—"

Brushed up and looking adorable, Ewan returned, still pouting. "I want me lover with me!"

"Aww, come here." Jason opened his arms.

Ewan cuddled against him, hiding his face. "Please come."

"Just to stand and watch? Then what about your voice lessons? I'd be a distraction and in the way." He wrapped around him, kissing his hair, and glanced up to see Adam

172

staring.

"I don't want you home on your own all day—"

"Not to worry, Ewan." Adam checked his voicemail messages again. "He won't be lonely."

Jason felt Ewan's body tense up. "He winding me up?" he asked Jason, still in his embrace.

"Yes, and no. He said he'd take me to see the beach."

"No!" Ewan shouted. "Oh, here we go!" He shoved back. "He's got it in for you, love! You and he don't need to spend alone time, yeah?"

"Ewan! Please, trust me." Jason grasped for his arms and brought him back to lean against his length. "I've got less than two weeks here and I do want to see something. On the days when I can go with you, I will."

"Bullocks!" Ewan whined, "Not alone with him, Jas..."

"Baby..." Jason kissed his face and made him look into his eyes. "Do you trust me?"

"Aye! I don't trust him!"

Adam laughed in delight. Hearing someone at the front door, he said, "Your car's here, Ewan."

Groaning in frustration, Ewan rubbed his hips against Jason for some last minute reassurances. "You said that your cock was mine."

"It is." Jason smiled at him sweetly. "Not even that wench back in Carlisle's touched it."

"We are going to dinner with Dennis together. Yeah? No excuses. After me lessons, you and me."

"And a whole night of shagging after." Jason nuzzled his nose playfully as Adam went to answer the door.

"Mine." Ewan cupped his hand over Jason's cotton shorts.

"Yours." Jason made sure they were communicating.

Sighing, Ewan lowered his head to turn and leave. Before he did, Jason yanked him back and kissed him passionately.

When Adam returned to hurry Ewan up, he stopped at the doorway and stared at Jason as he wrapped his muscular

173

arms around Ewan like a guardian angel.

Hearing him come into the room, Jason blinked open his eyes, met Adam's hungry leer, and then finished up with his kiss. "I'll see you later."

"Right." Ewan squeezed his hand and spun around. Seeing Adam there, he pointed a warning finger into his face. "You leave him be! He's not interested! Yeah? If I find you've been handling him, I'll have ya!"

"Yes, Mr. Gallagher," Adam laughed, then nudged him to go, both his hands on Ewan's tight bottom.

Jason and Adam stood at the door as Ewan carried his sunglasses and baseball cap with him into the limousine.

Seeing Ewan's little boy frown, Jason smiled sadly and waved, throwing him a kiss.

Adam watched the exchange. "You really love him, don't you?"

"Yes. Ever since I laid eyes on him in the casualty room."

Ewan leaned out of the window as the car pulled away, his disappointment overwhelmingly obvious.

"Ewan told me. He said he was hit by a car." Adam closed the door.

"He was. Fractured his left tibia." Jason ran his hand through his hair, remembering that day with perfect clarity.

"Love at first sight?" Adam walked around the house, shutting lights and getting them ready to leave.

Jason laughed to himself at that old cliché.

"You ready?" Adam took his keys out of his pocket and jingled them.

Checking his back pocket for his wallet, Jason nodded, "Ready, boss."


The convertible top down, a pair of Ewan's sunglasses on his nose, Jason felt the warm sun and air with a sense of triumph. He could live here. This weather! No rain! No icy cold! And it was so incredibly beautiful. The coast road they were flying down rested upon cliffs overlooking the water and white sand.

The music blasting, the earpiece from his phone attached to his head, Adam spoke to more than a dozen clients on his way to the beach.

Jason was experiencing a sense of freedom he had never felt before. Carlisle, the stifling claustrophobia of that area of North England, felt like the pit in a castle keep. Not that it wasn't lovely in England. On the contrary, it was very picturesque. But it was what the sterility did to his sense of self that was the problem. It smothered him. Living in that shadowy mansion with that mousy woman was killing him— Aging him before his time, weakening his spirit.

But this? This sun! This fantastic BMW! That view of sand and surf? Oh, yes! Yes!

He never wanted to go back. What if he didn't? What if he just stayed? Like Ewan had said, make arrangements from afar, could he do that?

Ending another call, Adam signaled and turned off the highway down a long exit ramp. As they slowed, Jason felt the air heat up and the sun rays scorching.

Lowering the loud rock music, Adam turned to look at Jason before they halted and then proceeded past a stop sign.

Adam seemed to have a specific destination in mind. Veering off the main road, sand under his tread, he spun dust behind him heading for the water.

A deserted expanse of land sat before the tidal waves. Finally pausing on packed sand, Adam shut the engine and unwrapped the telephone earpiece from his head.

"Lovely." Jason smiled broadly, gazing at the horizon where sea blue met sky blue.

"Let's go." Adam climbed out quickly and waited for Jason to do the same before setting the alarm.

The moment his feet hit the sand, Jason took off his shoes and socks. Digging his toes into the velvety softness, he groaned in pleasure.

"Does England have beaches like this?" Adam led the way to the water's edge.

"No. Not like this…well, Cornwall does have some nice beach areas, but the sand isn't quite this soft."

"Cornwall?"

"Southwest," Jason clarified.

"Right." Adam nodded. "And Carlisle?"

"Northwest." Jason laughed, making his way to the hard packed wet sand that was left behind by the waves.

When his toes touched the Pacific Ocean for the first time, Jason felt like it was a milestone. He wished Ewan were there to share the excitement. "The water is so warm. It's unbelievable." Jason inhaled the clean air deep into his lungs.

"It gets even warmer later in the year. I'm a lightweight. I don't think it's very warm right now." Adam leaned down and dragged his hand through it.

"Warmer than this? Oh, you're joking. This time of year you have to wear a wetsuit in Cornwall or you'll freeze your bullocks off."

Adam chuckled. "Christ, I love your accent. It's different from Ewan's. In the beginning, I couldn't understand a word he said. That was why we got him elocution lessons. But your accent I can understand."

"Well, though I was brought up in the same place as Ewan, my parents were from the south of England. I suppose my accent is more like a true Londoner than a northerner."

"Well, whatever the reason, it's very elegant." Adam smiled affectionately.

Trying not to tread anywhere near the possibility of attraction between them, Jason walked along the lapping waves, allowing his ankles and feet to get wet as he gazed out at the horizon. Jason felt Adam watching him.

He headed for a mound of grassy dunes. Setting his shoes down, Jason pulled off his shirt and laid it out on the dry sand, then sat on it.

Adam joined him, both staring west into the bright sky.

"I could live here, I really could," Jason mumbled, mostly to himself.

"Then live here." Adam leaned back on his elbow, staring at him.

"It's complicated." Jason pushed the sunglasses up on his head and wrapped his arms around his knees.

"The wife?"

"Aye. The wife, the sham marriage."

"You wouldn't be the first gay man to marry for appearances, or money."

"No. Perhaps not. But, it's still my dilemma."

"What are your plans, if you don't mind me asking."

"No. I don't mind." Jason sighed and twisted his knees to face Adam directly. "It's just that I don't clearly know what they are myself. I'm working on keeping the money and getting rid of the baggage."

"I expected that much." Adam laughed softly.

"It's…it's just complicated," Jason repeated, then found the sun too bright and dropped the glasses back on his nose.

"You know, at the moment, Ewan is making enough to support you."

Gazing out at the horizon again, Jason inhaled deeply, not answering.

"Too proud to have a man support you?"

"Something like that, yes," Jason whispered.

"So, back to England, back to the wife you go?" Adam pulled a long blade of grass out of the ground to play with.

"If and when I do go back, it'll be temporary. I just have to get my affairs in order." He wondered how he had done at the Sotheby's auction. He was certain it was yesterday.

Adam began tickling Jason with the fluffy tip of the grass.

Jason jumped, thinking a bug was on him. When he found the tuft of grass and the smirk, he laughed, "What are you playing at?"

177

"Just toying with you, doctor." Adam used the furry end to stroke Jason's leg hair.

"That tickles." Jason nudged it away and rubbed his skin briskly to rid the sensation.

Adam tossed the grass aside and moved closer to him, almost touching.

"Love—" Jason knew his motives. "I can't. You know I can't."

"You drive me crazy!" Adam stroked the soft hair on his leg. "That fucking accent! Your body! Face! Those green eyes! Christ, Jason, you're so fucking appealing!"

"I am flattered. Honestly. But you know the way Ewan and I feel about each other."

"He's a kid!" Adam moved closer. "He's only twenty-one!"

"I'm well aware of his age, Adam." Jason looked behind him in order to see if he could move back from him.

"Yes, he's sexy and wild, but he's got the brains of a kid! He's still growing!"

"Look, bad mouthing Ewan is not the way to get into me knickers!" Jason scooted back.

"Then what is?" Adam got to his knees and then leapt on top of Jason, trapping him underneath.

"Adam! This is well out of order!" Jason nudged him to get up.

"Kiss me!"

"No! Look, I don't want to fight with you or harm you—"

"Good! Then kiss me!"

"Adam!" Jason gripped his shoulders, pressing him back. "Be sensible!"

"No one is on this beach! It's deserted! No one needs to know!" He ground his hips into Jason's.

"I'll know! It's bad enough I'm married! I won't have an affair!"

"One kiss!"

"No. All right, enough. Get up." Jason was losing his

humor rapidly.

Hesitating, Adam finally sighed and slid off slowly, rubbing against Jason's body. As Adam sat back, he allowed his hand to drop to Jason's chest, then dragged it over his crotch before sitting up.

Jason was not stupid. He felt every grope and knew they were desperate attempts. Finally allowed to move, Jason stood, brushing off the sand. "I should have known this would happen. All I wanted was a pleasant day out. I should have known." He lifted his shirt from the sand and shook it off.

Getting to his feet as well, Adam sighed wearily. "I won't make apologies, Jason. You knew you wanted Ewan when you first met him. Well—"

"Oh, don't be absurd!" Jason put the shirt on and grabbed his shoes in irritation.

When they sat down again in the hot convertible, Adam sighed, "Ewan, you are one lucky fucker."

Jason ignored it and stared out of the windshield at the water splashing against the sand.


His helmet under his arm, beads of sweat on his brow and upper lip, Ewan took a break from the motorcycle training and flipped out his cell phone. "Oi! Adam! Answer, you git!" Getting his answering service, Ewan was about to disconnect when he reconsidered. "Adam, it's me, you with Jas? Call me!" He hung up as his instructor appeared before him. "Ready, Ewan?"

"Aye." He stuffed the phone in the pocket of his leather jacket, then put the helmet on.


They were silent.

Adam stuck his earpiece back in, then checked his messages. He heard the one from Ewan.

His attention on the scenery, Jason seemed to have

179

nothing to say.

When they headed in the opposite direction as the house, Jason cleared his throat in the awkward silence and asked, "Are you kidnapping me?"

Adam burst out laughing. "Don't tempt me! No, I feel badly for what I did. I've a surprise."

"A surprise?" Jason asked sarcastically.


Shoving his sunglasses back to the top of his head, Jason followed Adam into, and out of the back of a building. The sound of revving engines greeted his ears. Seeing a leather-clad beauty on a powerful motorbike did cheer him up considerably.

Jason watched as Ewan was flagged down to end the session. Ewan shut the ignition and shoved the heavy bike up on its kickstand. When he took off his helmet and shook out his long damp hair, Jason lit up at the handsome man, staring at him with lurid thoughts racing around his head.

Smiling, Ewan swung his leather leg over the bike and deliberately appeared to stalk his lover.

"Oh, bloody hell..." Jason hissed, his eyes glued to that vision as Adam observed from behind.

"Excuse me, mister," Ewan play-acted to tease him. "Is there a doctor in the 'ouse?"

"Christ, you're horny." Jason sucked a breath of air in between his teeth.

"You've a thing for leather?"

"I didn't. Till now." Jason swept his eyes over his length once more.

Seeing Adam behind him, Ewan said, "How long 'ave I got?"

Adam checked his watch. "An hour."

"Cush—" Ewan grabbed Jason and dragged him inside the building.

The instructor tilted his head to Adam. "Who's that guy?"

"Some married doctor he's got a hard-on for."

"Oh! Too much information!" The instructor held up his hands, and went back to tend the bikes.

Staring in the direction they had left, Adam sighed and went back to his phone.

In the locker room, behind a shower curtain, Jason had Ewan's leather jeans yanked down his thighs, and was pumping his hips between them.

Squeezing Jason tight, trying to give him enough friction without penetrating, since they had no lubrication, Ewan finally reached between his legs to grip Jason with his hand, urging him on.

Thrusting into that tight palm, Jason came, jamming his hips against Ewan's bottom. Before Ewan could take a breath, Jason had turned him around, then dropped to his knees to suck him.

His fingers covered in semen, Ewan leaned against the tiled wall, closing his eyes as his lover tried his best to get him to climax.

Tiptoeing in, Adam could hear their heavy breaths and grunts echoing in the empty room. Moving past the vacant stalls, through the toilets, he paused, knowing he was close.

As Ewan went into a spasm of pleasure, shivering in delight, Jason swallowed him down, moaning as he enjoyed Ewan's orgasm. Finally sitting back, Jason got a good look at that sight; the open leather jeans, the open leather jacket, and the long hair surrounding the face of an angel. "Oh, look at you..." he hissed, "Ewan, you are fantastic."

Catching his breath, Ewan opened his eyes to Jason's overflowing affection. "Aye, love, and now knackered!"

Standing up, Jason pressed him against the shower wall

and made for his lips. With his left hand smoothing over the exposed skin of Ewan's chest and abdomen, Jason dug his right hand through Ewan's long hair.

The edge of the curtain left a gap. Adam stood still, peering through.

After they had kissed, loving the gentle pressure and lapping of their tongues, Jason set back to smile dreamily at him. "I love you, Ewan."

"Oh, you say all the right things to me, doctor." Ewan sighed wearily.

"Do I have to get you decent?" Jason indicated Ewan's exposed genitals.

"Aye, love. Elocution lessons for me northern tongue."

"I love that northern tongue." Jason kissed him, teasing Ewan's lips with his own.

"Oh, I want to go home and shag all day. This is bullocks…" Ewan moaned.

Knowing he was making it worse for him, Jason stepped away from him and tried to close his leather slacks and jacket.

"Don't bother, love. I've got to get me jeans on again."

"Aye…right." Jason nodded and moved aside.

Adam started out of his dream and slipped out of sight.

When they came out of the locker room, Adam was standing near the door with his phone to his ear.

"So, I should get home to shower and change before dinner." Ewan held his hand as he walked out.

"I'll catch a nap and some exercise." Jason checked the time.

"Right. So glad you showed up," Ewan purred.

"Thank Adam. I had no idea I was coming by." Jason tried to meet his eye unsuccessfully as he continued to converse on the tiny phone.

"Aye, I will, love. Let me go." Ewan found the driver waiting.

Jason pecked his lips and stood back as he walked away.

Ewan waved once more, then disappeared around a bend.

Flipping off the phone, Adam tilted his head for Jason to follow him to his car. "You look terrific. I see hot sex agrees with you."

"Oi! You peeking?"

Unlocking the doors with a chirp, Adam climbed in. When Jason did as well, he said sarcastically, "Would you care if I did?"

"Naughty! Naughty!" Jason couldn't believe it. "You didn't watch us!"

"When you can't get any, being a voyeur is your only option." He started the engine.

Trying to get over the shock, and wondering if he was upset about it, Jason stuck the glasses back on his head as he was driven back to Ewan's house.

Thinking Adam would just drop him off and leave, he was a little annoyed he followed him in. Still on the phone, talking as he unlocked the door and opened the light, Adam headed for the kitchen and some liquid refreshment.

Jason climbed the stairs intent on a work out. When he caught sight of a little woman in one of the rooms he jumped out of his skin. "Hello?"

"Jello!" She smiled and waved, a dusting cloth in her hand.

"Oh, are you the cleaner?" Jason asked.

"Si!" She smiled sweetly.

"Carry on!" Jason smiled back and waved.

"Yes, I took care of that." Adam poured some lemonade into a glass of ice. "Jack, don't worry. I'm at Ewan's place now. Yes...he's here." Adam smiled and flickered his eyes to the ceiling and upper floor. "I did. Got him alone on a beach. Jumped his fucking bones. Nothing. He's really hung up on Ewan." Sipping the glass, he nodded. "I will. He's set to meet with him at seven for dinner." Another swallow of lemonade and he said, "Right. Did you see the paper? Yeah? The Associated Press picked it up? You're kidding. Well, that will show up in England no doubt. Yeah, right. I will. See ya." Dialing again, he carried his glass with him to the upper floor. "Yes, hello, this is Adam Lewis, may I speak with John Keller, please..." He passed the bedroom and waved to the maid, then continued down the hall.

Jason was in a pair of gym shorts pummeling the leather bag when Adam peeked in.

Pausing outside the room, watching from where he was, Adam finished his call and made another one, leaning against the doorframe. Thirty minutes and six calls later, Adam took a break as Jason removed the boxing gloves and climbed onto the treadmill. "Jesus Christ," Adam shook his head in awe.

Jason spun his head to where Adam stood, then he started the treadmill to warm up his legs. "How long were you standing there?" Jason asked.

The empty glass in his hand, Adam entered the workout room and shook his head at him. "You're a machine!"

As Adam watched, Jason brought the speed up quickly and had it moving at about seven miles per hour. "You should do a bit," Jason said.

"Why? You think I'm out of shape?" Adam leaned on the bars of the treadmill.

"A bit soft. How old are you?"

"Thirty-two." Adam poked at his own mid-section curiously.

"It wouldn't hurt, mate." Jason laughed, then increased

the speed to seven point five.

"Is that why you're not attracted to me? Because I'm out of shape?"

"No, you git. You're lovely. I'm just spoken for." After a few minutes where Jason was puffing and Adam just staring, Jason asked, "Don't you have anything to do?"

"No. Not at the moment. I do most of my work via phone. I just call clients and set up appointments or get them services they need. I don't necessarily have to be there, unless they're new, like Ewan, and want me there. But right now, Ewan is our newest client. Actually, Jack said he wanted to stop picking up new people. We've a ton of clients and really make plenty on them. It was just that Ewan was irresistible. Jack had to have him."

"Don't put it that way," Jason growled, increasing the speed to eight miles per hour.

"Right. Well, we've stopped right now. Ewan will be our last until we either lose some of ours or they die," he laughed. "Hang on," flipping out his phone he said, "Hello?"

As he talked he moved away from the whining noise of the machine.

Pacing down the hall, avoiding the rooms that were being vacuumed and the noise from the gym, Adam got busy again.

When he was through, Jason stopped the machine and wiped the sweat off his face with a towel. Shutting everything down, he passed Adam in the hall on his way to the pool.

Adam instinctively followed, still babbling on a call.

Out in the sunshine, Adam watched as Jason rinsed quickly in an outdoor shower, then dove in and started swimming laps.

When he did, Adam's mouth hung open. "Hold on," he cupped the phone. "Are you insane? If you're trying to impress me, you have! Stop! I'm exhausted watching you!"

It appeared Jason hadn't heard him. Soon he met the

end of the pool and spun under the water to push off from it to swim laps.

"Yeah, I'm here. Just watching some incredible athlete work out. Christ, makes me feel like a fat pig! What? I am not soft!" He poked his belly again. "Shut the fuck up. Now, look, who did you want me to call again?"

After Adam counted about twenty laps, Jason stopped and caught his breath. Wiping the water from his eyes he found Adam on a lounge chair staring at him.

"Lazy git." Jason laughed sadly. "You'll be as fat as Jack soon." Doing a push up on the pool rim, Jason climbed out and stood over Adam, who shaded his eyes even with sunglasses on.

Squinting as Jason dripped, both hands on his hips, his chest moving to recuperate his breath, Adam sighed, "I can't do what you do. It would kill me."

"You start slow." Jason sat next to him on another lounge chair, stretching out his legs.

"Want to be my personal trainer?"

Jason chuckled softly and shut his eyes to rest.

"I'm serious! You know how much money those guys make? Some up to two hundred dollars an hour!"

"Is that right?" Jason kept his eyes closed, seemingly lulled by the warm sun, which was drying his wet skin quickly.

"See? I'm thinking about your well being. If you stay, give up the money to the ex, and don't want Ewan to support you, then you have a new career."

"I'll think about it." He rose up off the lounge chair.

"What's next? Riding the stationary bike?"

"Nope, shower and nap."

Adam moved to stand.

"No! You can't come!" Jason laughed in amazement and walked away.

"You're mean!" Adam shouted, "Mean and vicious!" Hearing Jason's laughter, he chuckled to himself and flipped out his phone.

*For Love and Money*

After a shower and before his nap, Jason checked the time and sat with the phone on his lap in Ewan's bedroom. Taking his wallet out for the information, he dialed the country code and number and waited for it to connect. "Hullo? This is Dr. Jason Phillips—"

"Doctor! I've been hoping you would ring! We've instructions not to call your home, is that right?"

"Yes, thanks ever so much for that, Faye. I just now got a chance to ring. How did the auction go?"

"Splendid! Oh, the museum purchased your Sir Henry Raeburn for four hundred thousand pounds!"

Jason closed his eyes and shouted 'Yes!' silently. "That is good news."

"Oh, it was an amazing crowd. They were packed in Sotheby's auction house, standing room only. The excitement was palpable!"

"I wish I'd've been there. Truly I do." Jason was so happy he could burst.

"I've the list of all the prices. Shall I get it?"

"Please, Faye, it would be a great help." When she left the phone, Jason rummaged around for a pen and pad. Opening the drawer, he found what he needed and got it ready for her amounts.

"Right. Still there?"

"Yes, I'm ready for you."

"The Stubbs, two hundred and fifty thousand; the Constable, four-hundred and fifty; the Duncan Grant, thirty-five thousand; the William Hunt, seventy-five thousand; the Waterhouse only made seventeen-thousand-five hundred, since it was just one of his sketches."

"Okay. I'm with you so far…" Jason was scribbling as quickly as he could.

"Right, the Allan Ramsey portrait, fifteen thousand; the Thomas Lawrence, seventeen; the William Blake engraving, five thousand; William Payne illustration, eighty-five hundred; Turner's watercolor, fifteen thousand; and the Gainsborough sketch for the portrait of Mr. and Mrs. Andrews went for ten thousand. And I think that is all. Minus ten percent for us!"

"That's a bit over one million one hundred thousand pounds." He calculated the math quickly.

"I don't have it here, but that sounds right."

"Did you deposit the check where I had instructed?"

"Oh, yes, doctor. It's all taken care of."

"I'm very pleased. Faye, you've done a wonderful job for me."

"Any time, doctor."

"I've got some period furniture, as I've mentioned. I'll ring you later in the month and set you up with them."

"Very good! I look forward to hearing from you!"

"Right, cheers."

"Cheers!"

He hung up, scribbling more numbers. "In this exchange rate, it's over two million American dollars." Scratching his head as he stared at the total, he sighed, "It's a start. I wonder how those bumbling idiots are getting on with the moving of the grave." Checking his watch, thinking of calling, he just couldn't do it, not wanting to even hear Priscilla's nasal voice. Setting the pen down, he closed the tiny lamp and lay back on the bed, taking a much needed rest.

"Hullo?" Ewan pushed back his front door and looked around. "Jas?" He wandered outside and found Adam sitting by the pool on the phone.

When Ewan cast a long shadow over him, he peeked up and held up his finger for him to wait, then noticed he had a bouquet of two dozen long-stemmed red roses in his arms.

"Where's Jason?" Ewan didn't wait.

When Adam ignored him to continue his call, Ewan left to search for himself.

"Jas?" Climbing the stairs, he opened his bedroom door and found him asleep on the bed. "Ohhhh, love," he sighed adoringly.

When Jason felt the bed shift, he woke trying to figure out where he was.

"Hullo, baby…" Ewan set the roses down and stroked his hair and cheek.

"Hiya, love. Let me come round. I was way out."

"All right. I need to shower and change." He stood and started taking his clothing off.

As he did, Jason rubbed his face and tried to wake up. When he glimpsed at the bed next to him, he found the roses, then immediately smelled their sweet perfume. "Flowers?" he laughed.

"You wanted a bit of romance, yeah?" Grinning adoringly, he purred, "So now I can have me way with you. Aye, doctor?"

"You wicked boy." Jason inhaled them deeply after raising the bouquet to his nose.

"Was Adam down at the pool all this time?" Ewan kicked off his shoes and dropped his slacks.

"Is he still here? Christ, he's like a bloody leech." Jason sat up to watch as Ewan got naked.

"Did he try it on?" Ewan tossed his shirt down on the pile and waited.

"No…" Wanting to keep that information back to use if he needed it, Jason thought lying was the wisest course. "He knows how much we mean to each other." Gazing back at the beautiful red roses, Jason said, "No one has ever bought me flowers before."

Ewan mumbled, "Yeah. He does know, Jason. And he better keep away." Turning his attention to his lover, Ewan crawled naked on the bed to him and purred, "Well, I'm glad to be the first to buy them for you. No sweets, though, I remembered your waistline."

Setting the roses on the table beside him, Jason wrapped Ewan into his arms and kissed his rough cheek. "I've missed you."

"Aye, and me you," Ewan sighed sadly.

"It'll get worse when you're involved in a film, won't it?" Jason pushed back the long hair from his eyes.

Ewan hesitated before he answered. "You could come on set. Yeah?"

"You mean, hang around while you act? Oh, I don't know, love. I'd feel very awkward and out of place."

"But, Jason, this is what I do!" Ewan squirmed on him, then leaned up on his elbows to speak to him. "With luck, I'll always have a project going. Yeah? That's what I wanted out of life. To be busy, to be in movies."

"I know. And I'm very happy for you, but—"

"Oh, no," Ewan sighed miserably, "You've changed yer mind! Yeah? You don't like living here with me!"

"Shhh, calm down." He petted him gently and kissed his face a few times. "Love, I want a quiet life. You know that. Out of the hustle and bustle. At one time I thought Carlisle was too remote and isolated, but, the older I get, the more I appreciate its peace."

"Oh, no…" Ewan moaned, "Oh, no…don't do this to me, Jas—"

"I'm not doing anything yet—" He squeezed him tight.

"I'm going to dinner in an hour with a producer to sign a contract, yeah? I'll be committed to filming! Jason, are you telling me not to sign?"

"I can't tell you what to do—"

"No…no!" Ewan attempted to get free and off the bed, but Jason was having none of it.

"Stop this! Stop panicking and let us chat like adults!"

"Adults?" Ewan took deep insult. "What the bloody hell am I? A wee lad? That's unfair, love! Just because you're sixteen years older than me! That's unfair!"

"Calm yourself! Don't get all wound up!" Jason struggled to keep him still.

"You got me wound up! You got me crazy! I was ready for a nice shag! Now I'm half mad!"

Unable to contain him any longer, Jason let go. Ewan sprung off the bed quickly and faced him, breathing fire.

Slowly, Jason sat up on the edge of the bed. "Can we talk rationally?"

"Yeah! Rationally! Like two old geezers, yeah?"

Rubbing his tired face, Jason patted the spot next to him. "Sit. Please."

Arms crossed, glaring at him, Ewan stood back stubbornly.

"Please." Jason patted the spot persistently.

Exhaling a deep breath, Ewan plopped down on it.

"I just rung my auction house. They said the sale of my artwork netted over a million pounds."

Ewan spun around to look at him, his eyes wide in the dimming twilight that seeped in from the veiled windows.

"That's almost two million dollars. That's also just the tip of the iceberg."

"So? What'll ya do with the wedge? Go back to your manor and your ugly wife?"

"Ewan, stop. Try and calm down." Jason ran his hand down his satiny back.

"I'm listening, as usual," he grumbled, crossing his arms.

"I'm not saying I don't want to be with you. I just hesitate living this high-life. I keep throwing ideas around in my head as to how I can have both; a nice quiet life and you. And in reality, love, I would be without you more than with you, even if I lived here. You'll be traveling around, shooting scenes all over the world. Or even just in a studio, away from me. Okay, granted, I can keep busy, work out, maybe find a hobby or something. But I won't see you. Like today, we'll have snippets of moments when I can be squeezed in. And to be honest, love, if I were a doctor in Carlisle, you would be doing that with me right now. In between my twelve to sixteen hour shifts, we'd have exhausted snippets. What kind of life is that?"

"So where does this leave us, Jas? You not wanting to

191

get a divorce? You not wanting to relocate?"

"No. Those two things you can count on. I will divorce Priscilla, and I will relocate."

"To where? Here?"

"I love the climate. And from what I've seen of the area, it's fabulous—"

"But not for me. Not to live with me."

Jason sighed and dug his hand through Ewan's thick long hair. "I can't live without you. I have to have you in my life."

"You want me to give up acting."

It was exactly what Jason wanted. But he simply couldn't say it.

"You do. Jason, be honest with me. Is that what this is about? Me lifestyle? Yeah?"

Put to it, backed up into the corner, Jason ground his jaw and though he promised himself he would not take over Ewan's life or make decisions for him, it was the truth. Twisting on the bed to cup that lovely face and make those eyes search his, Jason sighed sadly, "If you want my honesty then you'll get it. I don't like Jack or Adam near you. They see you as a piece of meat, love, something to ogle and hold up to the highest bidder. And that's the men who are familiar with you and I. This entire industry scares me. I don't want you involved with actor types. I don't want other women and men thinking you are single and fair game. And I can't always be at your side. I can't live my life vicariously through you."

"I knew it. I had a feeling once you came out, saw the reality of this work and the people I have to associate with, you would tell me you did not fit in. So? Do I need to quit? Give up me career and go live in north England? Is that what you're saying?"

"Not necessarily live in England—"

"But give up acting. Yeah? Is that it?"

"No...not acting, love. I know you love that. But...it's this place..." Jason turned away first. How could he ask

Ewan to leave? It was infinitely cruel.

"What will we live on?" Ewan asked. "You think you have enough? That once the inheritance deal is broken your parents won't take it all back? You're mad if you think you can get away with it. Selling the paintings, being sly…" Ewan shook his head. "Oh, Jas, they'll catch on. Yeah? They'll catch on and you'll be coughing it up to some solicitor. You wait."

Jason shivered at the thought. "No. They will never take it from me!"

At that tone—that lusty greed for what he felt he was entitled to, Ewan asked, "Who are you?"

"Who am I?" Jason was startled by the question.

"Yeah. Remember me asking you the same thing? In Windermere? In the log cabin over a year ago?"

He paused to think. He did. It was when they had a proper weekend away, Ewan still had a cast on his leg and he told him about his aunt's estate.

"So, I ask you—who are you? Are you a greedy git who has to have the money? At any cost? Like you once did?" Ewan whispered, "Or will you trust me? Trust me that we will get everything we desire?"

It was the exact same deal. He failed miserably the first time. Hesitating, deathly afraid of taking that leap of faith, Jason could not help but stare at this naked seraph and decide his fate.

The last of the outdoor sunlight was fading and the tiny lamp by the bed needed lighting. But in that transition from dusk to night, Ewan's skin was glowing with an ethereal beauty.

"How— How much—" Jason swallowed audibly. He was a pragmatic man. He needed figures. "How much are you worth right now?"

A slight ironic smile passed over Ewan's lips. "The house is worth about five and a half million."

"Good—"

"But—" Ewan added, "But, I don't own it, Jas. I rent

193

it."

"Rent it?" Jason gasped in disappointment.

"Aye. Jack didn't know if I was going to be a flash in the pan, love. So it's temporary living quarters. And I had to make sure I had an extended work visa. Which I now hold. The agency pays for it. See? This roof over me head, the furnishings. That's why Jack and Adam feel so at home here. They've let clients live here on and off for years."

"No equity in the house." Jason was shattered.

"No," Ewan continued, "I got two-hundred thousand for the first movie, *Murphy's Hero*." He paused to watch Jason's expression. "That's in a U.S. dollar account."

"That's it?"

"I did a few small jobs before that. So, add another ten or so."

"Oh, love, that's not enough—"

"But," he cut Jason off, "when it goes to pay-per-view and then video, I get another payment of eight grand. Then, six hundred thousand each up front before taxes for the next two pictures. After they come out, I can do advertising, and interviews for more."

The numbers were still pathetically small as far as he was concerned.

Ewan read it on his face. "It takes time to be a multi-millionaire, love. But I will be. One good endorsement contract with someone like Calvin Klein or Oakley, and I'm there."

"No...no, love..." Jason was shaking his head in agony. "It's more than that...it's the degrading associations with the likes of Jack Turner, not just—"

"Ewan?" There was a knock on the bedroom door. "Ewan, are you dressed yet? We've got dinner with Dennis in a half hour! So, climb off Jason's back and get ready!"

With the clock ticking, Ewan sighed. "Aye. I'm getting ready," he shouted to the door. Standing scuffing to the shower, his head was hanging in defeat.

As if someone had passed a knife through his back,

Jason slumped over in the gloom. Only a few hundred thousand here and there? That was it? Didn't movie stars make millions right away?

The shower started. Jason knew Ewan would sign a contract tonight for a movie. He had no choice. He didn't have enough to stop working.

Rising up tiredly, Jason needed to splash his face and get ready as well. When he entered the bathroom, he only glimpsed at the blurry form through the sliding doors. Turning on the taps, Jason filled the basin and splashed his face, then brushed his teeth.

Finished, the faucets silent, Ewan opened the door and a blast of steam poured out. Finding Jason in the room brushing his hair, he grabbed a towel and pouted sadly. "I love you. I can't stop loving you."

At the soft sound of Ewan's voice, Jason spun to see him. His eyes seemed too large as they filled with water. "Oh, love, come here." Jason opened his arms.

Ewan fell against him, his heart breaking. "It's enough, love. Please. If we're patient, it's enough."

Jason wasn't patient. He had dreams of retiring in his late thirties. The last thing he wanted was to exchange the lifestyle he had now with one of needing to be dependant on Ewan, or worse yet, working in an emergency room in some hospital in LA, knee-deep in blood, treating gunshot and knifing victims. "I'll get us the money, love." Jason kissed his damp neck. "I'll make sure we have it all."


Victoria held the original will in her hand as she and Paul sat with their solicitor. "It clearly states he has to be living in the estate for at least five years before selling the contents, and he is to have one child."

"Does it mention how long he must be married?" The solicitor adjusted his eyeglasses and reached over the desk to read it for himself.

"Oh." Victoria scanned the confusing legal verbiage.

"Give it to the man!" Paul took it out of her grip and handed it over.

Shooting her husband a scolding look for embarrassing her, she then brought her attention back to her solicitor.

Mr. Wood examined it carefully. "Nothing about the length of time he must be married."

Paul replied, "I'm stunned. That's merely an oversight!"

"Well, whatever the reason, it's not in print." Mr. Wood read on. "Have they a child?"

"No," Victoria answered quickly, "He claimed to Priscilla he was impotent!" then she scoffed at the absurdity.

Lowering the paperwork, Mr. Wood met her eyes. "If he can get a medical opinion on that, then I would think that clause could be null and void."

"What?" Victoria shouted. "He can get any of his old work associates to write that up! This is nonsense!"

Setting the will down, Mr. Wood removed his glasses and tried to gain their complete attention. "May I ask you a very direct question?"

"Yes, of course." Paul nodded.

"Why do you want to remove this estate from your son so urgently?"

Immediately, Paul rubbed his forehead and averted Mr. Wood's eyes as Victoria shifted uncomfortably.

"I only ask," Mr. Wood continued, "because a judge will. Your son possesses this estate and its contents currently. Having him removed from the premise, making him return any money he may have accumulated whilst living there, well, it's taken very seriously." When again he did not hear an answer, he said, "Has he committed some sort of crime?"

"Only a crime on morality—" Victoria mumbled angrily.

Raising his eyebrows, Mr. Wood whispered, "You mean, like pedophilia?"

"Oh, good heavens no!" Paul choked in shock.

"Then I must ask myself what the man has done to upset you so greatly." He put his glasses back on his face after rubbing them with a soft cloth. "Remember, it's not because I am prying. I have to lay this case out before the court. I assume Dr. Phillips will fight it."

"Oh, he will!" Victoria shouted in irritation.

Mr. Wood sat back patiently and waited, moving his gaze from one to the other for an answer.

Seeing his wife would not speak up, Paul finally said, "He's a homosexual."

Waiting to hear more incriminating evidence, Mr. Wood gestured for him to go on.

"That's it." Paul bit his lip, feeling like a heel.

Growing annoyed, Mr. Wood lifted the paperwork once more and asked, "Did he marry to deceive anyone?"

Paul waited for his wife to answer. Suddenly she chose to keep completely silent. "No," he said, "We arranged the marriage for him."

"I see." Mr. Wood appeared to be getting more irritated by the moment with this horrible claim. "Do I have it correct then? Dr. Phillips married someone you had chosen, stayed married for a year to this woman, and finally he has done something to upset the arrangement?"

"Yes!" Victoria shouted.

"And you're surprised?" Mr. Wood handed them the will.

"What are you doing?" Victoria shoved it back at him. "There must be something you can do!"

"Oh, I can try and get your poor son kicked out of his home because of his sexuality!" Mr. Wood snarled. "I can force him to either stay in a loveless, sexless marriage for another four long years or go without his home and estate!"

"Leave it…" Paul heard enough. "Victoria, let Jason have his way. I don't like the sound of this battle. It's getting more unseemly every moment."

"I won't! Paul, I want grandchildren! I want him to be respectable! This is an outrage!" Victoria's veins were protruding in her neck. "If Mr. Wood refuses, we'll find another solicitor!"

"Mrs. Phillips," Mr. Wood interrupted, "Even if you find a solicitor who is anti-gay, he still has to prove to a judge that there is justification for removing him from his home. Let me advise you, the court is loath to do that unless there are extreme circumstances—" He held up his hand before she shouted that there already were, "And being gay simply is not enough of a reason to be expelled from your home! On the contrary, my dear lady, in this current air of political correctness, a judge could come under terrible scrutiny for that type of decision!"

"But he's breaking the contract!" She shook the paperwork at him.

"A contract that blackmailed the man into marriage? I think that's a bit suspect in the first place." Pausing. looking straight at Paul, he added, "If you love your son, let him be. You've punished him enough for his crime, haven't you?"

"Come on, Vicky, let's go." Paul rose up and shoved past the chair towards the door.

"Oh, this is absurd!" Victoria shouted. "I can't believe our own solicitor is allowing Jason to make a mockery of this will! Marge would be furious!"

"Come. Let's go." Paul tapped her arm.

She couldn't resist one last dig, "I hope you're happy! I hope one day one of your sons is gay and you see the agony of his decision."

"Vicky!" Paul grabbed her arm and physically dragged her out.

When they were out in the hall, Victoria ranted, "I will not let this go! He will not humiliate us by prancing around Hollywood with that tart!"

"Enough." Paul stormed out to the parking lot.


"Cilla?"

"Yes, Charles?" Sitting in the lounge in front of the

television, Priscilla ate chocolate and sipped tea.

"Did you say Jason had these paintings cleaned?" He held his feather duster over the frame of the William Hunt Shakespearean scene.

"Yes, why?" She was distracted by the news on the television, wondering why he was shouting to her.

He mumbled, "It hardly looks clean at all," squinting closer to peer under the glass reflections.

Her curiosity getting the better of her, she managed to get to her feet and found him in the hall, gazing up at one of their masterpieces.

"He did have it cleaned, remember? He removed them all." She stood next to him and tried to find the significance.

"Look at the texture, Cilla." He pointed to it. "The ridges are actually flat. Like it's a photograph of the original."

"Really?" She leaned closer and tried to see it. "What does that mean, Charles?"

"I don't think this is the original painting, Cilla. It appears to be a copy."

"A copy? Do you think Marge knew they were copies?"

"No. Not Marge, I reckon when Dr. Phillips had them cleaned, perhaps they were taken and replaced by copies."

"So, the people who cleaned them stole them?" she gasped.

"Perhaps…but, it seems odd Dr. Phillips wouldn't have noticed them when he picked them up."

"Should we call the police, Charles?" She bit her nail.

"I should like to speak with Dr. Phillips before I cast any aspersions on the gallery that has done the work."

"What gallery did it?" Priscilla struggled to see a difference in the paintings.

"I don't know. I would have to search through the doctor's paperwork."

"Why not wait until he rings?" Priscilla shrugged indifferently. "He said he would ring."

"Did he leave you with any information on which hotel

he was staying at?"

"Why, no, Charles. He just said he'd ring."

"Oh, Cilla, my dear," Charles sighed tiredly, "I think your Jason is up to no good."


Ewan brushed his hair in the mirror silently while Jason stood near the door in the bedroom, waiting.

They hadn't spoken to each other since the debate. Adam was impatiently goading them to speed it up.

Throwing the brush on the sink, Ewan lowered his eyes to walk passed Jason to the hall. Before he did, Jason stopped him, holding his arms, turning him to face him.

Reluctant to meet his eyes, Ewan stared at his feet.

Shaking him gently, Jason wanted Ewan to look. "Baby..." he sighed.

Finally, Ewan raised his dark eyelashes. "What do you want me to do, Jas?"

It didn't need to be reiterated. And Jason had not been able to put it into words for it sounded so cruel and manipulating.

Growing impatient, Adam stomped up the stairs, shouting, "What the hell's keeping you two? You're like a pair of fucking women!"

Ewan twisted out of Jason's hands and dropped down in defeat on the bed.

"What's going on?" Adam asked, crossing his arms and checking his watch. "Can it wait?"

"Jas doesn't want me to sign the contract."

"What?" Adam twisted to him in anger. "What the fuck are you trying to do?"

Unable to defend himself verbally, Jason raised his hands as if fending off the blow, but said nothing.

Ewan continued, "He thinks we won't see each other. Yeah? He sees me involved in two films and never being around. And...he's right, Adam."

"Right?" Adam screamed in anger, "So that's it? Fuck

your career?"

"I don't know what to do." Ewan rubbed his eyes tiredly.

"I knew you coming out here was a mistake!" Adam pointed a loaded finger into Jason's face. "I knew it the first minute I set eyes on you in London you were trouble!"

Instantly, Jason riveted his gaze to Adam's brown irises. "Did you!? Was that the same moment you fell in love with me?"

"Wha-at?" Ewan jumped to his feet.

"You son-of-a-bitch," Adam breathed in fury.

"You what?" Ewan rushed over to confront him.

"You want me to tell him about the beach or should you?" Jason's voice was measured and precise.

"The beach?" Ewan was near hysteria. "What about a beach?"

Adam tried to calm himself down, then met Jason's cold stare and said, "You really want to ruin him, don't you?"

"No. On the contrary, I want to save him. This whole business is nasty and unwholesome. Beginning with Jack. That nasty piece of work. How dare he make Ewan suck his cock—"

"Jason!" Ewan shouted. "Someone better tell me about this beach bullocks or I'll get violent, yeah?" He flicked the hair back from his eyes and took up a fighting stance.

Jason paused, waiting for Adam. When he realized Adam was not going to reveal his actions for the consequences were suddenly dire, Jason decided to be blunt. "He drove me to a deserted beach. The moment I sat down to enjoy the view, he came on. Then when he couldn't get me interested, he shoved me down and insisted I kiss him, telling me he fell for me the moment he met me."

"No, Ewan—" Adam shook his head in panic.

"I knew you were sniffing 'round!" Ewan shouted, "Is it true?"

"More lies, Adam?" Jason spoke calmly.

Adam looked helplessly from one to the other. His cell phone rang, adding to his confusion.

"Is it true?" Ewan shouted. "It's not a flamin' trick question, Adam!"

Taking his phone out, seeing it was Dennis Foreman probably waiting at the restaurant, wondering where they were, Adam appeared dumbfounded.

Jason shook his head. "Do you see him denying it, love?"

"Get out!" Ewan roared.

"No! Ewan! You're making the biggest mistake of your life!"

"Get the bloody hell out of me face! This whole flamin' business is full of bullocks! I'm through, Adam! I can't live here and I sure as shite don't want to work here! You're all a bunch of fucking wankers!" Ewan pointed for him to go, about to throw him out.

"Fuck you, doctor!" Adam growled as he backed away from them slowly. "You think fucking up Ewan's career will bring him closer to you? He'll resent you forever!"

"Get out!" Ewan screamed, covering his ears.

"It's not me he'll resent, Mr. Lewis. Blame your own bloody libido."

Still backing out, Adam began dialing Jack's number frantically. "Oh, maybe at first, but when his career is over, it'll be you!" As he walked down the stairs the men heard him shouting, "Jack! If you get this message, call me!"

Following to make sure he left, Ewan slammed the door and put the chain on it, resting his head on the cool surface to try and calm down.

Jason twisted on his heels to pack. He had no idea what mess he had left behind in England, but, knowing that twit, it would be a disaster.

202

# Chapter Seventeen

"So, what do you think I should do, Daddy?" Priscilla stood with Charles as she spoke on the phone in the lounge.

"Where the devil is he?" Crispin asked angrily.

"He went to a convention in the United States."

"And he didn't leave you a contact number?"

"He said he would ring. But he's been gone four days and hasn't yet. I do hope nothing has happened to him."

"Put Charles on the line, Priscilla."

"Yes, Daddy." She handed him the receiver. "He wants a word."

Charles took it and said, "Yes, sir?"

"What's this business about the paintings?"

"Well, sir, I was dusting them. The doctor had just had them cleaned. When I looked at them, to try and see if they looked any brighter, I found they appeared flat. I did the honors of taking one down and out of its frame, simply to verify, and well, sir—"

"What? What, Charles?"

"They are merely photos of the originals."

"Photos? And you're quite certain?"

"Oh, most definitely, sir."

"Do you believe the gallery switched them?"

"At first, it was my thought, sir."

"And now?"

"Well, to be honest, sir, the doctor hasn't been a proper husband to your daughter, sir. And I do believe he may have had them sold, in preparation for leaving Cilla. She told you about moving Margerie's grave, sir."

"Yes. A very tasteless subject."

"I'm sorry to burden you, sir."

"What about Jason's parents?"

"I'm hesitant to tell you about that over the phone." Charles made eye contact with Priscilla. She was biting her nails, looking confused.

"Well, you had better."

"Yes, sir. They stopped over, night before last. They brought the *SUN* newspaper with them."

"I fail to see the significance, Charles!"

"Well, sir, on the front page was a photo of the doctor."

"Jason? On the *SUN*? Whatever for?"

"It seems whilst he was on his trip abroad in Hollywood, he was seen—" taking a deep breath, Charles said, "seen kissing a male actor."

"WHAT?"

"I'm sorry to be the one—"

"Put my daughter on!"

"Yes, sir." He handed her back the phone.

"Hi, Daddy."

"Why on earth didn't you tell me about this incident the moment it happened!? I want you packed and out of there immediately!"

"Oh, no, Daddy. I can't leave Charles."

"Why on earth not!?"

Beside her, Charles was shaking his head no, trying to get her not to reveal any information.

"Because I am in love with him! And pregnant with his child!" she announced happily.

Hearing he was a father-to-be, Charles almost fainted.

"You what?" Crispin gasped.

"Well, Jason is impotent! So, one night when I was feeling very lonely…"

Rubbing his face in agony, Charles expected Mr. Prescott to have him drawn and quartered.


In reality, Ewan didn't have much, just some clothing and a few personal items. As he closed and locked the door, Ewan was silent. He'd been let down on so many fronts, he didn't know what was right any longer. But, one thing he had to admit, the two men from his agency were cads. As he and Jason loaded their bags in the back of a taxi cab, Adam narrated it over the phone to Jack who was trying to get there before they left.

"Oh, they're leaving!" Adam shouted sarcastically, "No, they just stashed their bags in a cab because they're staying! Jack, I'm standing here watching them!" Knowing it was futile, Adam shouted, "Jack wants you to wait! He's only a few minutes away!"

"In that case, we're going." Jason opened the back door of the taxi and gestured for Ewan to climb in.

Without any expression, Ewan ducked into the back of the car.

"He's leaving, Jack—" Adam moved closer to the cab. "No, I'm not kidding. I'm watching him leave. Yes! He packed his fucking bags!" Adam leaned down to shout through the open door, "You're making a big mistake! You're breaking your contract! Jack said he would sue!"

Before Jason climbed in, he grabbed Adam by the scruff of the neck. "If he causes us any aggro, I'll make damn sure he's exposed for his abuse to young men. In the closet, is he?"

"You're bluffing!" Adam held the mobile phone out as Jack's voice was heard shouting at him in the background.

Jason glared at him, not saying another word, and climbed into the car.

As it vanished from Adam's sight, he whined, "Forget it, Jack. Just forget it."


Victoria was pounding on their front door. "Charles! Charles!" she shouted, bruising her hand.

"Give him a minute, Vicky! The poor man!" Paul shook his head in irritation.

"Together we'll figure out what we can do—" When the door opened she shoved her way inside.

"Where's Priscilla?" Victoria attempted to sniff her out.

"Packing, Mrs."

"What?" Both Paul and Victoria shouted in harmony.

Pushing him out of her way, she raced up the stairs to find Priscilla in her bedroom packing a large suitcase. When she heard Victoria come into the room, she smiled sweetly. "Oh, hello, Mum."

"What are you doing?" Out of breath and exasperated, Victoria braced herself on the doorframe.

"I spoke to Daddy and he thought I should go back home for now."

"What?" she panted. "Divorce?"

"Daddy says I should file now that I'm in love with Charles." She folded one of her frocks neatly.

"In love with—" Victoria fainted just as Paul came up behind her to catch her.

As he stood over her, fanning her, Priscilla smiled at Charles who had poked his head in to see what was happening. "I'm so pleased Daddy is helping us, Charles."

"Yes, Cilla." He turned to speak to Paul. "Should I make some tea, sir?"

"Yes, Charles. That would be lovely." Paul shook Victoria to wake her up.


Jason handed his ticket to the flight attendant. Behind him, his baseball cap and sunglasses in place, Ewan gave her his passport and ticket silently.

Thanking the woman, Jason touched Ewan's shoulder, allowing him to walk in front of him down the corridor to the 747. Seated in first class, Jason again nudged Ewan to sit by the window then sat next to him, staring at him, then again, trying not to stare. "You all right?"

Peering over the sunglasses as if the question was completely absurd, Ewan didn't answer, just removed his leather coat and settled in for the long flight.


Both their bags were packed and set by the front door while Priscilla spoke calmly, "Oh, yes. Charles and I are in love." She batted her lashes at him. "I know it's a bit out of the ordinary, but you can't always control where your heart goes, can you?"

"You're pregnant?" Victoria's tea cup was shaking in her hand.

"Oh, yes. I've missed my menstrual cycle. I've never done that before." She nodded, then checked the time. "Daddy should be here at any moment."

"I'll see to locking up." Charles rose to his feet and had a look around the house to secure it.

"And all this time Jason still has not rung up?" Paul set his cup down, getting to his feet.

"No. I would like to talk to him. It is odd not having him know I'm leaving." Priscilla set her cup aside and stood, brushing her dress off to get the creases out.

There was a pounding on the door.

"That must be Daddy!" She smiled and danced over to answer it.

Crispin burst in, his anger getting the better of him. "Has he contacted you yet?"

"No, Daddy, but his parents are here." As he rushed by, Priscilla noticed a work van had pulled up. "Who is that, Daddy?"

"Never mind!" he growled and found Paul and Victoria

in the lounge. "What kind of son did you raise?" he shouted, "Kissing men across the bloody pond?"

"Oh!" Victoria reacted in shock. "And your daughter is any better? Becoming pregnant by her sixty year old valet! Oh, do be sensible!"

"I think we should all calm down." Paul held up his hands.

Crispin grabbed Priscilla and asked, "Where is Jason's room?"

"Upstairs, Daddy, second door on the left."

"Whatever are you doing?" Victoria followed after him as he stomped his way to the upper floor.

Like a mad bull, Crispin burst into Jason's private quarters and immediately found his desk. On top was a small stack of paperwork with a tiny brown porcelain mouse resting on it. As he grabbed the papers, the mouse tipped over on its side.

Not finding what he was looking for, he went for the drawers. They were locked. Shoving beyond the small gawking crowd, he shouted down the stairs to the open front door to a man who had been working on the lock.

"Up here! Could you come up here!?"

The man in the white overalls nodded, bringing his tools up. Crispin pointed to the locked drawers and file cabinet.

Paul reacted immediately. "Oh, this is out of order, Crispin! Searching through my son's personal papers?"

"Your son!" Crispin roared, "has sold off some of the oil paintings of this estate and replaced them with copies! I want to know if there is anything else he has done to my daughter!"

"They signed a prenuptial!" Victoria shouted.

"Open his files!" Crispin ordered.

In moments the locksmith had everything standing open.

"I don't like this..." Paul held onto Victoria. "I don't like this one bit, Crispin."

"I don't give a rat's arse what you like!" He tore through files, tossing unimportant paperwork on the floor carelessly. Finally finding what he was looking for, he held up the paper as evidence. "A signed contract with an auction house!" he shouted, "Look at the list of items!" He went on the read the names of the artists. "Then, he replaces them with photographs! Opens U.S. dollar accounts! Of all the sneaking—"

"They are his!" Paul argued. "Crispin, they are his to sell!"

"It's all unsavory!" Crispin shouted. "Until my solicitor can investigate what he has done, I want everything frozen! All his assets! This house locked up! I'll tie him up in so much litigation he'll never see any of this estate!" He nodded to the locksmith to continue his work on the doors.

"You see!" Paul shouted at his wife, "You see this nonsense? This is what you wanted! Our Jason having his legacy taken from him! You see it now?"

Victoria did. And though it was what she wanted originally, it felt very wrong suddenly.

Standing in the hall eating a piece of cake, Priscilla said, "I just keep eating! Perhaps I'll gain some weight!"

The crowd in the room paused to stare at her in amazement as she shoved chocolate cake into her mouth.

Eleven hours later, exhausted beyond measure, Jason located his Mercedes in the airport parking lot. Behind him, Ewan was a zombie, scuffing his feet and shivering at the cold temperature.

Unlocking the boot, Jason dumped his case in it and then turned to get Ewan's. Seeing his worn appearance, Jason reached for him. "Come here, love."

Moving towards him in a numb dream, Ewan fell against him, closing his eyes.

"Soon we'll be in a nice warm bed and sleeping," Jason assured him.

"How ya going to sneak me in, love?" Ewan yawned.

"You let me worry about that." Kissing his cheek, Jason nudged him to the side of the car. "Get in and relax."

"Aye…" Ewan dragged himself to the door and plopped down on the leather seat.

Closing the trunk, Jason climbed in and started the engine, blasting the heat. "Hang in there, love. We'll be home soon."

Ewan nodded, closing his eyes and stretching out his long legs.


Jason pulled into the rutty gravel lane, his headlights making little difference to the blackness of the estate. It seemed oddly dark. No light was coming from anywhere. He wondered if they had a power cut.

Pulling in front of the entrance, Ewan asleep beside him, Jason kept the engine running and the lights on to be able to see. Taking out his house keys, he stuck them into the lock. When he twisted them, nothing happened. Struggling for a few minutes, he couldn't get the door opened. Not wanting to wake the household up, Jason had resisted knocking. But, seeing as his key was not working for some reason, he had no option and thought about an excuse to get Ewan in. He pounded the front door loudly.

At the noise, Ewan woke as Jason stood on the front step beating the wooden door.

"This is absurd!" Jason's patience was worn to a thread. He just wanted to sleep.

Ewan leaned out of the window. "What is it, love?"

Giving up temporarily, Jason walked back to the car and climbed in, turning the heating up again. "My key isn't working, and there doesn't seem to be anyone at home!"

"Uh oh…" Ewan breathed.

Spinning to look at him in terror, Jason hadn't even thought about anything sinister. Until now. "Oh, no…no!"

"The locks been changed?" Ewan shook his head. "Oh,

Jas…"

"No!" Jason rushed out of the car again and tried his key, then he went to each front window and squinted into the pitch black interior.

"Jason!" Ewan shouted. "Come on, love! I have to get some kip!"

"I'll kill her!" Jason gnashed his teeth in rage. "I'll bloody kill her!"

"Let's go to me mum's." Ewan yawned again.

"I should break in," Jason shouted, trying to decide which window to smash.

"The alarm will ring and we'll have the Old Bill to deal with. Not tonight, love. Let's get some sleep, yeah?"

Going completely mad, Jason was very reluctant to leave his home for any reason.

"Jason!" Ewan whined, "I want to get in bed!"

"Bloody hell!" Jason gave up and climbed back into his car. "I don't know what she's done, but she is going to pay dearly for this." Shaking, slamming it into gear, Jason tore out of the gravel drive and headed to Ewan's mother's flat.

As they parked in front, Ewan checked the time. "Oi, she may still be at work, love. It's just about closing time at the pub." Ewan climbed out of the car tiredly.

"I'll kill her," Jason muttered under his breath, homicidal thoughts racing through his mind as he shut the engine and walked mechanically to the rear of the car.

Ewan had the front door open before Jason brought the bags up to him.

"Hullo? Mum?" Ewan called out, then lit the overhead light. "Not home. Come to bed, love."

Leaving the bags behind, they climbed the stair and had a look into Ewan's old bedroom. There were a few things on the bed. Packages Siobhan hadn't tended yet. Ewan shoved everything off and peeled back the spread. "Good. She's got sheets on it, love. You go and get washed up first." He nudged Jason to the bathroom.

After Jason scuffed away, Ewan gazed at the Lord of

211

the Rings posters he had up all over the walls. "I never thought I'd be back here…" he sighed unhappily.

Once they were both cleaned up and naked under the duvet, Ewan curled around Jason's warmth and snuggled up. Before he closed his eyes, he noticed Jason's wide open in the dim light.

"Jas, please get some rest. You need to be alert tomorrow to face the mess, yeah?"

Exhaling a deep breath, Jason tilted to Ewan, "I'm so sorry, love. I thought I was bringing you back here for a life of leisure. I'm so, so sorry."

When a tear moved slowly down Jason's cheek, Ewan wiped it off. "You don't worry, love. As long as we have each other, we'll get by."

'Get by'. Those words echoing in his temples like purgatory on earth, Jason closed his eyes finally and got some much needed rest.

# Chapter Eighteen

A dream had hold of him. In a darkened tunnel, Jason was set before a magistrate to explain his life's mistakes. "Heaven or hell?" The magistrate had horns and a tail.

"No!" Jason shook his head violently.

Blinking his eyes, then squinting at the sunlight pouring in from his window, Ewan tried to come out of a very deep slumber.

Jason was in the midst of a terrible nightmare.

"Oh, crikey," Ewan shook his head sadly. "Jason. Love." He rocked his shoulder gently.

With a swift inhale of air, Jason opened his eyes and woke up, panic stricken.

"All right. It's all right, love." Ewan brushed his damp hair back from his forehead.

Springing up, Jason shouted, "What time is it?"

With an effort, Ewan raised himself on his elbows and found the clock on the nightstand. "Ten, love."

Throwing off the duvet, Jason hurried to the bathroom to wash up.

"I'd've preferred a nice slow shag!" Ewan shouted sarcastically, then found his mother peering in, holding two cups of tea. "Oh. Hullo, Mum." He yawned and rubbed his head tiredly.

"When I got home, I found your bags in the foyer! Should I be worried? I never expected you to come home so soon!" She set one cup down on the stand and handed Ewan the other.

"Ta," he nodded thanks and sat up to sip it.

Siobhan sat on the bed near him and asked softly, "What's happened, love?"

"Ohhh, Mum, everything at once." He sighed in anguish.

At a noise behind them, they looked up to see Jason rushing back in. When he found Siobhan, he froze and covered himself up quickly.

She smirked at his expression. "No need to be shy with me, doctor!" Then tilted her head to the nightstand. "I brought you a cuppa."

"Cheers, love." He reached for his clothing and came up with his cotton shirt. Slipping it on, the tails hiding his crotch and bottom, he scampered down the stair to retrieve his case, then hauled it back up, set it down on the landing and dug through it for clean clothing.

Siobhan looked at her son, who was smiling at the sight of Jason's nearly naked body. She winked at him knowingly then asked, "I don't mean to pry, love—"

Tearing his gaze away from his lover's long legs, Ewan sipped his tea and then said, "No. No need to. We made a mess of things in LA"

"We?" Jason stood at attention, holding a clean pair of briefs in front of him before slipping them on.

"Me?" Ewan asked tentatively.

"Adam!" Jason shouted in rage, then turned his back to them as he jumped into his cotton briefs.

They both got a good glimpse of his bottom.

"Isn't he a lovely bit of stuff, Mum?" Ewan sighed.

"Aye, that he is…" She giggled, then brought back her attention to her son, "Who's this Adam bloke?"

"I need a phone." Jason, in his briefs and cotton shirt, stood on the landing in confusion.

"One here, love," Ewan nodded to the nightstand, "…or down the stairs in the hall."

"Cheers." Jason chose the lower level.

When he left Siobhan moved closer to Ewan. "Tell me about it, love."

Inhaling a deep breath before he began, Ewan told her the tale.

Standing in his underwear by the front hall, Jason dialed his parents' number. His father answered.

"Dad?!"

"Jason! Where the devil are you!?"

"In Carlisle! What the bloody hell happened? I tried to get in my house last night and the flamin' locks were changed! Where's Priscilla and Charles?"

"She's back at her father's estate, with Charles."

"Why the hell did they change my locks? This is an outrage!"

"Long story. Where are you? Can we meet up?"

Looking around the tiny flat, Jason paced as far as the phone cord would let him. "Aye. We can. I'm at Ewan's mum's flat."

"Where's that?" Paul asked.

Jason gave him the address. "But don't bring Mum! She's been 'orrible to me!" he warned.

"No. Just me. Give me a minute."

Jason hung up, fretting terribly. When the postman shoved some mail through the door slot, Jason jumped out of his skin. Seeing the letters, he calmed down and grabbed them, carrying them back up the stairs.

As he came in, he overheard part of their conversation. Pausing, he waited for them to acknowledge him before entering the room.

"What cheek!" Siobhan shouted in anger. "Trying to pull Jason behind your back!"

"Aye, Mum. Oh, you don't know half." He finished his

tea, then nodded to his lover. "You all right?"

"Dad's on his way. I hope it's not a bloody nuisance." He sat on the bed next to Siobhan.

"You stay as long as you like." Siobhan patted his naked knee.

"Cheers, love. I feel like hell at the moment." Jason rubbed his face tiredly.

"Between the jet-lag and your troubles, I don't doubt it." She laughed sadly.

"They locked me out of my own house!" he cried in frustration. "That estate is everything I own!"

"You'll work it out. You just wait to see, yeah?" Siobhan rubbed his furry thigh affectionately. "I just want the two of you to be together. That's all that counts, love. Everything else is nothing. All right?"

"Thanks, Siobhan." Jason reached to hug her.

She fell against him happily, rubbing his back. "You don't worry, yeah? You just don't worry."

Over her shoulder, Jason found Ewan's unfocused gaze. When he winked at him, Ewan woke up and smiled. "Aye," he said, "As long as we're together. Right, Jas?"

"Aye. Right, love." Jason smiled at him adoringly.

The front bell ringing startled them. "My dad!" Jason stumbled off the bed and searched for his trousers.

"You calm down! I'll see to it." Siobhan hurried passed him. "I'll make him a nice spot of tea. You take your time!"

His pants half on, Jason stared at Ewan who had climbed out of bed and dug for his blue jeans from the pile of clothing beside it. "I can't think straight. I'm so upset."

Sliding on his denims, Ewan zipped them up and walked over to where Jason stood. "You don't worry. I'm here with you. Yeah?" He helped Jason on with his pants and fastened them for him.

Paul didn't want tea. "Where's Jason?" He rubbed his hands nervously and looked up the staircase.

"Dad." Jason descended quickly to see him, Ewan right behind him.

"Christ, you look like hell." Paul shook his head at his son's disheveled appearance.

"What do you expect?" Jason shouted. "I just spent an eternity on a plane, then I come home to find my house locked up!"

"Go into the lounge." Siobhan nudged them to sit down.

As he found a seat on the settee, Jason said, "Dad! What the hell's going on?"

The minute Paul spotted Ewan coming into the room, he became distracted.

Averting his eyes shyly, Ewan crossed his arms over his chest defensively, allowing his hair to cover his face.

Jason noticed where his father's gaze was riveted at the moment. "That's Ewan, Dad. Ewan Gallagher. His mum's name is Siobhan."

Instead of any sort of polite greeting, he focused back at his son. "Cilla is having an affair with Charles."

"I know." Jason leaned over his knees as he spoke. "So, that gives her the right to take my house?"

"She's pregnant, Jason."

"Wha-at?" Jason choked in shock.

Both Siobhan and Ewan took a quick intake of air at the news.

Jason rubbed his face roughly. "Wait, wait...she's a bun in the oven from my pensioner valet, and I lost my house? Someone help me get this into my head!"

"The house being locked up was Crispin's idea," Paul said quietly.

"Crispin?" Jason roared.

"Who the bloody hell is Crispin?" Ewan whispered.

"Her father!" Jason spat.

Pausing until he got his son's attention back, he continued, "He found out you had sold some of the paintings—"

"Those were mine to sell!"

"Regardless, he felt it was unsavory and wanted his solicitor to investigate it."

217

"He can't keep me from my home!" Jason was near tears.

"He's promised to tie it all up in litigation. Even if you have rights to it, son, he's going to make it very hard for you to just re-occupy your estate temporarily until all the paperwork is seen to by a judge."

"We signed a pre-nup!" Jason jumped to his feet. "He can't do that! It's not her property!"

"Jason…" Paul implored, "Sit down."

Seeing his lover fall apart, Ewan wiped at his eyes as they filled. Slowly, but most assuredly, they were being crushed from all angles.

Gradually sinking back onto the cushions, Jason rested his face in his hands in anguish.

"When we found the photograph of you kissing Ewan on the front of the *SUN*—"

Both Jason and Ewan's head bolted up as they shouted, "What?"

Paul stopped to stare at them strangely. "You didn't know?"

"The *SUN*?" Ewan gasped.

"Oh, no…oh, no…" Jason moaned.

"Last Monday, front page," Paul explained. "It had Ewan in his ball cap and sunglasses standing out front some restaurant, and you and he kissing."

"No…no…" Jason rubbed his red eyes.

"That bastard!" Ewan shouted. "That was Adam again!" he told Siobhan.

She shook her head sadly. "You're well rid of that one!"

"Your mother went mad when she saw it," Paul continued over his son's whimpering moans. "We were in Tesco's when we found it. She had a right go at me."

Massaging his rough jaw, Jason tried to get over the shock and listen to what his father was saying.

"She took it right to Priscilla," Paul said. "I couldn't stop her, Jason." When all he received was his dull gaze, Paul kept going, "Priscilla was under the impression you

218

were impotent. She told us you never consummated your marriage to her."

Siobhan peeked back at her son and he nodded it was the truth. "But, he's not impotent. Oh, not half!" When both Paul and Jason stared at him tiredly, Ewan waved, "Sorry. Carry on."

Paul took a deep breath and faced his son. "It just went from bad to worse, Jason. Charles noticed the paintings and of course was alarmed. He originally wondered if the gallery had done it."

"You think I wouldn't have noticed it?" Jason snorted in irritation.

"No. I thought as much. But, the topper was moving Marge's grave. I knew then what you were up to."

"Dad," Jason cried, "You see her? She's a twit! I can't stomach the sight of her! You made me marry her! You forced me to! You blackmailed me!"

Hearing what his own solicitor had said, Paul cringed at how immoral it sounded.

"You what?" Siobhan shouted. "You did that to our Jason! You made him marry a woman and stay away from my Ewan? How dare you!"

When it appeared she was going to slap him, Ewan held her back. "Mum…please. Let Jason handle him."

Leaning back over his lap again toward his father, Jason said softly, "Isn't that what you did? I marry that hairy, skinny thing, and then I get my estate? Do you know what that did to me and Ewan, Dad?"

Paul glimpsed at the handsome young man with the long hair quickly, then turned back to his son. "You have to understand, Jason—"

"No, Dad—" he interrupted, "I do not have to understand any longer! I don't care if you take my estate!" Jason shouted. "I won't leave him again! Do you hear me? You can make me penniless, skint! And I will not give up my lover again!"

Ewan's eyes grew very wide at that confession.

219

"You had that choice once before, son," Paul reminded cruelly. "What did you choose?"

"I've learned something in that year, Father," Jason spat angrily. "I've learned how few people there are in this world who love me, respect me, and would do anything for me."

A sob choked Ewan as he stood listening.

"One man, Father! Not you! Not Mum! Not Auntie Margerie! Just my Ewan! He's the only one who has loved me without fail since we met!"

"Oh, Jas…" Ewan fell apart, tears streaming down his face.

Hearing him cry, Jason rose up quickly and reached out to him, embracing him, rocking him in his arms.

When Jason and Ewan embraced, Paul twisted away and tried to get his emotions under control.

Siobhan rubbed Jason's back warmly. "I love you, too, Jason. You don't worry about that, my love."

"Cheers, Mum." Jason smiled at her, tears in his eyes, then tilted back to his father while still holding his sobbing lover. "So, keep your bloody money. Keep your nasty wench. I intend on divorcing her immediately."

Rising up slowly, Paul kept his chin lowered as he approached them, headed to the door. "I'm glad you've finally made your mind up, Jason."

Squeezing passed them, Paul didn't look at anyone, disappointment written all over his face.

Jason never said good-bye as he left, holding his lover tightly, and kissing his tear-stained face. "I'll never let anything come between us again, lover," he whispered into his ear. "Not family nor money. Never again."

# Epilogue

Dr. Jason Phillips set up a small practice. In two rooms of his modest home he had a reception room and an examination room. A small comfortable handful of patients came to visit him daily. His working hours were only six per day, maximum.

In the Red-Green Room theater, Ewan was the new associate director, helping produce the latest new plays.

"Marcus, love!" Ewan shouted to him on the stage.

"Yes, boss?" Marcus smiled adoringly at him.

"A bit more sex, yeah? You're supposed to be hot for his cock, yeah?"

"Aye! Me pleasure, boss!" Marcus saluted him happily.

"Good boy!" Ewan laughed, "Oi, Darren," he shouted.

Darren hustled over to him quickly.

"Get us a cuppa, would you?"

"Yes! Yes, of course, Mr. Gallagher."

"One sugar!" Ewan shouted as he scurried off.

Marcus moved to the edge of the stage while Ewan wrote something into his notes. "Ewan!"

"Yes, Marcus, love?" he scribbled quickly.

"You and the Doc going to invite me for tea at your

estate?"

Ewan smiled to himself, then looked up at his friend. "As soon as we get it back, love. If we get it back. To be honest, we're not too bothered anymore. We're just content as we are now."

"No matter! I'd not mind an invite to your little cottage!"

"Then we will do, love! We will do!" Ewan laughed, "Now read your bloody lines!"

"Right, boss!"


"Do you think it's serious, doctor?"

"No. I shouldn't worry." Jason patted her shoulder softly. "I'll write you up a prescription of some tablets. You take them and let me know how you get on."

"I will, thank you, doctor." She stood up and noticed the collection of mice on a shelf. "How sweet!" She took a closer look.

Jason tilted back to his little fetish and smiled. "Aye, it started with one—"

"And grew!" She laughed. Lifting one up gently, she held it in her palm and admired it. "He's charming!"

Signing the prescription first, Jason rose up to have a look. A little brown mouse on a green leaf was smiling at him. "You've picked my favorite of the lot."

"I can see why. He's lovely!"

Looking beyond her to his desk, he found a photo of him and Ewan together. As he sighed happily, he said, "Aye, he is truly lovely indeed."

## The End

## About the Author:

Award-winning author G. A. Hauser was born in Fair Lawn,
New Jersey, USA, and attended university in New York
City. She moved to Seattle, Washington where she worked
as a patrol officer with the Seattle Police Department. In
early 2000 G.A. moved to Hertfordshire, England where she
began her writing in earnest and published her first book, *In
the Shadow of Alexander*. Now a full-time writer in Ohio,
G.A. has written dozens of novels, including several best-
sellers of gay fiction. For more information on other books
by G.A., visit the author at her official website at:
www.authorga.com.

Other works by G.A. Hauser:

Leather Boys (Men in Motion Book Four)
Driving Hard (Men in Motion Book Three)
Cruising (Men in Motion Book Two)
Mile High (Men in Motion Book One)
The Boy Next Door
When Adam Met Jack
To Have and to Hostage
Giving Up the Ghost
Capital Games
Love you, Loveday
Exposure
Secrets and Misdemeanors
Naked Dragon
The Kiss
A Question of Sex

# Recommended Read:

## Winds of Change by Lee Rowan
(Book Two of the Art of War Series)

The ruggedly handsome Lt. William Marshall of His Majesty's Navy carries a secret close to his heart, one that is more important than either his loyalty to England or his devotion to duty. His shipmate, Lt. David Archer, is not only his best friend, he's been his lover for over a year. The penalty should their relationship be discovered? Death, by hanging.

Both men control their passions and exercise discretion aboard ship as best they can, but the ship's quarters are close, shore leave is infrequent, and in the military…nothing is permanent.

A transfer to a new ship leads to danger as Will and David are caught in a web of intrigue. Ordered to masquerade as lovers in order to flush out and help capture a saboteur who is known to use blackmail to achieve his ends, they face possible discovery of the truth. Then a murder attempt leaves Davy near death while Will is sent off, without knowing his lovers fate, to command a captured French vessel.

Will and David have always known the risks, known that death might take either of them at any time. Their chances of staying together were never high...could it be that their luck has finally run out?

This is a publication of

Linden Bay Romance

WWW.LINDENBAYROMANCE.COM

LaVergne, TN USA
21 August 2009
155621LV00004B/13/P